INCUBASTARD

CHARITY B.

Editor: Kim BookJunkie
Formatting: Champagne Book Design
Cover Design: Opulent Designs

BROKEN
SPINE
PRESS

AUTHOR'S NOTE

If you've read my previous work, you may have come to expect extremely dark content. This book, though, is not quite as dark as my more recent releases. However, if this is the first book of mine you've encountered, please read the content warnings and take them seriously.

Incubastard is my very first PNR, and I had such a blast writing something so far out of my normal content.

Names of otherworldly locations, objects, divine creatures as well as their abilities are not in English or any human language since it was inspired by Enochian. I have included a decoder at the beginning if needed. I truly hope you enjoy the journey and thank you for choosing to read my story.

Content Warning

This novel contains graphic scenes depicting blood and gore along with sexually explicit content and violence. For mature audiences only.

I want to make it clear: there are subjects discussed pertaining to religion. The witchcraft used is made up and not based on or a reflection of actual practices. Everything in this novel is purely fiction. If you feel you may become uncomfortable by a story containing religious elements and Christian lore, then this is one you should skip.

There are incestual themes, although I don't personally think it counts because it's between immortal beings, but if that's going to bother you, please don't read this book.

Get the complete list of content warnings here: www.authorcharityb.com/warnings/incubastard
Complete list may contain spoilers.

For my Babydolls. This has been an incredibly rough year for me, but you have stuck with me through all of it. You truly have no idea what you've done for me. When I was struggling, questioning everything and drowning in self-doubt, you were there to have my back. There's no way I'd be where I am without you, and I owe you more than I can ever repay. I love you guys, and as always, embrace your weird!

Term Decoder

Aldonitas Comselh /al-don-ee-tass comm-sell/: Land of Greed (Kingdom of Mammon)

Aldonitas Orseiinak /al-don-ee-tass or-sin-ack/: Daemon(s)/Demon(s) of Greed

Ammalok Qew/ am-mah-lock kew/: Book of Seven

Bransg /bronz-g/: Shield (Invisibility)

Cronug /craw-nugg/: Infernal Beast

Drilpa Nalvage /drill-puh nall-vij/: The Beyond (Immortal Realm)

Emetgis /em-ett-giss/: Seal

Farzem Rings /Far-zimm/: Hardened Rings Beneath the Penile Skin

Formurifri /for-murr-ree-free/: Archangel(s)

Gohed /go-ed/: Divine Pendant

Ialpr / ee-all-purr/: Liquid Fire

Ialzo /ee-all-zo/: Liquid Air

Invigil Comselh /in-vij-ill com-sell/: Land of Envy (Kingdom of Leviathan)

Invigil Orseiinak /in-vij-ill or-sin-ack/: Daemon(s)/Demon(s) of Envy

Levithmong Comselh /le-veeth-mong comm-sell/: Land of Gluttony (Kingdom of Beelzebub)

Levithmong Orseiinak /le-veeth-mong or-sin-ack/: Daemon(s)/ Demon(s) of Gluttony

Madriiax /mah-dree-ax/: Heaven (Paradise/Silver City)

Maelprog /moll-progg/: Hell (Realm of the Damned)

Murifri /murr-ree-free/: Angel(s)

Orseiinak /or-sin-ack/: Daemon(s)/Demon(s)

Otiopag Comselh /ot-tio-pogg comm-sell/: Land of Sloth (Kingdom of Belphegor)

Otiopag Orseiinak /ot-tio-pogg or-sin-ack/: Daemon(s)/ Demon(s) of Sloth

Ovoarslondoh /oh-voor-slon-doe/: Purgatory (Middle Realm)

Pashbab /posh-bob/: Lust Kingdom Torture Chamber

Priidzar /pry-idd-zar/: Camouflage (Human Form)

Rorvors Comselh /roar-voors comm-sell/: Land of Pride (Kingdom of Lucifer)

Rorvors Orseiinak /roar-voors or-sin-ack/: Daemon(s)/ Demon(s) of Pride

Saziamiin /soz-ee-a-meen/: Tattoos/Markings

Shigmir /shig-meer/: Teleport

Unphic Comselh /oon-fik comm-sell/: Land of Anger (Kingdom of Satan)

Unphic Orseiinak /oon-fik or-sin-ack/: Daemon(s)/Demon(s) of Anger

Zibiidor Comselh /zi-by-a-door comm-sell/: Land of Lust (Kingdom of Asmodeus)

Zibiidor Orseiinak /zi-by-a-door or-sin-ack/: Daemon(s)/Demon(s) of Lust

Zildar Tiantas /zill-darr tee-on-toss /: Wandering Beds

Zodinu River /zod-i-noo/: Burning River in Maelprog/Hell

"The hell in your soul will always find heaven in mine."
Jenim Dibie, The Calligraphy of God

Black Baby Booties

MISHKA
Portland, Oregon

This is it. The day my life changes.

Raindrops explode against the windshield in tune with the drumming of my heart. The anticipation for this moment has made me jittery all day. Jumping out of my car, I tuck the gift bag beneath my jacket to protect it from the elements. If I hadn't needed to finish the custom order at the doll shop, I probably would have been here hours ago.

I've been fantasizing about this for weeks, driving myself mad keeping it a secret. After tonight, though, I can tell anybody I want. My best friend, Leena, will likely have a few colorful words to say about me not clueing her in earlier, but it's only fair Harry hears it first.

Originally, I had planned to wait until this weekend, but last night, I finished crocheting the black baby booties I've been working on. There's no way I could make it till Saturday.

I'm truly hoping this will be what helps him see me as an adult instead of the 'teenage girlfriend' his colleagues tease him about. I'm far from a teenager. I just look young, and he's more than a decade my senior.

He won't be off work for a few hours, allowing me plenty of time to set the scene, and depending on what he has in his kitchen, maybe make dinner.

Standing on his porch, I use the housekey he gave me to unlock the door, dropping my purse and jacket on the glass entryway table. The scent of his linen plug-in air freshener is so intense, it irritates my nostrils.

I mentally run through the checklist of details that will make this night extra special. Lighting some of the candles he keeps in the closet for storms is a no brainer. I'll make sure my makeup looks nice and put on some of that pretentious classical music he likes.

While climbing the staircase, daydreaming about the out-come of the evening, I'm jolted from my planning by a *thud, thud, thud.* I freeze mid step, my pulse accelerating to the point my head becomes fuzzy. Is there someone upstairs? It's a fancy place, never anything out of order. It would be the perfect tar-get for a home invasion, and I know for certain the vault in Harry's room holds his grandmother's diamonds. Looking over my shoulder, I reprimand myself for leaving my phone on the table downstairs.

With the pace of a sloth, I creep to the top landing, try-ing my best to keep my steps silent. My hand wraps around the first thing I see, Harry's ugly Chimaera statue. I gently touch my fingers against the wood of his bedroom door, attempting to crack it open.

Should I be making an escape right now instead of searching for the source of the scary noise? I question if I'm acting like the dumb bitches in those horror movies Leena and I make fun of. What am I really going to do with this stupid statue anyway? As my internal voice continues to debate with itself, I get the door opened enough to see the source of the sound.

My body sways, and my mind fights to make sense of what I'm seeing. The scene in front of me filets my heart, causing it to fall dead at my feet. Bile burns my throat when I stare at Harry lifting and lowering his bare-naked ass, rutting himself into Nicolette, the coworker he swore to me was 'only a friend.'

Her fingers are tangled in his thick, red hair that I've always loved. "Oh, God! Don't you dare stop."

Rage and sorrow braid together in my gut, making me queasy. "Fucking asshole." My voice is a whisper yet apparently loud enough to have him whip his head in my direction, his green eyes widening at my presence.

Choking on my own sob, I drop the giftbag and the statue, spinning around to get away from both of them immediately.

With slurred words, he hollers behind me, "Mishka, wait! You don't understand!"

Tears make everything blurry, the acceptance of his betrayal erupting from my throat when I look at him. "What don't I understand, Harry?! Is she sick, and you're just checking her temperature with your dick?"

Light freckles sprinkle across his pale body, causing the memory of him laughing at me whenever I'd connect them with a pen to force its way to the surface. His erection, still shiny from Nicolette's arousal, bounces as he reaches toward me. He didn't even wear a condom.

His hand grasps my arm, but he just lost the right to ever touch me again. I jerk away from him, sprinting down the stairs. The sound of him yelling my name intensifies what has become familiar nausea. I wish I could mute his voice. Snatching my jacket and purse, I run out of the house into the wet, gray evening.

After fumbling with my keys, I start my car, peeling away from the home I thought would be mine one day. Tears fall faster than I'm able to dry them. I scream at the top of my lungs, cursing his name now that I'm alone.

How could he do this to me? Why didn't he break things off if he wasn't happy? And if he was, then why the hell did he cheat? I've never once denied him sexually. Half the time, I was the instigator.

I honestly don't understand what I did wrong. What could possibly have made him deceive me this way? I don—

Clouded lights flash across the car's windows. The world flips around me, my body slamming against something hard every couple of seconds as I'm weightlessly hurled through the air. Sharp pain shoots through my abdomen before an unbearably bright light blinks on and off across the backs of my eyelids. Sounds I can't decipher accost my ears as my disorientation seeps into darkness.

What is with the incessant beeping? I wish someone would make it stop. A chemical smell tickles my nose as panic consumes me, causing a layer of sweat to make my skin sticky.

Where the hell am I?

I hear a gasp before a hand squeezes mine, steadying my

breathing. Looking down, the tattoos on the inside of our forearms press together, hers of a baby blue rib cage against my own pink inked human heart. Leena's gotten more tattoos over the years, but the heart is my only one. We got them around the time we moved into our first apartment together. A heart is tender, and a rib cage is strong, but each are a necessity for the other.

Of course she's here. Her role ascends beyond that of a best friend. She's the only family I have.

"Jesus, girl. You sure know how to scare the shit out of someone." When our eyes meet, my tears garble her face. "You nearly died, you bitch! Do you..." She waves her hand around her head, attempting to coax out the words she wants to say. "How do you feel?"

From the sounds of the machines and the bed I'm lying in, it's obvious I'm in the hospital. Anxiety intermingles with heartbreak, making my question difficult to choke out. "The baby. Is the baby alright?"

She drops her head, and I don't need to hear her say it to know I'm not pregnant anymore. "Oh, Mimi. I can't believe you didn't tell me."

I rub my sore forehead, attempting to retrieve my memories, but all I can recall is the sound of Harry's pleasured moans as he fucked another woman. "Wh-what happened?"

She rests her head against mine, her blue and green locs falling in curtains around my face when she softly kisses my nose. Since she prefers the term 'locs' over 'dreadlocks' that's what I call them too. The stale smell of smoke from her cigarettes opens my throat allowing me to breathe. Unlike most people, I don't mind the aroma. Actually, since she's been a smoker for all the years I've known her, its familiarity has become a comfort.

"The hospital called me a few hours ago. All they told me

was that you had gotten into a nasty accident." Her bracelets *jingle* when she leans back to stretch her arms and release a yawn. I wonder what time it is? Looking toward the window reveals an ashen sky, raindrops pelting the glass. "I didn't know I was still your E.C. I thought for sure Harry would have that honor by now."

Letting out a slow breath, I tug on my fingers. "How did you find out? About the miscarriage, I mean."

She points her thumb over her shoulder, nodding toward the hall. "Not long after I got here, I overheard the loud-ass nurse mention it. That's when I called Harry to let him know what was going on. What happened with you two anyway? He's under the impression you don't want to see him."

Memories clog my brain. The very thought of saying it out loud has my stomach shriveling itself into a useless knot. Every time I close my eyes, all I see are visions of their naked bodies writhing against each other in the bed I thought only we shared. Another wave of grief threatens to suffocate me, so I cough in an attempt to prevent more sobs from escaping. "I went to his house to surprise him with…" My breath trembles with my heavy exhale. I can't even say it. "I found him having sex with Nicolette. From his work." Leena's jaw hangs open while her brown eyes stretch so wide beneath her false lashes they're bulging.

Scoffing, she throws her sea-colored hair over her shoulder, revealing fish-in-a-bag earrings. "That piece of regurgitated ass vomit." The colorful beads in her braids knock together when she shakes her head, pursing her shiny lips. "I swear to God, if I ever see him again, I'll cut off his pecker and feed it to his mother in a casserole."

I don't know how she does it, but even when I'm at my lowest, she still finds ways to make me laugh. "You're so eloquent."

She tilts her head with a sad smile. "I've got you. Always. Even if you don't want me to." My hands tremble as more tears trail down my cheeks. "I'm so sorry about the baby. I wish I would have known."

Struggling to sit up, my body screams in protest. "I wanted to tell Harry first."

She uses her fingers to comb through my fine, blonde hair, which feels terribly tangled. "I get it, I do." She stands to straighten her purple cropped jacket before leaning down to kiss my forehead. "Let me check on the ETA of your discharge from this depressing shit hole so we can get you home."

As she walks away, I whisper, "I thought he was going to propose soon."

Her shoulders fall as her knee-length heeled boots stomp across the hospital tiles to get back to my bed. "You're twenty-five, baby doll. You've got plenty of life left, which will be much better without that micro-dicked fecal stain. I promise."

Even amidst my inner torment, I smile. "You should really consider poetry."

Winking, she leaves me alone with the maddening beeps of the hospital machinery.

Lust the Lock

MISHKA

10 days later

My bed dips with added weight, yanking me out of my dream about being attacked by a bird. The rank smell of sage offends my senses when Leena claps her hands in my ear.

"Alright, my little vanilla glazed ho-nut. I've been cool about you hiding out in this room for too long now. It's time to get your pasty, smelly ass out of bed, and I mean that in the most loving way possible. You've had your moment to wallow in despair. Now it's time to remember you're a moth-erfuckin' queen, and Harry damn Hickinbottom is sure as hell not going to be the one to dethrone you." She theatri-cally shudders. "Can you imagine if you would have married that skid mark?" *Click-clacking* her acrylics with a grimace she adds, "Your name would have been 'Mishka Hickinbottom.'" I glare at her because she's clearly amusing herself. "Gross."

Groaning, I roll over so I can bury my face in my pillow. "Go away."

Shittles, our little, white sphynx kitten, jumps on the bed with us, biting at my hair. "Noooope!" Leena picks up the hairless cat before standing to her feet, but I'm not delusional enough to hope she's finished with me. "I gotta whole night planned. Wine, ice cream, a kickass playlist, and everything we need to manifest someone who can dick you down so hard, the only Harry that will matter anymore is Harry Styles."

Chilled air violates my bare legs, making me screech from the shock. "Give my blanket back, whore!"

Laughing, she wraps my green spiderweb comforter around herself and Shittles. "If you want it so bad, come get it." The bedspread hits me in the face when she spins on her heel, skipping into the hall. She's lucky she's my platonic soulmate, and I'm not much of a fighter, or I'd kick her ass.

I give in, lowering my feet to the blue shag rug. The front door slams shut, a telltale sign that Leena's taking a smoke break. Cursing her under my breath, I sniff myself, scowling at the odor. She's right. I am getting pretty ripe.

Walking over to the window, I move my sheer pink curtains aside to look at the clear night sky. The full moon hangs among the stars, appearing enormous tonight.

Once I'm clean from my shower, I pull on my pink, casket print shorts and crop top tank before walking down our hallway lined with framed artwork we've accumulated over the years. I still laugh to myself when I pass by the painting of Steve Buscemi's head on a cat body. Now that I'm free of multiple days' worth of grime, I feel more revitalized than I have in a while.

Passing through the beads dangling from the archway to the living room, my eyes find the candles flickering on every available flat surface and the wildflowers that adorn the floor in a giant circle, creating a five-pointed star in the center. For the last few months, Leena's been dabbling in witchcraft. She's determined to teach herself because the one and only seasoned witch she ever came across apparently needed, and I quote, 'anti-bitch lotion for her pompous ass.' I've even humored her a few times, letting her practice reading my tarot, but tonight, I'm hardly in the mood.

Personally, I've always been a sceptic about religion and folklore. I just can't make myself believe in things like magic and spells, creatures and deities, gods and fucking monsters.

Leena's locs drape over her right shoulder, her pink Starbucks Frappuccino earrings dangling by her jaw while she focuses on the pages of a book I've never seen before.

Without looking at me, she points to the RuPaul pillow positioned at the star's top point behind a candle. "Sit there."

I do as she instructs, grabbing the wine off the coffee table to drink straight from the bottle. "Have you seen how big the moon is tonight?"

I sit amongst all her ceremonial tools. There is shit everywhere. A goblet, a wand, bowls of herbs, a small cauldron, mortar and pestle, a notebook, and a glass jar of what appears to be cigarette ash.

"At least use a cup, peasant." She jerks her head toward the coffee mugs sitting on the table behind me. Picking up the jar of ash, she whispers words over it I can't understand. "And of course I did. It's a supermoon."

That must be why she picked tonight to do this, because of the moon. The book she's reading has no title. It looks so old and brittle, I'm surprised the pages aren't falling out. "When did you get that?"

Caressing its binding, she sets it in front of her on the floor. "A little over a week ago. There was a metaphysical shop in Salem going out of business. The owner died or something. It cost me an entire paycheck, but look at how badass this thing is."

Bobbing my head to Vize and Leony playing in the background, I watch Shittles batting at the flower petals while I drink my wine from my *Full of Anxie-Tea* mug. Leena holds out a notebook and a white feather quill, impatiently waiting for me to take them.

"Write down the qualities you want in a pound pal with this." She places an ornate goblet in front of me. "When it dries, rip it up, and drop the pieces into this jar of ash."

Gulping down the rest of the wine in my mug, I dip the quill inside the goblet. As I touch the tip of the nib to the paper, I almost drop it at the sight of thick, red liquid. Coagulated liquid. "Is this blood?!" I cringe, trying not to barf. "The literal fuck, Leena?!"

She waves me off. "Chill. It's yours."

Relief calms my shock for exactly half a second before what she said actually clicks. "Wait. It's my blood? How the hell did you get that?"

She bites her bright pink lip, smoothing out the fabric of her satin joggers. A telltale sign she knows she's done something questionable at best. "Don't be mad. You've been a wreck. When I bought the book, I got the idea, and…"

It dawns on me like a rock landing on my head. I think I'm going to be sick. "Oh my God! That's why you kept taking out the trash? For my pads?!" This is extreme even for her. I don't even want to know how she extracted the blood.

"I'm sorry! The spell requires blood, and everyone knows virgin blood is the best, so I figured miscarriage blood would be the closest we could get. It's not my fault your ho train left the station in middle school." Gritting my teeth, I remind myself her heart is in the right place. It's her mind that's completely insane. This is so messed up. "Not to mention, it's a sexual spell, so blood from your penis fly-trap is ideal."

Sometimes I want to strangle her with her own hair. "How about maybe telling me the truth next time?"

"You never would have gone for that."

Her being absolutely right isn't the point. "How did you keep it so … moist?"

"The fridge."

"That's fucking gross, Leena."

She waves her hand at the notebook. "Just make the list, okay?"

Hooking up right now is the last thing I'm worried about, so it takes me a minute to come up with anything. Gagging at the blood dripping from the quill, I write the first traits that come to mind.

1. Sense of humor

2. Low-key

3. Mischievous

4. Exotic accent

5. Bit of a dark side

I hand Leena my list before pouring more wine. She clicks her tongue. "You didn't write a single thing about looks." She grabs the feather quill and dips it into the goblet. "Specifics are important or else you'll be railing a four-foot, hairy hobbit."

She hands the list back to me, to which she added:

6. Tall

7. Sexy

8. Huge dick

I smirk, tossing the paper onto the floor to dry. "Okay... I'm pretty sure you put this," she shakes a bottle with yellowish, shimmery liquid inside, "on your temples and between your brows." After doing as she says, I watch her mix the herbs inside the mortar, sprinkling them into the jar of ash. "Alright, rip up your list. Once I put the candle in the jar, start dropping in the pieces and repeat after me. Got it?"

"Whatever. How long is this going to take?"

She squints at me. "Until it's done." Crossing her arms, she waits for me to finish shredding the paper. "You know, I'm doing this for you. A little gratitude wouldn't kill you."

Is she serious? She just made me write a hookup wish list in my own vagina blood. "Thank you, Leena."

Ignoring my sarcasm, she straightens with a smug smile. "Looky there. You're not dead." She lights a white candle to lower into the jar. "Ready?"

I nod, picking up one of the paper scraps.

"Say what I say while focusing on the flame, and you have to mean it, so at least try to make an effort." She works her hands and stretches her neck before chanting, "I implore the flame: guide him to me."

The paper falls into the jar, landing near the flame which makes its edges glow orange. "I implore the flame: guide him to me."

"Lust the lock, passion the key."

"Lust the lock, passion the key."

"From the deepest of depths to the highest of skies."

"From the deepest of depths to the highest of skies."

At some point, I become entranced by the candle, unable to look away if I wanted to. Watching each piece of paper being consumed by the burning tendrils is hypnotic.

"Answer the call from between my thighs."

Her ludicrous words snap me out of it. "Are you serious?"

"Shut up. I worked hard on this. Just say it."

I curse under my breath before continuing. "Answer the call from between my thighs."

Over and over, we chant the words, Leena's voice getting quieter each time. Even when she's gone silent, I repeat the words in my head.

I implore the flame: guide him to me.

Lust the lock, passion the key.

From the deepest of depths to the highest of skies.

Answer the call from between my thighs.

"Picture him in your mind's eye, and repeat the enchantment three more times," Leena instructs.

I close my eyes, attempting to conjure an image of my perfect man until I hear the *hiss* of the flame being extinguished. Opening them, I see Leena pouring the remaining drops of my blood into the jar, and I grimace.

"That's so disgusting."

Flipping me off, she stands to her feet. "Welp, that's it. Help me clean this shit up. Then we'll finish that bottle, get our chocolate chip cookie dough on, and binge *Sweet Tooth*."

We place everything in a box she calls her 'ritual chest' then wait for the candles to cool. As dumb as this was, it did make me feel better. If nothing else, it got my thoughts off Harry for a bit.

Once our living room is back to its normal hodgepodge of randomness, Leena sits next to me with the tub of ice cream and two spoons. Shittles settles between us while Leena twirls a blue loc around her finger with a dramatic sigh, her not so subtle signal she has something she wants to talk about.

I hand her a mug before tapping mine against it. "Cheers. Now spill it."

She shifts on the couch to face me, crisscrossing her legs, Shittles giving her the side-eye for moving. "Okay, so the night everything went down with you and Harry, I was with Tim." I waggle my eyebrows. She's been crushing on this guy since they met two months ago. Last I heard, they were only friends, mainly because she's hesitant about how he'll respond to finding out she's a trans woman. Which is understandable, especially considering how her own parents reacted. "Well, he finally made a move, but I freaked out the second he tried to kiss me. I like him so much. I wasn't ready for us to be over yet, you know? He kept trying to calm me down by hugging me and saying all this sweet shit."

"Well, he sounds like a decent guy." Shoving a spoonful of ice cream into my mouth, I moan at the chunk of cookie dough deliciousness.

"It was too much. I ended up blurting out that I'm trans." She sticks out her bottom lip in a pout, giving Shittles the head scratches she's *meowing* for.

"Wow," I say around another big bite.

It's clear she's frustrated from the way she scavenges for the biggest dough chunks. "Honestly, though? It went better than I ever expected. He said while he wasn't sure how to feel, he really likes me. By the end of the night, we ended up fooling around. It was amazing."

I shove her shoulder. I can't believe she's been holding this in. It must've been driving her crazy. Just more proof she's the perfect best friend.

"That's awesome. What's the problem?"

Her smile drips off her face when she stabs the ice cream with her spoon. "He's ghosting me. No texts, no calls, not even a PM. I'm past my self-respect quota based on how many times I've already messaged him."

This shit pisses me off. He could have simply walked away, but instead, he gave her false hope first. My fingers are twitching to call the asshole to tell him how much of a pussy he is. While I'll never fight with Leena over a guy, I'm always willing to go off on a guy for her.

For the next hour, I listen to her overanalyze every comment he made, every minor action, and every facial expression he had that night. By the time the bottle's empty and the ice cream remnants are melted, she's concluded he did her a favor by not calling her back.

Before she begins to talk herself back around to him being a sweet guy who's confused, I say, "It's his loss, baby girl."

She yawns, stretching her arms over her head. "I know you're right." Leaning forward to kiss me on the cheek, she hops off the couch with Shittles on her heels. "I'm gonna go to bed. Goodnight."

"Night."

The beaded curtain strings knock together as her and Shittles disappear into the hallway, leaving me alone with the cashed wine bottle and empty ice cream carton. For the first time since the accident, I check my phone, regretting it instantly. I knew I was probably unemployed after more than a week of no-call no-shows, and the last of the three emails from my boss confirms it. There are a few DMs from my now ex-coworkers asking me what's happening along with multiple texts from Harry, spinning some bullshit story. The truth is, I think I'm handling the miscarriage better than I am his infidelity. I can barely think about it without feeling sick with the urge to cry. I hate that I'm letting him do this to me. Torturing myself until my eyelids are too heavy to stay open, I finally shut the phone off.

I carry everything into the kitchen, putting the mugs in the dishwasher and tossing the empty ice cream carton in the trash. How am I so tired after sleeping for more than a week straight?

Rubbing my hands over my face, I turn around to go to my room. My stomach lurches up to my chest, yet it still takes a second to register that there's a hooded stranger with crossed arms leaning against the counter a mere few feet from me. As I open my mouth to scream, he lifts his head enough to show his devastatingly beautiful face wearing an impish grin.

Before a single sound can leave my lips, my skin pulsates with tingling waves that crawl down my arms and legs. I lose the ability to use my knees, forcing me to turn my back to him and grab the edge of the counter. Attempting to hold myself up, I involuntarily moan while tides of supreme ecstasy roll from between my legs. My hand slips, crashing a plate around my feet, but I can't seem to care. The prodigious pulsing continues for such an inordinate amount of time, I think I may pass out. It's an orgasm on LSD.

After what feels like an eternity, the frenzied vibrations begin to ebb, allowing my stiff fingers to release the counter. Somehow, I momentarily forgot about the man in the room with me.

Spinning around, I find him still standing there, wearing the same wicked smile. "You're welcome."

With darting glances, I search for something sharp. My mind finally catches up with the knowledge that I just had a spontaneous mega-orgasm in front of an intruder who may or may not be here to kill me. "Wh-what do you want?"

He scoffs, standing straight to reach his full, impressive height. "You called me, remember? I'm here to do whatever you desire."

I don't dare take my eyes off him while my hands continue fumbling behind me, nearly crying in relief when I wrap my fingers around the handle of a knife.

Seeing as I most certainly did not call him, he's clearly off his meds. I try my best to keep my voice soft in a desperate effort to placate him. "I think you're confused." Attempting subtlety, I take tiny steps toward the kitchen doorway.

His chuckle makes my nerves snap one by one. "I'm clearly not the one who's confused." With tattooed hands, he tugs on the sleeves of his black leather jacket, walking toward me. I hold the knife out between us, clueless if I have the guts to use it. Narrowing his dark eyes, he reaches up to lower his worn brown hood, revealing more ink scrawled up his neck in weird symbols. "That's not going to do shit to me, but you're more than welcome to have at it. Although, it would be a bit rude, seeing as, like I said, you fucking called me."

If my heart beats any harder, I'm going to blow chunks. "Please don't kill me."

His eyes narrow as if I insulted him. "Not allowed. Besides, I'd much rather fuck you."

The way he speaks is incredibly odd, with an accent I've never heard. My gaze falls to his strange pants. What appears to be different tones of distressed leather are fused together into a unique patchwork. It's also odd that his jacket looks brand new, yet the hood beneath it appears as weathered as his pants.

I shake the useless thoughts from my head, focusing back on the threat in front of me. His questionable fashion choices are not what I should be thinking about. If only I hadn't had so much wine. There's a psychopath a few feet away who could very possibly rape me or worse, and I can barely stand up straight.

The need to preserve my life overcomes any critical thinking I may possess. Taking less than a second to process my thoughts, I bolt out of the kitchen, sprinting for the front door. Right when I'm about to reach the handle, I run smack dab into his solid form before falling back on my ass. He doesn't even sway from the impact.

Tears wet my face in defeat. How on earth did he beat me here?

Dark, straight hair falls over his face as he crouches down to my level. My stare lifts to the two twisted braids above his left ear when his harsh voice commands eye contact. "You incited Maelprog flames with death blood, using the Ammalok Qew to call upon me by name. What could you have possibly expected to happen?"

The words I understand have my chest heaving. "L-Leena's spell? It worked?"

His unnerving laugh pushes me closer to the edge of my sanity while he stands, towering over me. "You clearly got enough right that I ended up here." His synthetic smile is tainted with a sneer. "What were you attempting to do, human?"

Human? Barely comprehending his question, I scramble to my feet. Even though a voice in the back of my mind whispers he's speaking truth, I can't accept it. This all has to be a stress-induced nightmare. "What are you?" I ask the question so quietly, I doubt he hears me until he winks.

"It'll be much more fun to show you."

I'm surely looking at him like he's unhinged when a huge grin stretches his face, revealing bright teeth and pointed canines. Covering my mouth to stop my scream, my insides lurch in horror. Symmetrical spots on his temples tear open into bloodless wounds with bones forcing their way out from his flesh. His tattoos burn away, only to be replaced with a glowing, orange substance moving across his olive skin as if alive. Thick, ivory horns with twisted threading that smooths out toward the tips now protrude from his forehead. He shrugs out of the black jacket, revealing a leather vest and the moving markings scrawled up his arms. A gust of heat hits my face, the scent of smoke burning my nostrils. Enormous, feathery slate wings spring from his back to stretch across my entryway. His gaze finally meets mine, the skin surrounding his solid white eyes, that have now lost their irises, has darkened as if a goth kid did his makeup.

It's impossible to take in the smallest of breaths. "You're … you're a … a …"

"A …a …" he mocks. "I am orseiinak. What you would call a daemon."

I can't prevent the manic laugh that tumbles out of my mouth. It's kind of comical, the way his head jerks back at my reaction. This is either an insanely vivid nightmare or he's not the one losing it. I am. It's much more likely that I'm seeing things than the lunacy of what's spewing from his sensual lips. With an unamused frown, he tilts his horned head, the glowing swirls reaching up to his jaw.

"I'm not sure what's so humorous."

I squeeze my eyes shut, murmuring to myself. "Demons don't exist. None of this is real." I repeat the mantra twice, breathing deeply each time. "One," inhale, "two," exhale, "three." Slowly peeking out of my right eye, I don't know whether to laugh or cry in reprieve when I find myself alone in the entryway.

"Hello?" I turn in a circle, making sure he's not silently

lurking somewhere. Dropping my head back, I push out a breath from my lungs.

My respite is short lived because I have no explanation for the delusion my brain just fabricated. I've never hallucinated without drugs before, and seeing people that aren't there is never a good sign. I've heard full moons can have a strange effect on people, but I've never bought into that. I am exhausted, though, and I have been since what happened with Harry. Maybe it simply boils down to my brain's reaction to trauma.

All I have the power to do is hope that's the case.

A Monumental Mess

Loch
Zibiidor Comselh, Maelprog

"Prince Loch?" Refusing to open my eyes, I attempt to disregard Murkus's incessant presence. I should flog him right now for disturbing me this early. "The King demands your assistance with the new arrivals." Last evening's bedmates shift next to me when I sit up to see the orseiinak slave standing in my doorway, assaulting my ears with his shrill voice. The chains on his wrists and ankles connect to his collar, *jingling* as he bows to me. He doesn't wait for me to request his elaboration. "A prison in Turkey was bombed moments ago, killing roughly four thousand. Over seven hundred souls have been assigned to Pashbab on top of the normal daily intake."

A smile spreads across my face despite the unwanted awakening. Every session I perform at the Pashbab cells, a torture chamber for those damned by their deplorable sins of lust, allows me to return the twisted perversion of pedophiles and rapists back on them in a fantastical game of immeasurable agony.

Climbing over sleeping princes and princesses, I toss on my necropants, made from the eternal flesh of execrated souls. I latch the buttons of my hide vest, sitting on the edge of my bed to buckle my ash-covered boots.

Semanedai's nude body scoots next to me, her teeth nipping at my shoulder. "Where are you going?" Brushing her dark curls off her shoulder, she arches her back, showcasing those superb tits of hers. I lean down to suck her dark nipple into my mouth. She's an Aldonitas orseiinak, a daemoness born of greed, notorious for being unfailingly insatiable in bed. Which is a large part of why she's been a reoccurring bedmate for so many decades.

Corlbin crawls across the bed to join Semanedai. "Stay with us, my prince." He's another favorite of mine, particularly for his incapability to be satisfied no matter how many times I make him come.

"Can't. I need to get to work. Father's orders."

Semanedai shifts up on her knees, grabbing my face to lick my cheek. "I hope I'll see you tonight."

Standing up, I slide two fingers inside her pussy to pull her body against mine. Her wetness coats my hand as Corlbin attempts to untie my pants. "You will. I want to see that thing you did with the crucifix again." She gives me a smoldering smirk while I remove my fingers to lick them. Reaching down to fondle the space between Corlbin's adorable ass cheeks, I wink at him. "Have this hole ready for me when I'm relieved of torment duty." He grins, combing his long, fair hair with his fingers. His attentions shift toward Semanedai who lies on her back, spreading her legs.

I bite my lip, watching his tongue flick at her clit, stepping out on my balcony before I become too aroused to be able to leave. Releasing my wings through the slats in my vest, I take the long way, flying alongside the twisted, black tourmaline castle. Ash falls from the inferno sky, raining down on my face until I reach the top level.

My father is Asmodeus, ruler of Maelprog's second circle, the Land of Lust. I'm lucky enough to have my living quarters located in the ninth highest wing of Zibiidor castle. The structure would be impossible by mortal standards. Six hundred and sixty-six levels with six hundred and sixty-six bed chambers on each floor. Residents are strictly limited to my father's descendants, their mothers, and our slaves. I'm far from the oldest of his children, however, my mother is revered as the queen of orseiinak, making me favorable amongst his offspring.

Arriving on the highest floor, I fly into the wide opening, absent of windows or obstacles, and retract my wings. As I walk through the obsidian pillars, flickering flames held in hematite sconces line the walls, illuminating my way. His insignia is everywhere in Zibiidor Comselh, but the one ablaze outside his office doors indicates he's inside. I've always thought it resembled a sideways trumpet with a pointed tail. Of course, I could simply shigmir, my ability to instantly travel between distances and appear directly in front of him, though, out of respect, I knock.

"I've been waiting for you, Loch."

Pushing open the marble doors, I cross the threshold, my footsteps echoing in the expansive room until I'm standing in front of his desk.

"I assume Murkus filled you in on the overflow?"

You'd think with his thousands of children, I would be obsolete to him. While he may not always be available to give me his time, he somehow makes up for it … one way or another.

"Yes, he did." Flames in iron bowls lick the air, their reflections flickering on the black pearl floor. I'm not able to make out who it is, since they're hidden beneath his desk, but I can see a head with short blond hair bobbing up and down in his lap. "Do you have an approximation of how many sessions I'll need to perform over the next few days? Just so I can plan my schedule."

He dips his pen, a sharpened baculum from a goat, into his inkwell. After a few moments of listening to it scratching on paper, he answers. "Expect about two to three hundred child molesters and approximately five hundred rapists." Dropping the pen on his desk, he places his hand on the blond, pushing down and making them gag. "You'll, of course, have many of your siblings to help you. If you require more, simply put in a request with one of the slaves." He drops his head back, growling with his release. When his body goes slack against his throne, he snaps his fingers, nonverbally ordering who I now recognize as my cousin, Biln, to crawl out from beneath the desk. He smiles at me, wiping his chin on the way to the door. My father waits until he disappears to ask, "Is there anything else?" Since I'm clearly being dismissed, I bow and close the doors before I shigmir out of his office.

"There's Mommy's pernicious boy." My mother emerges from the corridor, the blue jewels on her black onyx horns shimmering amongst her dark, curly hair. The train of her midnight dress drags across the shiny floor while Ors, her pet cronug, flies low to the ground behind her, flapping his membrane covered wings. The massive creature's long tongue sticks out of his hound-like head, wagging his reptilian tail.

She scrapes her long, black nails beneath my chin and gives me a kiss on the head. "How's your morning, wickedling?" I'm nearly one hundred thousand years old, yet at times, she still treats me as though I'm three hundred.

"It's starting earlier than I'd prefer."

She pouts, her hand gently caressing my horn. "You deserve a break. I'll talk to your father about giving you some time off after the Decennial Ball, okay?" Her nails tap together before she holds up her ring-laden finger. "When Lucifer and I return from vacationing in Ovoarslondoh, that is." I'll never understand why she enjoys the middle realm so much. The one time I went, I found it incredibly dull. "Speaking of the Decennial Ball, do you have a guest in mind?"

The Decennial Ball is nothing more than a giant scale pissing contest between my father and uncles. After about ten thousand of them, they've lost their appeal. "No. I haven't given it much thought."

Her smile reveals her fangs, the jewels of her horns glittering in the firelight. "Mammon's daughter, what's her name? Semanedai? She's quite vicious, and you two have been entertaining each other frequently the last few years."

Ors flies close enough that I'm able to pet the infernal beast across his large back. "I'll think about it." Kissing her on the cheek, I release my wings. "I need to get to work. I'll see you later."

She returns my affections, softly pressing her lips between my horns. "Of course, my dear."

I make my way to the edge of the massive opening, stepping off the ledge while forcing down my wings to propel me upward. Flying up near the flaming sky, I'm able to see all of Zibiidor Comselh along with the outskirts of Rorvors and Levithmong Comselh, the kingdoms ruled by my Uncles Lucifer and Beelzebub. Each kingdom has its own perks depending on what mood I'm in, but some of my fondest and wildest nights have been spent here, in the streets of Zibiidor Comselh.

Pashbab's gargantuan size is apparent from even this high up. The merlinite structure is home to hundreds of millions of souls and is the third largest torture hollow in Maelprog.

Once I arrive, I make my way to the meet hall where my brothers and sisters are receiving their location orders. It's forbidden to intermingle sexually during work hours unless it's part of a punishment session, so we mostly keep to ourselves while we're here. Cronugs roam between the iron cells, which is commonplace in every torture hollow. Ripping the immortal flesh from dead sinners is a favorite game of theirs.

My name is engraved across the marble plaque above my job files. Looking over the list of today's playfellows, I make my way to the first cell. It's impossible not to grin at the festivities another day of torment can bring.

I allow the heavy door to slam shut behind me when a woman shrieks. "Who are you?!" She's perfectly primed for my performance, upside down and naked with her legs spread.

Wrapping my hand around the blooming flower, I lift the heavy implement from the table. It's affectionately named for such a horrific device. It's larger than my forearm while closed, yet once I crank it open for dramatic effect, the razored segments are reminiscent of a flower in bloom. Simply imagining the possibilities has my cock straining in my trousers. For someone who abducted women off the streets so she and her husband could rape them and film it for profit, she's already showing quite the lack of tolerance. I wait for her screaming to subside before answering her question with a bow.

"I am Prince Loch. I'll be your source of insurmountable agony and incomprehensible persecution during your first day of eternity."

"Stop! PLEASE! You can't keep doing this!"

This is my thirty-fifth session today, but I wish it had been my first. This particular piece of shit was a psychiatrist for children during his time on Earth, using the vulnerability of his patients along with his position of power over them to brutally rape, molest, and manipulate the innocents in his care. Oddly enough, his love for his young daughter was pure.

Distorting his soul's eye, I force him to watch the illusion of his beloved child being violated with red-hot pokers and jagged daggers. Her nonexistent blood pools around his dirty feet, sticking to his toes as she's peeled apart, small pieces at a time. His screams have me stroking my erection over my pants, and although the scene is all fiction, the malevolent beauty of it is, he has no idea.

As I bend down to his level, I whisper my question in his Turkish tongue. "Remember Caria? The four-year-old you abused so viciously, she came close to dying from internal bleeding?"

"I'm serving seven years for that! I'm paying my dues for her!"

That humors me to the point of a smile. He hasn't even begun to suffer for his sins. His eyes can't leave my brother, Sephilen, raping and mutilating the mirage of his child, when in reality, he isn't doing anything besides stroking himself, waiting to assist me with anything I may need. It's amusing how long it sometimes takes the new arrivals to even comprehend they're dead.

"And Demir? The ten-year-old who killed himself because of what you did to him?"

"STOP! I'm … I'm so goddamn sorry! I … I don't know why I did it!" he coughs on his sobs, snot and spit dripping from his chin. "I couldn't control it. You just ... you have to STOP!"

Kneeling in front of him, I grin, tasting the sugary bliss of his suffering. Fucking antichrist, I love this shit. His belief that there will ever be an end to this is pathetically comical. "Are you not enjoying yourself?" I scoff in mock disbelief. "I thought this would bring back fond memories. This is what fills your balls with yearning, is it not?" His screams echo and bounce around the large cell. Here in Maelprog, the emotional distress of the damned is one in the same with their physical pain, each increasing the other fifty-fold.

Untying my pants, I release my erection, yanking him by his scalp to force myself down his throat. He chokes with bulging eyes while still staring at who he thinks is his child.

As if happening a few feet away, I watch his memory unfold. He sits with his daughter at a small table, laughing when she clips barrettes in his hair and paints his face with rouge. *Do you want some more tea, Daddy?* He smiles at her, holding up his cup. She pours the pot, though no liquid comes out. Even still, he acts as if it's delicious. *Thank you for playing with me. I love you, Daddy.*

"Daddy! Why won't you help me?! It hurts so badly! Please help me!" the imaginary girl bellows, bright red droplets dripping off her fingertips.

Every time he attempts to pull back, I thrust harder, the chair of thorns puncturing deeper into his immortal flesh. He screams around my cock until his jaw goes slack. Eventually, his mouth becomes monotonous, so I pull out to cover his tear-stained face with my semen.

"Daddy! Please, make him stop!"

I nod to Sephilen who is fondling the genital fileting implement, leaving him to finish off our prisoner's first day.

Stepping out into the hall, I scratch one of the cronugs

under the chin when he licks my face. The door to the cell holding the next soul I'm scheduled to disembowel squeals from lack of maintenance. The moment I step inside the room, I'm brought to my knees by a high-pitched shrieking I can only assume means one thing.

Screech! Screech!

"Ah!" Blaring soundwaves attack my ears and consume my brain, threatening to bring me into a fetal position. My vision blurs while bile burns my insides. Is this seriously happening? Of all the orseiinak in Maelprog ... fuck!

The overbearing agony in my head makes it impossible to even shigmir. I clench my fists, compelling my strained wings to carry me alongside the fire rise, the burning stream that flows upward from the Zodinu River into the flaming gates above.

The longer it takes me to answer the call, the worse the symptoms will become. I can barely keep myself upright with how dizzy I am. My cousin Rendia, a guard of the gates, looks at me with an arched brow. "What's the matter with you?"

I press my palms against my eyes, attempting to alleviate the anguish in my head. "A summoning." Even speaking is excruciating. "Inform my ... father ... will you?"

She slaps my back, just about making me pass out. "Sure, I'll tell him when I get off my shift. Have fun."

The burning ceiling opens wide like the mouth of a beast as Rendia's booted foot lands against my back, kicking me out of Maelprog. I claw my hands down my face as I spin and fall through Drilpa Nalvage.

The very moment I cross into the mortal world, the squealing in my ears dissipates. My vision clears, and just as I exhale in relief, shivers roll across my skin from the wretched cold atmosphere of this realm. I pull up my bransg, shielding me from the eyes of mortals. It takes a moment to get used to, considering I haven't used it since I was a young orseiinak learning to control my abilities.

I lift my head toward the neon sign with a white stag right above my head.

Portland

Oregon

Old Town

This place doesn't look old. I wonder how different it is from the new town. Whoever called me is southeast of here. An invisible string tugs at my chest, guiding me toward my summoner. This is undoubtedly the work of the Ammalok Qew. That abomination of a book shouldn't have existed in the first place. I've never personally been unfortunate enough to be subjected to the human realm before, though through the memories of the damned souls I've watched the evolution of Earth over time.

Until I know exactly where I'm going, I'll have to follow the pull between my ribs. Buildings made of brick and metal line the paved street. I can't believe my luck when I pass one that houses clothing. I shigmir inside, searching for something to warm me in this freezing realm. Mortal garments seem to become more hideous with time, so I'm grateful to find a black overcoat that will work once I fashion holes for my wings to slide through.

The sun has traveled to another side of the globe. I should be shrouded in darkness, but the electric lights illuminate my way as I continue following the unseen rope across a steel bridge. Pulling my hood up around my face, I keep turning onto different streets until I sense the femininity of my summoner's essence. The yanking sensation in my chest dissolves the moment my feet step onto the unkempt grass in front of a modern cottage. Climbing up the steps, I peer inside an open window to see the back of a woman. She's standing in what

I assume is her cooking quarters, her wavy blonde hair falling past her shoulders. My eyes trail down to her ass, visualizing what it would look like outside of those short trousers she has on. She's clearly who called me. Inhaling the freezing air, I close my eyes. When they open again, I'm standing right behind her.

Less than two seconds after lowering my bransg, she turns around. Her eyelids stretch around golden irises, the sourness of her shock dancing on my tongue.

Instead of introducing myself verbally, I give her a sample of the pleasure she has awaiting her. Forcing accelerated stimulation across the nerve endings of her clitoris, I compel pressure against the walls of her pussy and the entrance of her ass while manipulating her nipples all simultaneously. Her response is almost instantaneous and quite erotic to watch.

If this is the view I'm going to have during my time here, then the mortal realm may not be so bad.

This isn't making any sense. How can this be the human who called me here? It has to be her, it's simply impossible it's anyone else. There's a part of me that hopes this isn't some sort of cosmic misunderstanding because I'm quite looking forward to dipping the wick into a mortal. It's been a bit of a fantasy of mine to experience laying with one of the temporary creatures, however, I assumed I'd be much more welcomed. I was invited here, yet she's acting as if I'm infiltrating her home.

Demon. The word is plucked from her brain, settling in mine. With clenched fists, she stands with her eyes closed, counting to herself for whatever ridiculous reason. Even if I couldn't smell or taste it, the tension of her body and shakiness of her breath makes it clear she's utterly terrified. Not knowing what I'm supposed to do, I lift my bransg back in place. This is nothing close to the summoning stories I was told growing up.

The tartness of her relief sticks to the back of my throat when she opens her eyes, believing her little whispering fit sent me away. She's still apprehensive, though, which is a refreshing palate cleanser.

"Hello?"

Unamused, I watch her search for me, half tempted to reveal only my voice so I can get another taste of her fear. I can't read her mind per se, but I am able to understand main thoughts and intentions, sometimes picking up a few words. *Sleep.* She must be planning to go to her bed chamber. Staring at her little ass cheeks peeking out from the bottom of her bloomers, I follow her while she flips switches, causing darkness to consume the house. I don't mind it, I can see perfectly fine in the dark. It's humans who don't have the best vision in the absence of light, so it's odd she would minimize her sight while she's still so anxious.

She eventually grabs a thick, mint duvet off the back of the couch, carrying it to a nauseatingly colorful room with pink furniture and twinkly lights strung up everywhere. Tossing the blanket onto her bed, she crawls beneath it, reaching up to turn off the lamp sitting on a small table. While the moonlight settles across her room, I scrape my tongue over the point of my fangs, watching her rock her body from side to side before eventually drifting off to sleep.

I climb on her bed to observe her. It's strange how humans are still in a form of consciousness during rest, which is what allows them to dream. The nostrils of her little upturned nose flare each time she exhales, her pouty lips slightly parted. Running my finger down her soft, ivory arm, I inhale her strawberry scent and consider making her come again whilst she sleeps. Instead, I choose to explore her home, hoping to obtain some answers as to why I'm here.

Since I've arrived, I've sensed another feminine life force in the home, informing me I'm not alone with this mortal. Walking down a hallway of bizarre images, I follow the other human's essence to a door. Behind it sleeps a beauty with colorful hair and rich brown skin. Maybe I'll also get the chance to become acquainted with her body. I lean down to smell her when a white feline arches her back at my presence.

I bare my fangs to the creature, backing out of the room and into the hall, stopping in front of a tapestry hanging on the wall. It's a needlepoint image of a cottage that reads, *There's some whores in this house*. Considering my encounter with the pale haired girl earlier, that seems inaccurate.

Once I return to the cooking quarters, I sniff at anything that might be edible. I, of course, don't require human food, though, some of it can be quite pleasurable to ingest. The table has papers sitting in a stack, and reading through them tells me nothing of import, but I do find a little box of what humans call cigarettes. Occasionally, I'll be able to find them in Levithmong Comselh, the Land of Gluttony, and I quite enjoy them. Pulling enough heat from my finger to ignite a small flame, I light it, breathing in the smoke. I'll need to be sure to acquire more of these during my time here.

The end of the smoking stick illuminates orange as I tilt my head to examine a photograph of my summoner and the other woman stuck to the giant box humans call a re-fridge-rator. I pull it off, turning it over to read the words on the back. *Mishka & Leena 2013 BF 4-EVER*. She mentioned Leena being the one whose spell they used earlier, so my summoner's name must be Mishka.

"Mishka." I say it out loud to feel it on my tongue. It's an odd name for someone residing in this part of the Earth. In

Russian it means 'bear cub.' I open the cold box, mistakenly snapping the handle off in the process. Shit. I forgot Earth has this effect on our strength. Since I'm unable to reattach it, I leave the handle on the counter. The cigarette has burned down to the stub, so I drop it into the hole at the bottom of the washbasin, lighting another before continuing my search.

Moving on to the sitting room, I notice a tele-vision. I don't fully understand the purpose they serve. From what I've gathered, humans simply stare at them. When I turn around, my eyes attach to a leather-bound book lying on the table. The Ammalok Qew. The desire to touch it is overwhelming, yet once I do, my fingertips are stabbed with sharp pinpricks, making it impossible to maintain hold of it. I try one more time with the same result. Now, of course, I'm even more de-termined to see exactly what's inside.

Careful to put everything back in its previous location and not break anything else, I search each room in the house until I find tools appropriate for the task. I eventually come across a set of plastic prongs in the cooking quarters and a pair of metal tweezers in the washroom. When the cigarette goes out, I close the remnants in my fist, using the heat of my flames to burn it to ash and wipe the residue on my trousers.

Kneeling in front of the book, I utilize the prongs to open the cover. The Book of Seven is an atrocity that's very exis-tence is offensive to orseiinak. About twelve hundred years ago, my distant cousin, Therveris, born from the offspring of Leviathan and Mammon, came to Earth as a gatherer, one who accumulates the blood of Earth animals. During his time here, he fell in love with a human man. He traveled inside his dreams, whispering the antiprayers for summoning an orseiinak from each of the seven families. The basic require-ments are all in the book along with variations depending on the desired outcome. Our Enochian tongue is translated to perfection along with sketches of each of my uncle's sigils drawn in exact detail. Since it's impossible to summon a murifri, only those born in Maelprog are at risk of being called. It's been so long since any of us were summoned, I had all but assumed the book had been destroyed.

Using the tweezers, I turn to the section specified for my father's descendants. A stark white piece of paper, much newer and sturdier than the other pages, sticks out from the gutter of the book.

As I read the antiprayer that brought me here, I don't know whether to laugh or be appalled. They didn't even spell my name right.

It isn't until I reach the back pages that I learn Therveris's lover kept the Ammalok Qew contained to his bloodline, passing it on to a chosen family member of each generation. According to the notes inscribed in the margins, approximately three hundred years ago, one of the chosen family members proclaimed the use of the book to be forbidden. From that day forth, whoever was in possession of Ammalok Qew was beholden to keep it protected and hidden. It appears the last person to take on the responsibility signed the book over forty years ago, so how did it come into the custody of these mortal women?

However they got their hands on it, it's clear they had no intention of pulling me from Maelprog, meaning my forced relocation was unintentional.

Unholy fuck. This is a monumental mess.

Demon Dickhead

Mishka

The aroma of brewed coffee is a powerful motivator to get the day started. I stretch my arms over my head, my eyes flying open when the memories from last night slam into my brain like a hammer to the skull. In a fit of paranoia, I toss off the blankets, jumping up to examine every inch of my room. I look under the bed and in the closet, even opening my drawers as if the six foot plus demon from my nightmares could be hiding in my Ikea dresser. The whole thing just felt so damn vivid, I'm having a hard time shaking it. Embarrassed for myself, I stare out my window, slipping on my short, pink robe with the white clouds on it. At least it's a pretty day today.

Leena's sitting at the table in her green bonnet, practicing her tarot when I walk in the kitchen. "Morning, hooker," I chime, realizing I'm in an oddly decent mood today. I haven't felt this normal since the Harry incident.

"Morning, skankylosaurus."

With a snort, I reach for my mug, realizing the room smells of cigarette smoke. I know she knows better. "Did you smoke in here?"

Tossing back her locs, she narrows her eyes. "No cigarette is worth your bitching. I was actually going to ask you about it because I could have sworn I had more in the pack last night." Prickles bounce across my skin like my whole body has fallen asleep when she adds, "And what happened to the fridge?"

My heart doubles in speed before it feels like it stops all together. The handle has been completely pulled off from the door and now sits dauntingly on the counter. While I despise lying, especially to my best friend, I also don't want to hint toward the possibility that I'm losing my grip on reality.

"Oh, yeah, it popped off last night."

She reaches out to scratch Shittles's head when the cat jumps on the table. "That's weird. It wasn't even loose. Oh well, I'm sure I can re-screw it in."

My body flashes hot upon realizing Shittles is batting at a black feather laying on the stacks of bills. Shit, shit, shit. I point to it, my voice raising an octave. "Where did you get that?"

Resting her hand on her fist, she presses her lips together, obviously questioning my mental state. "In the entryway. I thought it was pretty. I've never seen a feather like this. The strands will usually separate." She takes it from the kitten to hold it up. "This is one solid piece."

My brain spins so fast, it makes me woozy, each breath more difficult to take. Swallowing another drink of my coffee, I count to ten in my head.

"Your friend has a nice cock." The steaming liquid goes down the wrong pipe from my attempt to gasp with a full mouth.

No. No, no. This isn't happening.

Slowly shifting my gaze down to the apparent demon from last night, I find him sitting under the table peeking up Leena's skirt. With a quirked eyebrow, he adds, "Do you ever let her..." He makes a *clop* sound with his mouth, disturbingly mimicking sex by sticking his finger into the hole of his fist.

I quickly turn to my oblivious friend who stares at me with blinking eyes. "Are you okay?" My intestines perform acrobats in my gut as my freshly swallowed coffee threatens to jump up my throat.

She doesn't hear him, and she doesn't see him. I really am going crazy.

The imaginary creature fabricated by my apparent psychosis vanishes from under the table only to reappear on top of it. The long, dark hair on the top of his head falls into his deep brown eyes, and he grimaces while sniffing at Leena's coffee.

"She can't see or hear me because I don't want her to. I'm not in your head." The symbolic swirls on his arms look like normal tattoos this morning, and I keep staring at them, waiting for them to glow the same way they did before.

"I'm fine," I respond to Leena. "I think I just went to bed too late last night."

"You wanna go to Spellbound Woodland for brunch? My treat. I've been dying to go since it opened."

My eyes are straining from how hard I'm trying to focus on Leena instead of looking at the man who only I can see. "Um, yeah, sure."

"What's on your agenda today anyway?" It's a struggle to listen to what she's saying, but she doesn't give me a chance to answer when she adds, "Because you need to find another job soon. And who knows? Maybe that's how you'll meet a guy?" Her phone *pings*, and she laughs at whatever it is, waving her manicured hand. "It's not like he's going to pop up out of thin air. That's not how the incantation works." I clear my throat as the man who may or may not exist pokes at Shittles. She hisses at him, and he hisses right back, sending her scurrying from the kitchen. "Crazy-ass cat."

"Do you want to whip out the Ouija board really quick?" I suggest. At this point, I'm willing to try anything to convince myself I'm not mental.

Leena slams her phone on the table, sitting up straight to stare at me with slitted eyes. "Okay, what is up with you today?"

It takes all my willpower to not make eye contact with the man sitting on the table. "Nothing. I … I've been feeling a bit … off since last night."

With an eyeroll and a dramatic exhale, she stands up to walk into the living room. "Fine, but then you have to stop being such a freak."

Following behind her, I glance over my shoulder to see an empty kitchen. She digs in the closet for the board, and when I cross into the living room, I have to clasp both hands over my mouth so I don't scream. The oddly normal looking demon is perched up on the hot pink, baroque throne chair Leena had to have yet won't ever let anyone sit in.

"Hey, where did this come from?" I force my eyes from his to see what she's talking about. In her hand is the leather jacket he had on last night.

The skin across my chest tightens with panic. My brain doesn't process under pressure. "Uh … maybe Harry left it here?"

She pokes out her bottom lip. "That doesn't seem ugly enough for him."

My laugh comes out choppy and unnatural as she sets the board on the coffee table next to the spell book from last night. Jumping off the chair to kneel opposite of us, the demon gestures to the Ouija, his eyes narrowed into slits, lacking amusement. "You can't be serious about this."

Leena places her fingers on the planchette, and I do the same, trying not to make eye contact with the man staring at me. "Alright, what do you want to know?"

Closing my eyes, mainly to calm my nerves, I ask, "Who is here?"

The second I feel the planchette being yanked across the board, my eyes fly open to see him pulling on the tip, bringing it to the *F*. My hands are clammy from how hard my heart is beating. He's going to tell me his name.

U. C. K. O. F. F.

Leena growls, standing up in a huff while he smirks at me from across the table. "I should have known. You never take this shit seriously." She storms off before stomping right back to move the planchette over the 'Goodbye.' "Just in case you're not screwing with me."

I consider telling her I didn't move it, but she would either not believe me or spend the next three months trying to rid the house of spirits.

"I'm gonna go shower and bathe Shittles. Let me know when you're ready to go," she snaps.

Once I hear the bathroom door close, I stare straight at the source of my sudden onset insanity. I speak softly, not wanting to alert Leena about my brittle mental state. "Shittles … she saw you. And Leena saw the planchette move."

He stands to his feet, evaluating my living room. "Animals have senses humans don't. My bransg doesn't work on them."

I shake my head because I'm barely able to understand a word he's saying. "Your what?" At least he's less scary in the daylight. Even the darkness around his eyes is gone.

"My bransg. It hides me from mortal eyes and ears."

This is all too much. I can't be buying this, but ... Leena saw the planchette move. Lacing my fingers, I inhale through my nose and exhale out of my mouth. "What is it you want?"

He rolls his neck, holding his hands out as if he's fighting the urge to choke me with them. "I'm going to speak incredibly slow so you can understand." Although he's being a bit of a condescending prick, he's not completely wrong that I'm struggling to comprehend this. "You. Summoned. Me. Okay? I saw your antiprayer. You know why you called me here. Even if it wasn't exactly me you were expecting. So when are we doing this?"

While he may appear normal right now, I keep getting flashes of his horns, the glowing marks ... the wings. My mind has picked the worst time to stop functioning. "D— doing what?"

He lets out a huff clearly packed with irritability. "You're a bit of a dense bitch, aren't you? Ground your corn, play rumpskuttle, poke the squid ... how many ways do you want me to say it?"

I don't know how to react to that, so being the awkward person I am, I laugh from the nervousness of being in over my head. "Look. This is clearly a misunderstanding. So I, um, I release you."

He clicks his teeth, standing closer to me than I'm comfortable with. "That's not how this works. I have to fulfill the terms of the summons before I can leave." With a lopsided grin, he crosses his arms. "Believe me, I'm more than qualified for the position."

On his last word, I almost lose the strength to sit upright.

My body tenses yet trembles with overstimulation. I can feel every muscle in my pussy pulsing with each crash of the orgasm. I hate hearing the sounds of gasping falling from my lips.

"See? And I promise you, little mortal, it'll be magnitudes better once I'm sliding inside of you."

As I catch my breath and regain my bearings, anger at my lack of control consumes my trepidation. He has no right to manipulate me or my body that way. "Stop. Doing that. Haven't you heard of consent, you asshole?"

He shrugs with an infuriating display of misogyny. "You called me by name. That's all the consent I need."

My eyes widen at his audacity. Attempting to keep my voice down, I speak through gritted teeth. "I don't even know your name."

Bowing like we're living in fourteen thirty-six, he says, "I am Loch. Son of Asmodeus, King of Zibiidor Comselh."

There are only a few words I recognize in that sentence, so I focus on what I can comprehend. "Loch? I…" My memory suddenly betrays me. That stupid spell. *Lust the lock, passion the key.* "Oh, fuck me…"

He rubs his hands together before his fingers begin to unfasten his hooded vest. "Now you get it."

Pointing a finger at him, I clench my jaw. "No, that wasn't what I meant. Stop!"

"Listen, tin nanba. I'm stuck here until we do this, and I'm immortal, so I have much more time than you do."

I massage my temples because he somehow went from terrifying to incredibly irritating in less than five minutes. "Okay. I don't understand half the words coming out of your mouth. Can you tell me, in plain English, how I reverse this?"

"You can't. However, since we're on the subject of bringing me here," he points his thumb over his shoulder toward our paint chipped coffee table, "how did two clueless humans come to possess the Ammalok Qew?"

"Are you talking about the spell book?" He nods as if he isn't speaking gibberish. "Leena bought it. Can we use that to send you back?"

"Unfortunately, no."

I don't know how to respond to any of this. What I do know is that he isn't staying here. "I truly am sorry you can't get home, but we," I gesture between us for clarity, "are not doing … *that*." Not to mention, I'm still having a difficult time accepting he's here in the first place. "And I'm gonna need you to find somewhere else to go until the spell wears off."

"That's not possible. It won't wear off until you're dead or the terms have been met. Then there's the troublesome issue that we now have a bond, so if I'm away from you for too long, I'll get ill."

Leena starts slamming cabinet doors, signaling she's out of the shower. "How long is 'too long' exactly?"

He bobs his head from side to side. "About twelve hours. Give or take."

"Twelve hours?!" I drop my voice to a whisper because that was loud enough for Leena to hear. "Are you serious?"

"Of course, I'm serious. I don't lie."

He's got to be full of shit. "You're telling me you're a demon, from Hell I'm assuming, and you don't lie?"

"That's more of a murifri trait."

I'm having a hard time keeping up as it is, and he keeps using these cracked out words. "And that would be?"

He looks thoughtful for a moment before recognition consumes his expression, and he snaps his fingers. "Angels. You call them angels."

Great. Now angels are apparently real too. Leena is going to be out here soon, and the last thing I need is for her to hear me talking to what will appear to be myself. "Right … well that's plenty of time for me to go to brunch, so stay invisible, and …" I huff, combing my hair away from my face with my fingers, "I don't know, do whatever it is you do."

Turning my back to him, I walk toward the bathroom when I hear his voice behind me. "What's a brunch?"

"Something you're not going to."

I slam the door in his face, and once I'm finally alone, I stare at my reflection in the mirror. If I choose to believe the massive amount of ridiculous information he just dumped on me, then I have no idea what I'm going to do.

I think I need a priest.

Miniature Mortal

Loch

I n all my millenniums, I've never encountered a situation
comparable to this one, and Mishka, my summoner, is a
bit of a bitch. Even if she is pulchritudinous.

Keeping my bransg in place gives me the opportunity to
observe her without her knowledge, granting her the illusion
of solitude. She's wrapped in a towel, flipping through her
colorful wardrobe, when I notice the scars on her back. It's a
shame for such pretty skin to have been blemished. Before
thinking better of it, I reach out to touch them, making myself visible to her.

"What happened here?"

She screams, jumping as she drops her towel. I don't get

a long look, but what I do see is impeccable. I can't wait to smell the little blonde bush between her thighs.

Scrambling to cover herself, her eyes dart from my horns to my wings. "What the hell are you doing?"

"What happened to your back?"

His touch. Hot. Her chest rises and falls rapidly. I must have caught her off guard because confusion flashes across her mind. "Shitty foster parents." Her gaze drops to my hands when she asks, "Why did you look normal earlier but now…"

"Because I'm not currently wearing my priidzar." Her cluelessness is apparent, so I translate. "My human camouflage."

"Well, can you put it back on and get out?"

I have no intention of leaving, but there's no reason for her to know that. Once she believes I'm gone, she drapes her towel over the back of a pink and white striped chair, causing me to nearly salivate at her pert ass cheeks. Covering them with green sparkly undergarments, she slips into a black blouse with a pink collar. The short sleeves allow me to see the pink anatomical heart inked on the inside of her forearm that I hadn't noticed until now. After putting on a pale blue short skirt with suspenders, she paints her face with rouge and colorful powders.

She said I wasn't invited to whatever a 'brunch' is, so it's a good thing I don't give a shit about what she says. While she finishes with the curls of her hair, I put on the black overcoat I acquired last night.

"Hey, are you ready?" the woman named Leena calls from somewhere in the home.

Mishka's lacing up her black boots as she hollers, "Yeah. I'll meet you outside."

Following her out the front door where Leena sits in a tiny green vehicle, I shigmir to the back seat and the car comes alive. The music they play is drowned out by their off-key

47

singing. I wish I had the ability to turn off my hearing the same way I can shield theirs.

Within a few minutes, Leena stops the vehicle, granting me reprieve from their torturous racket. I follow them into a building attempting to mimic a castle but doing a terrible job of it. *Spellbound Woodland* is written on a sign above the large wooden doors of the entrance.

We are immediately met by a woman, who I think is meant to be dressed in garments from the thirteenth century. However, if authenticity is what she's going for, she missed the mark by a great deal. Leena covers her mouth in complete awe of this ghastliness.

"Welcometh ye weary travelers. Wouldst thee pref'r a table'r a booth?"

What mutilated syntax is that supposed to be? I notice that she isn't the only one in historically inaccurate clothing either. It seems everyone besides the patrons are dressed in a similar fashion.

"Can we sit by the waterfall?" Mishka asks.

"Well, of course. Followeth me, ye lovely lasses."

I don't know how long I can listen to this. I trail behind the girls, looking at the walls painted to seem as if we're standing in the middle of a thick forest. Deer, rabbits, birds, and a mix of other rodents are not only depicted among the giant mural of trees, but there are also stuffed ones sprinkled between the plastic foliage and scattered around the square wooden tables. The floor appears to be made of cobblestone, yet it's smooth, meaning it's also synthetic.

The woman leads them to a table in front of an actual waterfall, probably the only authentic thing in this place, before laying a plastic bill of fare in front of each of them.

"Thy server shall beeth with thee sooneth."

I perch myself on the edge of the table, watching Leena

ogle the offensive décor, "This place is better than I imagined." Clearly the girl's taste leaves a lot to be desired if this is better than she imagined.

Mishka's pretty pink lips, which I should have already felt around my cock at least twice by now, lift into a smile when a man, or a large child—it's not easy to tell human ages—greets them. "Hail lasses. My nameth is Jordan. What can I bringeth thee to drinketh?"

His gaze lingers on Mishka longer than it should, even while Leena orders her ale. *Nice tits.* Everything I pull from his thoughts centers around his attraction to her. The second he walks away to give them time to choose their food, Leena's mouth spreads open wide. Tiny guillotines dangle from her earlobes as she leans toward Mishka. "He was totally checking you out."

Even though it's mild, I can taste Mishka's flattery, and it makes me want to gag. I'm not jealous of the mortal boy, I don't experience jealousy, but how dare she consider a suitor while I'm stuck here waiting for her to allow me between her legs?

Moments later, the boy returns with a plate of bread, smiling at her. The taste of lust is usually delicious, yet coming from this rodent, I wish I could spit it out.

"Art thee lasses content to order?"

Mishka points to the list of food. "What's better? The fish or the fowl?" He leans down to look, close enough to touch her shoulder. As if he doesn't know what the damn restaurant serves. The pink of her cheeks and quickening of her pulse irk me. Whether she wants to be or not, she's technically mine until my duty has been fulfilled.

I think it's time I remind her of that.

Forcing the stimulation of her every erotogenic nerve, I orchestrate her body like a harp. Her arms tremble, and her eyes roll back in their sockets. Not only are humans much more sensitive than daemons, if they're anything like Mishka, they're also exponentially more entertaining.

I can see on her face the exact moment she realizes I'm here. *Loch.* My own name is loud in my mind. She grips the edge of the table, the earthy ambrosia of her fury and bliss are intoxicating on my tongue.

She really is an arousing creature. She attempts to conceal her gasps, yet eventually, the overwhelming frenzy I'm giving her is too much, and she releases what is possibly one of the sexiest moans I've ever heard.

Jordan's eyes widen, and there may even be some tenting in his trousers. I can't really blame the fool. It is quite mesmerizing to watch. The other people eating at their tables turn to stare at her, almost making me feel bad when the spiciness of her humiliation coats my throat. Leena's green eyebrows rise at her friend's show of pleasure before Mishka breathes heavily, casting her gaze to the counterfeit cobblestone. One thing I'm reading very clearly is she's furious. *Fucking Loch.* Apparently, with me.

Brushing the stray hairs from her face with a shaky hand, she's still breathless when she says, "I need to use the bathroom. I'll be right back."

As she shoots to her feet, Jordan stumbles through his absurd lingo. "Th-the chamber pots are uh … back there."

She scurries across the establishment so fast she's borderline sprinting. I shigmir to the washroom, waiting for her on the sink counter painted to mimic meadow grass. She storms in with such vigor that the wooden door bangs against the wall. Her livid mumbling makes my cock throb as I watch her peek beneath the stalls.

Seemingly satisfied that they're empty, she spins around, screaming at the ceiling. "Loch! Show your stupid demon face right now, you son of a bitch!"

Her attempt at an insult is amusing, so I'm grinning when I show myself wearing my priidzar. "She definitely can be."

She stomps over to me, using both hands to hit my chest, proving to be much less strong than she is feisty. Her caramel eyes are alight with her anger, making them brighter. "You're such a goddamn bastard! Do you know how mortified I am?!"

I cross my arms. "You don't get to throw yourself at human men while I'm still here, biding my time. For you."

Asshole. Her eyes narrow with her laugh, although it doesn't seem to be because she finds this funny. Her offense tastes so exemplary, I lick it off my lips.

"You know what, you piece of shit? Do whatever you want. You can stay on Earth until I die for all I give a fuck."

Sticking up both of her middle fingers, she storms past me, once again slamming the door. Fucking antichrist, humans are melodramatic. It was only an orgasm.

Since Mishka is in such a tizzy and this will hopefully be my last visit to this realm, I make the decision to explore what fun I can get myself in to.

Even though Mishka and her friend have their own home, there are many humans who appear to live in cloth houses or have no shelter at all. They're dirty, tired, and reek of hopelessness. If I've learned anything from seeing the worst of mortal souls, it's that desperation can create violence, and I could go for some violence right now. The best way to find it is to sniff it out. Mortal feelings give off distinct aromas. The problem is, with so many humans grouped together in the same area, it's hard to pinpoint exactly where each scent is coming from.

Finally, I catch the cinnamon scent I'm searching for. Zipping up my jacket in an attempt to shield me from the cold air, I'm led to a large building much more unkempt than Mishka's. Missing bricks, broken windows, and cracked concrete gives it a dilapidated facade. I've wandered farther from her than is comfortable, the invisible string causing an unpleasant prick in my chest. Just when I consider giving up to go back to her, I hear it. The enraged voice of a man immediately followed by petrified screams.

As I walk inside the structure, the *crash* of objects being broken becomes more distinct the farther I go. The hallway is lined with doors, not terribly different from the cells at home. The stronger the smells of ire and terror become, the louder the noises are.

What stops me mid stride is a cry clearly coming from a tiny mortal. Very young humans don't come to Maelprog. It's impossible to perform acts of evil without the ability to comprehend them.

Cunt! The single word screams across my thoughts when I visualize myself on the reverse side of the door. Once inside the room, I turn around, my gaze scanning the living quarters which are in repugnant disarray.

A tele-vision lays shattered on the brown, stained floor, bowls overflowing with cigarette butts. I inhale the scent of thick fury coming from a large, sweaty man slamming his fists against the face of a naked woman with tangled hair sitting on the floor. He hurls threats and insults, roaring that she's a useless whore who's done nothing besides ruin his life. Blood pours from her nose and down her thighs as she chokes between her wails. The smell of her pain is strong, indicating the massive extent of trauma her body has endured.

Attempting to protect herself, she crosses her arms over her face, and he immediately screams at her, "Move your fucking hands!" Her palms press against the wall above her head, her dirt caked nails scraping at the torn wallpaper as if she's trying to dig her way out of the room. The concoction of her agony, panic, and horror smells of vinegary chocolate.

The woman's bloodshot eyes keep flickering toward the little human who's covered in shit, crying inside a small cabinet with a clear door. Emotions from children have a strange flavor, not bad exactly, but they are so undeveloped they taste acidic.

Kneeling in front of the cabinet, I lower my bransg as well as take off my priidzar for the child. Instantly, her tears stop. I hold a finger to my lips before giving the miniature mortal a smile.

Standing to face the malevolence next to me, I step directly behind the man a second too late. In his fit of rage, he slams his booted foot against the woman's fragile skull, smashing it against the wall, creating a bloody hole in the sheetrock. Even though I am still hidden from them, I reach for her. "No!"

Clenching my fists, I watch her iridescent blue soul float through the air, disappearing into whichever realm she is destined for. If I'd been a millisecond sooner, I could have prevented her unnecessary death.

The man's shoulders heave, still unaware that he has a divine being in his home who will make him atone for his deplorable actions. My wings spasm in my back as he leaves the small child and dead woman alone in the living area to walk through the door leading to the cooking quarters. I follow him, watching as he calmly pops open a can with his bloodied fingers.

Revealing myself to him, I step closer, removing my overcoat and vest, draping them on the back of a chair. Without the jacket, I'm free to release my wings.

"Do you feel better now?"

The beverage drops to the linoleum as he turns around, sudsy liquid splashing onto his dirty jeans. His eyes bulge from their sockets, and he trips over himself, falling to the floor. He doesn't have so much to say now.

"Wh-what—who—wh—wh…"

My wings cast a shadow over the coward, holding his hands out like he believes it will save him from what's inevitable. I'm unable to take the life of whomever summons me, however, this piece of shit is fair game. The same rush I get from my work at home burns through my body, and fucking antichrist, I'm rock hard.

"What did she do? Burn dinner?" I smirk at him, swallowing his terror as I close the distance between us. I've heard human flesh is so brittle, I could easily tear out his heart with my bare hands, but I have something much more fun in mind.

Evil. His eyes snap from my horns to my wings, scanning my form. "Are you … Satan?" He speaks in a raspy whisper as though every syllable is painful. I take a deep inhale to appreciate the delicacy of his horror. It's simply marvelous.

Spotting a pack of the smoking sticks on the counter, I pick it up, dropping one into my hand. "No. That's my uncle." I slip the cigarette between my lips, lighting it with the tip of my finger. "You'll get to meet him real soon. Don't worry." This sack of meat is undoubtedly going to Unphic Comselh, where Uncle Satan reigns.

My touch can range from comfortably warm to rivaling the flames of Maelprog. With the cigarette hanging from my lips, I place my hands on him, slowly cooking his flesh while enjoying the music of his tortured wails along with the aroma of melting human skin. After a long drag, I stop before his nerve endings disintegrate completely. Bending over, I ram my right horn into his chest, thrusting it in and out. My cock strains in my trousers at the warm sensation of his wet insides.

As I untie my pants, his trembling hand reaches into his pocket, retrieving a blade. I allow him to make his attempt at stabbing me, laughing at the gargling sound he makes upon seeing the useless weapon *clatter* to the floor.

Crimson drips from my horn when I remove it to slide my erection into the wound it's created. Once my smoke has burned down to a butt, I use my fingers to hold his lids open. I snuff it out on his eye, watching the slimy membrane bubble around it. Dropping the butt on the soiled floor, I hold his face against my stomach while the blood gushes onto my legs and abdomen. His struggle beneath my grip has all but stopped, the taste of his pain and fear becoming bland.

With two fingers, I scoop up a pool of the scarlet liquid to suck into my mouth. I've never had human blood before. It could easily become addicting. The *squelch, squelch, squelch* sounds have my dick twitching inside his chest cavity, causing me to pump harder.

Fuck, I really needed this.

Even after his blackened soul has moved on to the next realm, I prod his body until reaching orgasmic completion, releasing my daemonic seed between his rib cage.

This happened much faster than I would have preferred, but there's a small child in the adjoining room alone with her dead mother. Next time, I'll be sure to allow myself the circumstances to not rush. Dropping his corpse on the floor, I fasten my trousers and leave his body to rot before returning to the pygmy person in the cage.

Pygmy. That fits. That's what I'll call her.

Now what am I to do with her? Washing the shit off her is a good place to start, then I'll ask Mishka.

The child hasn't cried again since I smiled at her. Kneeling on the floor, I open the door keeping her imprisoned. She simply babbles and chews on her hand. Not very intelligent at this age it appears.

"Come on, Pygmy. You can come out now."

Eventually, she crawls on all fours, taking her ages to get a mere couple feet. Being immortal doesn't keep my patience from having its limits. I pick her up, holding her far away, so I don't get her excrement on me while I carry her to the cooking quarters. Standing next to the dead man, who I assume was her father, I spray her off in the sink, using a wooden spoon to push down her soiled bottoms.

Once she's clean of fecal matter, I hold her against my chest, her father's blood smearing between us. I pick up my vest and coat from the back of the chair, touching my fingertip to her nose. "I think we're going to both need a proper wash."

There aren't any distinct words coming from her mind, assuming because she isn't able to speak yet. All I can make out is, *Mobby*.

With the naked child in my arms, I hold the imprint of Mishka's bedchamber in my mind and shigmir the both of us next to her bed where the white feline scampers off and out of the room. I'm going to need some fresh garments, but in the meantime, I search through Leena's drawers until I find a pair of pants that will have to do.

Since Pygmy's babbling seems joyful when she sees me in my true form, I keep my priidzar off. Setting her on the floor of the washing tub, I use the spraying water to rinse her father's blood off us and out of her curly dark hair. She keeps moving away from the spray, fussing in protest, so I hurry to get us clean before turning off the faucet and wrapping her in a towel.

"There you go, tiny human. All done."

Leena's pants are much too small, and the only reason I'm able to get them on at all is courtesy of the stretchy waist band.

While I attempt to scrub the red splatter off my necro-pants, Pygmy crawls around the washroom floor, leaving the towel behind. I have no idea how often these creatures release their waste, so I pick her up, searching for something to put on her.

In the cooking quarters, I find a cloth bag strangely filled with yet more cloth bags. After slipping Pygmy's legs through the handle holes, I wrap it around her, fastening it with clips I find in a drawer.

With both of us clean and at least partially clothed, I carry her into the living room, letting her sit on the couch as I stare at the Ammalok Qew. There must be a way for me to get rid of it.

Shaking out my hands, I glance at Pygmy chewing on her fist, blinking at me with big blue eyes. "Wish me luck."

Pulling the flames from my hands, I slam them down on the book in an attempt to set it on fire. Immediately, the sensation of a hundred blades piercing my palms has me jerking away. All that's burning is the table it sits on along with the ridiculous spirit board.

"Damn it."

After snatching up Pygmy, I shigmir to the cooking quarters, filling a pitcher with water to extinguish the flames. The book is left untouched while everything around it is now charred.

I growl in frustration while Pygmy keeps gnawing on her hand, making me wonder how frequently something so small needs sustenance. Every day? It likely wouldn't help my cause with Mishka if she came home to find me with a dead child, so I better feed her to be safe.

Rummaging through the cabinets in the cooking quarters, I find an orange bag I'm pretty sure is food. "Alright, Pygmy. I hope you like…" I read the bag since I don't really know what it is. "Chee-toss."

ƎLƐP
6

Handy Holy Water

MISHKA

'Mad' isn't sufficient enough to describe how I feel right now. I refuse to make eye contact with anyone in the restaurant as I reluctantly return to our table. Even though 'dying from embarrassment' is nothing more than a turn of phrase, it seems one hundred percent likely right now.

"You wanna tell me what in the jalapeno popper fuck that was?" Leena whispers across the table.

I take a big gulp of water, shaking my head. How would I even begin? Even if I told her about Loch, there's no guarantee she'd swallow that pill. I'm still not even sure if I can. "No. Just drop it."

Our waiter is much less flirtatious when he comes back,

pissing me off even more because Loch's bullshit got the result he was going for. At least Leena is enjoying herself. Plus, the food is extremely good.

"Hey, can you take an Uber home? By the time we get done here, I'll need to get to work. I have a cut and color at twelve-thirty."

I'm grateful for the escape plan because the last thing I want is to give her a chance to bring up my mortifying display again. Once the food is gone and the bill is paid, we go outside where Leena kisses me on the cheek, leaving me alone to wait for the driver.

As I keep checking my phone for the Uber's location, a light goes off in my brain with an incredible idea. It's so obvious. The car barely stops before I jump in the backseat.

"Can you drop me at Holy Trinity Books and Gifts on Stark instead, please?"

The driver agrees, and twenty minutes later, I walk inside the first religious place I've been since that one summer I was forced to go to vacation Bible school by the foster parents I was with at the time. A bell chimes above my head, instantly making me feel like an imposter for merely being in here. Walking between rows of books and religious home décor, I find what I'm searching for. A bottle of holy water. A triple blessed one at that. It's even in a handy aluminum spray bottle.

The shop isn't too far from my house, and I spend the entire walk home fantasizing about sending Loch straight back to Hell.

Unlocking my front door, I step inside, clutching the bottle in my hand. "I'm not in the mood, you demonic douche, so if you're here, you better tell me."

"I need your help." He appears in front of me so fast, I scream before pulling the lever and drenching him with the blessed water. To my absolute horror, he doesn't shriek in pain or writhe in agony, he simply wipes his face with his hand. It's then that I realize he has an awkward hold on a toddler who's reaching for his horns. "What was that for?" His white eyes find what's in my hand, causing him to deadpan. "Wow, really? Holy water?" I can't move. My brain can't figure out what to process first. That the water didn't work, or that he's holding a very young child. "That shit only hurts low level orseiinak, and even then, it won't send them home. Don't you think I would have suggested it if that's all it took?"

"Did you steal a child?!"

"I didn't steal her, calm down. I saved her." He groans, adjusting the kid to lift her higher. His voice is deeper when he looks this way. I think his accent may be thicker too.

For what seems to be an eternity, all I can do is stand there and blink like I'm having a stroke. It's a miracle, or I guess whatever the opposite of that is, Leena had to go into work. How would I have explained this? At least the kid seems okay. She has what I think is a little Cheeto dust on her face, but she's smiling and babbling.

What the hell is she wearing?

"Is she diapered in a Whole Foods bag?"

He scrunches his nose, staring at her as if he doesn't see the problem. "I could have let her shit all over your house. So how about, 'thank you, Loch?'"

I swear, he attacks every single one of my axons just to fray them. "How about, fuck you, Loch?" He ignores my comment, more interested with smiling at the kid. "What if Leena had come back with me?" Speaking of my friend, I see that her night pants are fighting for their life on his obviously toned thighs. How on earth did he even get those on? I force myself to avert my eyes from the very prominent bulge below his waist. It doesn't help he's shirtless, revealing more of the strange markings across his frustratingly defined chest and abs. "Puttin' a lot of faith in those sweatpants, aren't ya? Where are your clothes?"

"They got dirty."

His wings are currently gone, making me wonder if he can pull them into his back. I hold my arms out to reach for the kid chewing on its own hand. "We need to take her back to where you found her."

He steps back, causing his hair to fall into his face when he jerks her away from me. If it weren't for him being a hell spawn, his frown and scrunched brows would make me think he's disappointed. "You don't want to keep her?" He pokes at her cheeks, making her giggle. "We could teach her tricks or something. Besides, she can't go back."

"She's not a stray dog you can train to fetch, dumbass." I'm seriously starting to consider screwing this guy if it will get him out of my life forever. "Why can't she go back?"

Pretending he didn't hear me, he says, "Well, I think she's happy here. Aren't you, Pygmy?"

"Her name is Pygmy?"

She wraps her little finger around his, cooing as if she's actually fond of him. "It's what I named her."

"Of course it is." I need this kid out of my house right now before I get arrested. "Where did you find her, Loch?"

"Somewhere dangerous."

"Fine. Don't tell me. It doesn't matter anyway." Watching him and the little girl playing out of the corner of my eye, I search on my phone for where I can take her without involving the cops.

This sensitive side of him is unexpected, and I don't think I'm a fan of it. Since I have no idea where he got her from, I decide the best place to take her is a Safe Haven drop. The only problem is getting her there without witnesses.

Shit.

"Can you do your teleport thing with other people? Like, can you bring us somewhere and still keep us invisible?"

Quirking a thick eyebrow, he gives me that damnable smirk. "Are you asking for my help?"

I can feel my nostrils flaring as I clench my teeth. "Can you do it or not?"

"Oh, I can do it. I simply want you to ask politely first."

The toddler in his arms is getting wiggly, and I need her out of my possession immediately. "Please, Loch, will you help be bring the child you kidnapped to the fire station?"

He nods at me, discounting my insincere tone. "Yes. I need to see where we're going, though. Do you have a map or coordinates?"

Holding up my phone, I show him the location. After placing the child on the ground, he disappears for less than a second. When he returns, he kneels in front of her.

"What are you doing now?" Without responding, he lifts the child's foot. By the time I realize what's happening, he pokes her with a needle from my sewing table. "Jesus Christ, Loch!" 'Pygmy' starts crying until he quickly brings her bleeding heel into his mouth to suck on it. I'm too horrified to move. "Seriously, what the hell?!"

"Lrasd dae lansh cas Maelprog ol allar aai de ol." He doesn't take his eyes off her as he rambles in whatever jacked up language he's speaking. Bopping her on the nose, he picks her up, holding his free hand out to me. "Ready? You're gonna want to hold on tight."

I don't know how much more of this I can psychologically take. My eyes have to be bugging out of their sockets. I point to the kid's foot. "What was that?"

"A binding antiprayer. Now I can find her whenever I want." His voice sounds bored, like what he's telling me is obvious and something I should have known.

"Do I want to know why?"

"I didn't save her for her to end up somewhere else unsavory.

Now I can check on her while I'm here in the mortal realm." Waving me over to him, he asks, "Are we going?"

My hands become clammy as it really hits me what we're about to do. Considering he seems keen on protecting the child, I doubt he'd do anything that would harm her, but teleporting isn't natural for humans. "Will it hurt?"

The slow shake of his head isn't exactly reassuring. "No. Now, hang on to me and don't let go."

Reluctantly, I wrap my arms around his waist, his firm body seeping its warmth through my clothes. This is the closest I've ever physically been with him, and my mind and my body are having opposing opinions on how I feel about that. "Why is your heart beating so fast?"

There's no way my face isn't red right now. "Maybe because I'm about to teleport across town with a demon and the child he stole."

Although his full lips lift into that stupid grin, he keeps his mouth shut for once. I press my head against his chest, holding on for dear life and listening to the snapping sound of his wings being released. His aroma is unique, a sweet spice I've never smelled before. The next thing I know, I'm wrapped in darkness, feeling the silkiness of feathers against my back.

"Is this the place?"

The chaos of traffic sounds in my ears as the cool wind whips my hair off my shoulders. I open my eyes, not realizing I'd closed them. I don't know if I'm more shocked he really did it or that I couldn't feel it at all.

"Wow." A laugh of relief tumbles from my lips, and I find myself smiling at him. "Thank you, Loch." What's crazier still is I actually mean it.

I wait for his smart aleck reply that never comes. He simply says, "Don't stop touching me yet, or else it will appear like you materialized out of nowhere."

Instead of the awkwardness of hugging his waist, I loop my arm around his. We walk to the drop box, and I point to it. "Okay, put her in there."

He doesn't make a move to do what I say. Instead, he furrows his eyebrows in a way that has no right to be as sexy as it is. "Are you sure this is safe for her?"

"It's literally called, 'Safe Haven.' She'll be fine." I point to the sign plastered on the little door. "See? An alarm will go off as soon as we open it and put her in. She won't be in there for more than a moment."

With a heavy exhale, he nudges the little girl's chin before resting his forehead to hers. It's such an odd sight with his horns. "I'll come see you soon, Pygmy."

It doesn't make sense for an actual demon to give a shit about a kid he doesn't know, but seeing the way he is with her nudges at my heart.

Even though she's a bit big for the box, she still fits. Loch closes her inside, running his fingers through his hair while I squeeze his arm and whisper, "Okay, let's go get you some clothes that fit." He's shivering to the point his arm is shaking. "Are you cold?"

"I'm not used to this climate." After a quick glance at the box, he straitens, holding me against his chest, and once again cloaking me in feathered blackness. Before I can tell him where to take us, we're standing in front of a shop I can tell is way out of my price range. How did he know about this place?

Shaking my head, I scoff. "Yeah, right. I couldn't afford a pair of socks from here."

I shift at the awkwardness of still holding on to him, even though I wouldn't dare let go with all the people around. He lowers his head so his nose is level with mine. Wow. His eyelashes are so long. "You don't need to pay for anything, I can shigmir inside and take what I need."

I'm so focused on his stare that it takes me a second to realize what he just suggested. I gape at him. "That's terrible. You're not stealing anything." Digging out my phone, I show him the directions to one of my favorite stores. "Let's go here."

We land in the alley next to a Sylvia Plath quote painted on the wall of the vintage shop. After I glance both directions to make sure no one is around, I step away from him. "Keep in mind, I currently don't have a job, so we're only getting you a couple outfits."

"I already told you, you don't have to pay for anything." He wraps his arms around himself, shivering as he follows me inside.

"And I already told you, you're not stealing." A woman standing in front of us turns around to look at me like I'm a freak. Probably because it looks like I'm talking to myself.

Since I can't respond to him anyway, I ignore his comments on how humans have 'an atrocious sense of fashion.' He ends up settling on two pairs of jeans and two long sleeve shirts that I'd be lying if I said I wasn't looking forward to seeing him wear.

With the shopping bag in hand, I walk in front of him, returning to the mural we arrived by earlier and check our surroundings. Once again reaching my arms around his waist, I hold my wrist, waiting for the sensation of his wings to cover me. I keep my eyes open, but it happens so fast, I still can't see anything.

Not a second later, he releases me. We're standing in the middle of my living room, music faintly playing from the speaker.

"That's a pretty insane skill, I gotta give you that."

I narrow my eyes at his smug expression when my coffee table having burn marks across the top of it catches my attention. "What the shit did you do?!" Dropping the shopping bag on the floor, I run my hands over the curled, charred paint.

He waves his hand toward the book on the table. "I attempted to destroy the Ammalok Qew, but not even my flames could harm it."

His flames? What the hell does that mean? Resting a hand on my hip, I jab a finger at him. "You can't be catching my stuff on fire, asshole!" After I throw away Leena's Ouija board and attempt to wipe down the table, I stomp my way to Leena's room, leaving the book on her dresser. I close her door behind me to find him standing with crossed arms in the hall.

I cross my own arms just the same with a huff. "I'll figure out what to do with the book, okay? But you need to leave it alone, and maybe try not to burn my house down." Who would have thought a demon could be such an incredible pain in the ass? "Now I have to figure out how I'm going to explain this to Leena."

He stands there completely unaffected that he's derailing my entire life. The moment I turn around to go to my room, I'm suddenly zapped with an exhaustion bolt, making my eyelids feel like they weigh ten pounds each. My body is tender and sore as if I haven't rested in days. The problem is, I'm not too comfortable sleeping with a rapey stalker who can literally make himself invisible which brings voyeurism to a whole other level.

"What's it gonna take for you to leave, and I mean really leave, so I can take a nap?"

He reaches out, placing a hand on either side of my head against the wall. "I've heard the first shigmir can be exhausting for humans. Don't worry, tin nanba. I'll let you sleep."

While I hate that he's calling me ... something, I'm too exhausted to care at the moment. I dip beneath his arm to back into my room. The last thing I see before he vanishes is that ornery smile, which doesn't give me a modicum of comfort.

บาล
7

Bad Idea Blowjob

Loch

It's happening much sooner than I expected. My wings ache, and my head throbs around my horns. I've always known going too long without release could make me weak, but I've never experienced it until now.

Watching Mishka sleep, I know I only have a couple options at this point. I either need to find a human to seduce, or quite literally, take this situation into my own hands.

I've never had to do that before. Slowly tugging on her blanket, I pull it down enough to reveal her breasts under the tiny top she has on. Her nipples poke up beneath the fabric, and that's all it takes for my cock to grow. I rub myself over my new heavy trousers, lowering the zipper to grip my erection. Her pink lips are barely parted as she breathes, making it easy to imagine what it would look like to slide myself between them. I take in her features, stroking at a steady pace. Her freckles are light across her upturned nose, only noticeable because her makeup has mostly worn off. Even though her breasts aren't large, they are plump and would fit nicely in my palm. I risk waking her up by softly touching the thumb of my free hand over a hardened nub, stopping when she shifts in her sleep.

Fucking antichrist, this isn't easy. I want to run my tongue from the dip at the base of her neck to the sweetness between her legs. The forced restraint is making my symptoms worse, and I'm nowhere close to coming. I stretch out my wings in an attempt to relieve the dull pain, moving my hand faster. Her blonde locks sprawl across her pillow, and while I shouldn't have touched her breast, I convince myself that fondling her hair would be okay. There are silver strands by her nape that fit her complexion well. I want so badly to wrap her hand around me and use it to jerk me, but that'd be taking it much too far. Fantasizing about her touch is intensifying the pain, my head thumping like it houses a tiny drum. If this goes on much longer, I'm worried I won't even have the strength to keep on my priidzar, much less my bransg, and that would be detrimental.

"Mishka? Are you here?"

Her housemate. Maybe she could be of assistance?

I shigmir outside to the freezing porch, knocking on the front door until Leena answers. The way her eyes take their time traveling down my body makes my dick jolt in excitement. *Hottie.* Good. She's already turned on. I can smell the syrupy scent of her lust.

"Can I help you?" she asks.

I sure fucking hope so. "I'm a friend of Mishka's. Is she here?" Asking a question I already know the answer to isn't a lie.

Her grin lowers ever so slightly. "I'm sorry, she isn't." Stepping back to open the door farther, she offers, "I know it's late, but you can wait here until she gets back if you want."

Responding with a nod, I step over the threshold. "Mishka never mentioned she had such a stunning friend."

Her eyelashes flutter with a shaky laugh. "She hasn't mentioned you either. How do you know her?"

"We're new acquaintances. She's helping me with something."

Her eyes narrow, obviously wanting me to elaborate. "Oh … okay. Would you like a drink, umm…?"

"Loch, and no. I'm fine." The savory course of sexual desire she's feeding me accelerates my condition, making it more excruciating.

"I'll grab some wine in case you change your mind. You can take a seat on the couch."

Each second is becoming endless. I need to get this going quickly if I have any chance of keeping on my priidzar. Returning with a bottle and two mugs, she stops at the sight of her burned table. "What the hell?" She runs her fingers over the blackened wood. "Shit. What did Mishka do to this? It's trash now." Setting the cups and wine down, she sits next to me. "What exactly is the deal between you two anyway? Are you … *talking?*"

She puts emphasis on the last word, indicating it means more than the actual definition. Her anticipation makes it obvious she's feeling out my availability. Assuming I'm reading her correctly, I say, "I'm not courting her, if that's what you mean."

Even with her lips pressed together, it's clear she's attempting to stop from laughing. "Courting? Who says that anymore?"

I don't have time to work up to this, so I lean toward her, testing my luck when I bring my lips inches from hers. "I do."

The beating of her heart and the word, *Kiss,* coming from her mind urges me to go for it. Pressing my lips against her mouth, I grip the back of her neck to pull her closer. She doesn't resist for all of two seconds before she's pushing me away.

"Stop. You need to stop." Shit. "What is happening here?"

"I thought it was fairly obvious."

She squeezes the bridge of her nose with a throaty laugh. "You don't even know my name."

The actuality that I do isn't something she needs to be aware of. I reach out to grip her chin. "Will knowing your name make me want you less?"

Although her complexion makes it more subtle, I can still see when her cheeks flush with embarrassment. "Well, maybe not my name, but there is something…"

I can sense what she's talking about, so I reach down to touch her erection over her skirt. Her gasp is accompanied by a jump of surprise as her shock tickles my throat. "How did you know?"

I kiss her again, never moving my hand. "Does it matter?"

She shakes her head and grabs my face. *Tim.* Who is Tim? "This is so insane." She moans against my mouth, her hips rolling into my touch, giving me the go ahead to slide my hand beneath her dress. The moment I wrap my fist around her solid cock, her breath hitches, and she reciprocates by reaching between my legs. Fuck, yes. It's already easier to wear my priidzar. She fiddles with the button then reaches inside my pants to pull out my dick, using her hand to massage me.

"I really want to feel that pretty mouth."

Giving me a shy smile, she lowers herself to the floor between my thighs, blinking up at me. *Slut.* The word is soaked in guilt, and that's not something I enjoy tasting. "There's nothing wrong with sexual pleasure."

She tilts her head, swirling her tongue around the tip. "I swear I don't ever do this with strangers."

I grip her hair, attempting to refocus her thoughts as I

push her head down. Her mouth envelops me, feeling so nice to fuck something wet. I buck my hips, being careful to not hurt her. I still make her gag, but she keeps at it. Her green and blue hair drapes over my thighs, her pink lipstick smearing across my human looking shaft. Every couple of minutes, she'll glance up at me with those big brown eyes.

"That's it. Keep sucking."

For a reason that makes no sense whatsoever, a thought nags in the back of my mind that what I'm doing is disloyal. Which is ridiculous because Mishka wants nothing to do with me, and I'll eventually be in too much pain to move if I don't come soon. I decide it's best that I keep this interaction strictly to the oral variety. Fucking her without Mishka's knowledge or permission could make this whole thing harder and messier than it already is. My laying with Mishka is mandatory if I have any chance of getting back home within a few decades.

I've passed the point of doubt, so for now, I'm going to enjoy fucking this girl's mouth and worry about my summoner later.

If this were a normal situation, I would take my time, letting my stamina do its thing. Right now, though, I just need to come and get back to feeling normal. My hands grip each side of Leena's skull, concentrating on being gentle as I thrust down her throat. She gags, her drool dripping into the dark hair at the base of my cock while I erupt down her esophagus.

She inhales a deep breath when she lifts her head, wiping the excess ejaculate from her mouth. "This is going to sound weird, but I've never had come taste like that. It's really good."

I've heard our semen can become somewhat addictive to humans if they absorb too much of it, so it having a pleasant flavor isn't surprising. With one hand on each of her arms, I bring her to my mouth, sliding my tongue against hers before pushing her onto her back. It's in bad form to not reciprocate sexual favors that have been given, and I've always been one for propriety.

My fingers grip her skirt, lifting it to her waist before spreading her legs. I pump her cock as I lower my head to flick my tongue over the puckered hole of her anus, sliding it inside to fuck her with it. Her erotic sounds are so loud, I'm worried she'll wake Mishka. "Oh, shit! Your mouth…"

Nails scratch at my scalp as she pulls on my hair. Removing my tongue, I finger her ass and lick up her shaft to focus on the little hole. When I suck her tip into my mouth, she arches her back, pushing herself farther between my lips. I lower to the base, relaxing my jaw so her cock can slide down my throat. With her hips bucking, I swallow her with ease, bobbing up and down. She watches me with dilated, glossed over eyes, pushing up her shirt to tug on her nipples. The effects of my seed are already taking ahold of her.

Fuck me. I'm already tempted to, and her pleas penetrating my mind make being inside of her even more desirable. Yet for reasons I can't explain, it feels like that would be taking things too far. Being with her this way is out of necessity. If I go further, however, then it's solely because I want to which may be something Mishka won't forgive. She can't blame me for survival, though.

Since Leena believes I'm human, I can't do half the things I want to. Still, it doesn't take more than a few moments until she's crying, "Keep going! I'm coming! Oh, God, I'm coming."

Once every drop is swallowed, I pop off, winking at her. "Definitely not God."

Doll Designer

Mishka

My eyes flutter open at the sound of music seeping beneath my door. The morning sun shines its rays across my bed, and I sit up to see the clock says it's already eight in the morning. Jesus, I slept for over twelve hours.

I don't see Loch, but that doesn't mean anything. I won't temp fate by whispering for him. Throwing on my robe, I walk out into the living room to find Leena dancing to Jxdn, placing crystals inside of what she calls her 'charging station.'

"You're in a good mood."

She spins around, a smile spreading across her face. "When did you get home?"

Something seems weird. I mean, she's usually cheery, but

it's amped up to full capacity this morning. "I've been here. I just went to bed early."

She arranges the last crystal, widening her eyes. "Oh…"

I tighten the belt on my robe and cross my arms. "Okay, I'm going to need coffee before dealing with whatever shoved a glow stick up your ass."

She giggles, following me into the kitchen and bouncing on her feet while I add milk to my cup. "Oh, by the way, what happened to the coffee table?"

I clear my throat, thankful I already thought of a lie. I'm getting sick of having to do it so much lately. "I'm so sorry, I knocked over a candle. I guess the varnish on it was really flammable. I'll give you some money to replace it. And to get a new Ouija board. Okay?"

She bites her lip, rocking on her heels. "That's fine. It's the last thing on my mind right now, to be honest."

I'll admit, she has my curiosity piqued. To give her credit, she waits until after I make myself comfortable on the couch with my caffeine to go off.

"Your 'friend' stopped by last night to see you."

I have exactly one friend, and she's currently spazzing out. "What friend?" The warm java hits my tongue, making me sigh in gratitude.

"The hot one with the neat accent. Loch."

One godforsaken name is all it takes to rob me of my simple pleasure and make me choke. "What?!"

"He said you're helping him with something." She waves her hand, the beads on her locs *clacking* against each other. "Anyway, you're never going to guess what happened."

If I appear as lightheaded as I feel, then I surely look like a ghost which is completely lost on Leena. "I can't imagine," my voice squeaks out.

Surely, he didn't tell her what he is?

"It was so weird. Just being around him made me horny. He wasn't even here for five minutes before I had his dick in my mouth. We didn't fuck, but he gave me the best head I have ever had. In. My. Life."

She might as well have kicked me in the chest with how fast my heart falls to my stomach. "He did?" Even I'm surprised by the stab of betrayal lacing my words.

The happiness melts off her face, her posture turning rigid. "H-he said you guys were just friends."

It doesn't make sense, me feeling this way. I hate him. I think. "He said that?" No, I definitely do. Especially now.

She shakes her head, covering her mouth with her hand. "Shit, Mimi. I swear, I didn't think there was anything between you, or else I never would have—"

I hold my hand up to stop her because while I am inexplicably angry, it's absolutely not at her. I'm not even sure if it's fair to be mad at him. "It's fine, Leena, there isn't."

She wraps her arms around me, squeezing me to her chest. "I am so fucking sorry. Please forgive me."

I push her back because she's hugging me so hard it's uncomfortable. "I said it's fine. Don't worry about it." There shouldn't be so much venom in my voice. It's stupid.

She keeps blinking, clenching her fists in frustration. "Why the hell didn't you tell me about him? Where did you meet him?"

I'm terrible at lying on the spot. I need time to fabricate a plan, and since I don't have one, I blurt the first thing that springs to life in my brain. "At the ... park. Yesterday." As soon as I start, the word vomit keeps leaking out. "He needs help with his ... uh, um sister. He wants me to make a doll for her."

I feel like an ass. Lying to her this much is going to come back to haunt me. I know it. The green hair of her eyebrows scrunches up. "What made you go to the park?"

"I wanted to go for a walk?"

"Are you asking me?"

"Jesus Christ. What's with the twenty questions?"

She leans back, tilting her head to the side as if I hit her. "You're clearly mad."

I close my eyes to take a deep breath, but when I do, all I see are the images my brain has constructed of them touching each other. "Look, I just woke up, and I need to find a job, so I'm stressed about that."

She purses her lips, squinting like she doesn't believe a word of my bullshit. "Well, if it makes you feel any better, he didn't ask for my number, and he didn't leave his. So I'm pretty sure it was a one-time thing."

I don't know if she's more hurt by that or my reaction. Either way, she stands up to pass by me. "I'm gonna put these out." She carries her crystals outside before returning to say, "I need to get ready for work."

Once I'm alone, I blow the air out of my mouth so hard, my bangs flitter. I'm gonna kill that asshole. Isn't he here for me? Why the fuck is he screwing around with my best friend?

"Your jealousy's quite the treat." I really, really hate that he can just poof out of the air like that. "Though there's no need for it. I can easily satisfy both of you." I have half a mind to smash this coffee mug against his horns to knock the smirk off his face.

"Do not go near her again, Loch. I swear to God."

Bending his leg, he turns to face me on the couch. "My grandfather couldn't give a shit if you swear to Him or not."

It's as if this whole thing is hilarious to him. He can't be serious for a single damn second. "I'm not kidding. She's off limits."

He laces his long fingers together, shrugging his shoulders. "What would you have me do? I get incredibly weak without sexual pleasure. I need it for survival, and you're not facilitating me in that capacity."

He can't be serious. "Are you actually expecting me to believe you'll die without fucking? That's more ludicrous than the blue ball argument."

"It's true. I already told you, I don't lie."

Rubbing my temples, I leave him in the living room. I can't deal with him right now. He doesn't follow me to the shower, but of course, when I get back to my room he's lying on the bed.

"What did Leena say about getting rid of the Ammalok Qew?"

At this point, I know he's seen me naked whether I knew he was watching or not, so I drop my towel without looking at him. "It didn't exactly come up." I hate the obvious snark in my voice.

Taking out a pair of panties, I shimmy them up my legs before drying my hair. Making the mistake of meeting his gaze in the mirror, I see his moronic grin. He really doesn't possess a drop of shame.

The moment I turn off the hairdryer, he says, "You were jealous, and you can't deny it." He taps his outstretched tongue that I hadn't realized was split. Like a snake. "I tasted it."

He says some of the stupidest shit sometimes.

"I think you're confusing the fact that I'm pissed at you for using my friend with jealousy. She's been taken advantage of enough in her life. I'm not going to let you do it too."

He opens his mouth just to close it again as if his voice was stolen. Too bad that's not the case. My phone *pings*, notifying me of the estimated time the Uber I requested will be here while I curl my hair enough to give it some volume. It's not until I'm applying my mascara that he does finally speak.

"That wasn't my intention. I was getting sick, and she

was willing to give me her body. I would have preferred if it had been you."

I spin around, pointing my mascara wand at him. "Don't do that. It's fucked up to compare us. We are both human beings, you dick. I know first-hand how you can arouse people."

He arches an eyebrow, quirking his lips. "Do you, now?"

"Shut up. I don't know how you're going to do it, and I don't care, but fix this." Finishing my makeup, I add, "And you better not make her feel like crap either."

After putting on a cap sleeve white dress with melting pastel rainbows on it, I zip up my black boots.

"Where are we going?" he asks, moving to stand in front of me.

I put my hand on his chest, which looks ridiculously good in his new gray sweater, to push him back. "We aren't going anywhere. I am going to kiss my old boss's ass and try to get my job back."

He sticks out his lower lip, turning his mouth downward as he crosses his arms. "Is that normal? Kissing asses to get work?"

I never know if he's being a smartass or serious. "Yes." Sliding my arm through my purse strap, I warn, "I better not come home to any more abducted kids. Do you think you can handle that?" He winks at me, and I roll my eyes, leaving him in my room.

"I'm headin' out," I call down the hall. "Wish me luck!"

Leena's head pops out from her room. "Good luck, strawberry cuntcake! I love you."

Good to know we're back to normal. "Love you too, skank."

A few minutes after stepping outside, my ride pulls up to my driveway. I slide into the back, falling against the seat with a huff. Now that I'm not wallowing in despair and sleeping all hours of the day, I realize how stupid it was to let my job go. If I would have simply explained my situation, I would likely still be employed. Ryan Innes, the shop's owner and doll designer, is a great guy. If he doesn't give me another chance, it'll be close to impossible to find another job I enjoy much less one that pays me the amount he did. I don't exactly have a glowing resume.

The shop's wooden sign swings in the wind, *Sewn To Death* written across the front. Taking a big mental breath, I push open the door to hear the familiar *ding*. Ryan's husband, Chase, is the first to see me.

"Mishka! We've all been so worried about you!" He puts down the sign he was fidgeting with on a display table to give me a hug. "Are you okay?"

Now I really feel like a jerk. I could have at least responded to one of their calls or texts. "I am now. Is Ryan here?" Smoothing out his apron adorning the store's logo, a profile view of a skull wearing a dark lace veil with a sewing needle pierced through the cervical spine, he motions for me to follow him. The walls are covered in gothic imagery. Framed skeletal images, both human and animal, are sprinkled between black, ornate accent mirrors, paintings of crows, and faux taxidermy. Glittery, black chandeliers lead the pathway to the back room where the dolls are made. Ryan sits at the sewing machine, finishing up the plush hybrid of an octopus and a bat with wooden button eyes.

"Hey, babe. Look who's here."

The machine stops, and Ryan turns to me, his face transforming from a concentrated frown to a full-blown smile. "Mishka! You've had me worried sick."

A nervous laugh slips from my lips when he hugs me. "I know. I really am sorry. Can we talk?" Chase leaves us alone, shutting the door behind him. "It wasn't fair of me to leave you guys high and dry. You've been an incredible boss, and had every right to fire me—"

"What happened? It was so out of character for you to disappear like that."

Falling into the seat next to the door, I drop my purse on the floor. "Remember those baby booties I asked you if I could make for a friend?" He sits back down, his forehead creasing with his nod. "The 'friend' was me." With wide eyes, his mouth pops open. "I was pregnant. The night I went to tell Harry, I found him in bed with someone else. I left so angry that I wasn't paying attention and got into an accident, causing me to lose the baby. I couldn't even get myself out of bed, never mind deal with anything else."

The expression on his face makes me feel worse for not contacting him. "Jesus. Why didn't Leena call me?"

"She probably didn't feel it was her place to share. Anyway, it was a horrible fluke of circumstance. If there's any way you would consider giving me my job back, I swear I won't ever keep you out of the loop again."

He squeezes my arm. "You will always have a place here for however long you want it." Scooting his chair back in, he resumes his work. "Besides, training a new doll maker is a pain in the ass."

My chest opens, allowing the oxygen to flow freely again. "You're amazing, Ryan. Thank you."

"Can you make it tomorrow morning? Ten o'clock?"

I couldn't stop my smile if I tried. Standing up, I squeeze his neck in a hug. "I'll be here."

Bloomers in a Bunch

LOCH

While I admit getting sexually involved with Leena wasn't the best idea I've ever had, the envy seeping from Mishka and her adamancy in denying it upset her makes my dick hard. The number of times the word *asshole* sprang from her thoughts over the last few minutes is amusing.

As she leaves the house, I consider following her to watch this ass kissing she was talking about, but when I hear Leena moving around in the hall, I figure it'll help my chances if I smooth this out with her before Mishka gets back.

After I shigmir outside to the front door, I lift my hand to knock. Seconds later, Leena answers, her neutral expression instantly lifting in surprise. "Loch! Hey, I didn't know if I'd see you again. Come on in."

I shove my hands in my pockets, attempting to make it clear things won't be going the same direction they did last time. "I need to talk to you." That's all it takes for her smile to fade. Humans and their emotions involving sex is proving to be exhausting. Do they not ever fuck for the sake of fucking? "Last night, I went against my better judgment. With you being so close to Mishka, it was in bad taste."

Crossing her arms, she squints at me. "So there is something between you two?"

I know I can't tell her why I'm here, however, I usually try to divulge as much truth as I'm able. "I want there to be."

Although there's still a dash of arousal coming off of her, she's mostly serving me disappointment. "Can you look me in the eye and tell me this has nothing to do with…" Her voice fades when her gaze casts downward.

"What? Your dick? Why would that matter?"

The smallest smile makes an appearance, giving me the impression she's going to make this much easier on me than I'd originally expected. "So if it wasn't for Mishka, then—"

"Then I'd be bending you over that couch right now."

Charming. She tosses her hair over her shoulder as she laughs, smelling of amusement. "Okay, well you fucked up royally. You know that right?"

"Do you think you can help me out with that?"

Shaking her head, she leans against the wall. "Mishka has been through some shit recently. I like you and all, but I don't have a problem kicking your ass if you pull anything like this again."

I hold my hands up, feigning submission. "As I said, while it was fun, it was a lapse of reason."

Fondling the small scissors dangling from her ear, she

snorts, "Since we're being honest, I did kind of use you to get my mind off another guy, so I guess we're even. Anyway, I hope you're good at groveling because I doubt she's going to let you off the hook as quickly as I am."

Unfortunately, I think she's right.

I stay hidden in Mishka's room, inspecting her undergarments. She has a pair in nearly every color and shape. Some of them are only a few scraps of fabric which don't seem very functional. Practical or not, I'd be willing to bet they'd be mouthwatering on her.

When Leena finally leaves, I move out into the main living room where the feline sits on the couch, hissing at the sight of me. There's nothing entertaining to do here without the girls, and after ten minutes, the tediousness threatens to become my demise.

I should go check on Pygmy.

Our bond leads me to a small, messy home where she squeals in delight when I lower my bransg for her. A woman, who I assume holds the role of the mother figure, stares at her in disgust, which brings my ire to the surface much easier than normal. How dare she look at Pygmy that way? Isn't she meant to care for her?

"Why are these foster kids always so fucking weird?" she mumbles, presumably to herself. A few moments later, I follow the woman into the washroom, watching her put drops of clear liquid from a small bottle in her eyes.

I return to Pygmy, but the woman doesn't. When I hear a door close in the hall, I lean down to pick up the sweet child, allowing her to pull on my hair and horns. "I'm sorry you have to be here," I say to her. Thankfully, she seems oblivious to her predicament, giggling as I lift and lower my wings. Placing her on the floor, I shigmir to different spots around her, making ridiculous facial expressions every time I stop so I can hear her merry laugh. She crawls across the carpet, stopping to sit up when she gets to the corner of the room. Kneeling beside her, I watch her little fingers reach for a small, black, triangle shaped box. It takes me a second to realize what it says because the black letters blend in.

POISON
Do Not Touch

"Pygmy, No!" I grab her hand, picking her up to carry her away from the box. My wings twitch as I look toward the hall. The woman still hasn't returned. What if I hadn't been here? I lower Pygmy into a little pen—one she should have been inside in the first place—before returning to the box so I can take it with me and dispose of it.

I hear the woman clearing her throat, and as I walk into the hall, I smell a strange scent coming from one of the closed doors. Stepping into the lavatory, I dump out the contents inside the little bottle the woman used earlier, replacing the eye solution for the acetone sitting next to it.

Since the woman chooses to use her eyes to give Pygmy dirty looks instead of using them to watch over her, I'll make it so she can't use them at all.

It's time I take my leave, so when I return to Pygmy in the pen, I bend down to kiss her forehead. "Bye, Pygmy. I'll see you later."

As soon as I shigmir to Mishka's room, I throw the poison box in the waste bin, waiting for the tug of distance between us to deplete and alert me to her proximity. When she opens her door, I land in her entryway where she almost drops the cup in her hand. "Okay, new rule. No more of this blinking into existence shit. You can walk like a normal person."

"But I'm not a person, and that is normal for me. I wouldn't ask you to stop snoring in your sleep."

Her face twists up, pushing past me to go to the cooking quarters. "I don't snore."

"Yes, you do. You sound like a bear. Is that how you got your name?"

"What are you—" she holds her hand up to my face. "Actually, I don't care. Just tell me there aren't any random children running around here."

She acts as if I've done that a hundred times. It was one child. "No, but I did speak to Leena like you asked."

Her keys *clatter* from being dropped on the counter next to the cloth bag she always carries around. "Does she hate you as much as I do now?"

I've tasted hate plenty of times, and what she feels toward me doesn't even come close. I won't tell her that, though. Her denial is kind of cute when it's not maddening. "No. She said she used me too, so we're even."

"She still doesn't know you're a..." I slough off my priidzar for a second, her stunned expression delighting me as it does every time she sees me out of my human camouflage.

"Your secret's still safe, I just don't understand why you need it to be. Didn't she help you call me in the first place?"

"Yes, but," I follow her out of the cooking quarters and into the hall, "I'm still struggling to wrap my head around your existence without bringing her into the mix. Speaking of, I really want to be alone tonight. Is there somewhere else you can go for a while?"

"If you'd let me fuck you, I'll be gone forever."

Not a trace of amusement crosses her face, yet she can't hide the momentary rise of her pulse.

"Tempting. Now go, and I mean for real. No creepy, invisible lurking shit. Go entertain yourself."

I know for certain she doesn't want me to do what she says. "The last time I did that, you got your bloomers in a bunch."

"Out, Loch."

Caught in the Cookie Jar

MISHKA

*T*he pointed tip of his horn trails down my naked chest that's heaving with excitement as he kisses the valley between my breasts. I arch my back, needing to be closer to him. My pussy clenches merely from the heat radiating off his skin. My legs fall open farther, giving him plenty of room to nestle between them. He brings a nipple between his teeth, white eyes burning bright.

"Are you ready?"

I nod in earnest, my body aching to be filled. "I want you inside me, Loch." He lines his cock up with my entrance, the sight so arousing that I cry out in ecstasy before his body is fully inside mine. Hot waves roll across my tingling skin while I come, every throb of my cunt sending me further into bliss.

With a smile that turns my body to jelly, he bites his lip, but when he opens his mouth, the most grating noise comes out. "Beep. Beep."

Beep.
Beep.
Beep.

My mind slides into consciousness, and I open my eyes enough to turn off the alarm. Still aroused from my unwelcome wet dream, I reach between my legs to feel the evidence of a very real orgasm. My finger rubs at my already tender clit, my hips rocking with the need to release the lingering tension. I quietly croon, hating myself for using Loch's face as my sexual inspiration.

"Did you sleep well?"

I jerk my arm out from under the sheets, my face burning in humiliation from being caught with my hand in the proverbial cookie jar.

"What the fuck, Loch?! I told you I wanted to be alone!"

"You know I would be more than pleased to do that for you."

I want to ask if he had anything to do with my dream, but that would require admitting I had it in the first place. "We really need to lay down some ground rules."

He's standing there in all his hellish glory, wings stark against the backdrop of my lavender walls. I imagine it must be exhausting, maintaining a human disguise. The same moment I toss off my blankets to get out of bed, my door swings open.

"Hey are y—" Leena's words are cut off by her blood curdling scream. Loch immediately disappears which has her eyes widening in terror as she tries to back up.

I scramble to my feet, rushing across my room to grab her

hand. "Leena, calm down." She keeps spinning around, her head jerking from left to right. "She already saw you, idiot," I snap at the space where he was standing a second ago.

When he becomes visible again, he's still in his demon form. Leena stabs her finger in his direction. "What the fuck?! What the fuuuck is that?!"

"Don't you remember me, lovely?" He presses his tongue against the inside of his cheek in an obscene gesture before flashing her a grin.

Dark brown eyes bulge from her head that she's jerking back and forth between us. I'm a bit worried she's going to faint from shock. She allows me to hold her hand to my chest as her breathing slows enough she shouldn't hyperventilate. "Okay, I need you to listen to me." Even while she nods, her gaze keeps flipping to Loch. I inhale deeply myself, not sure how to put this into words. "So ... you know the spell you got from that book?" Her lips part, and she freezes, appearing catatonic. "It ... um ... it worked better than anticipated." A nervous laugh falls out of my mouth because I can hear how absurd this sounds.

She pulls her hand back, balling it into a fist. "Are you saying we *summoned* him?"

Loch snaps his fingers. "Look at that! You're much quicker to the draw than Mishka was."

I glare at him. I wish he would shut his dumb mouth for one freaking second. She slowly crosses the room, circling him. "Is this because of the supermoon?" Her fingers hesitantly reach out toward the feathers of his wings, but she yanks them back without touching them.

"Your moon is still part of your realm. It has nothing to do with Drilpa Nalvage."

She glances back at me. "What's dreel paw Nollvaj?"

I shrug because I have no idea what he means by half the shit he says.

"The beyond. A land outside of this one. A realm of immortals."

When her eyes fixate on his horns, her face softens to an expression of awe. For some unexplainable reason, I wish he would put on his ... whatever he calls the thing that makes him human. Her seeing him this way feels intimate, and it makes me uncomfortable.

"Wow," she finally breathes. "This is incredible."

I cross my arms. "If by incredible, you mean incredibly inconvenient, then yes, it is."

Loch's smile shows his fangs. "Come on, tin nanba. I'm growing on you, and you know it."

"No, you're not, and stop calling me that." It's killing me to not know what it means.

"You speak Latin?" Leena asks.

"I'm pretty sure that's not Latin."

She spins back on me, realization shifting her temperament. "You lied to me, feeding me some bullshit story about meeting him at the park. I knew that was sketchy as shit. We're keeping things from each other now?"

The way she's looking at me smashes my heart to mush. "Leena, he's not a random guy I met. He's an actual demon, here to make my life hell until—" I cut myself off because the whole thing is monumentally ridiculous.

"Until what?" Her voice sounds angry, but her eyes are sad. Even though, of course, it wasn't my intent, I hurt her.

"Until she lets me part the pink sea," Loch pipes up from behind me.

I scowl at him. He has zero decorum. "You're disgusting."

She holds her hands up to stop us. "Wait ... is he saying you have to fuck?"

"It was your stupid spell that summoned a lust demon!"

Her head whips back in his direction. "You're an incubus?" He holds his arms out with a subtle bow of the head, and I scoff. Incu*bastard* is more like it.

She stands there silent for so long, it's almost awkward. Finally, she says, "Holy shit! I blew a demon."

He holds up a finger. "Unholy shit is much more accurate."

I really hate being reminded they touched each other that way. "Shut up, Loch."

Leena calls in to her job because she says it will be impossible to deal with moronic clients after finding out demons are in fact real. I, however, need to go in since this is my first day back since being rehired.

It makes me much more uneasy than it should, knowing Loch and Leena are home alone together. I don't truly believe Leena would hook up with him again, and since he's not around to cherry pick my thoughts, I can admit he has a bit of a charismatic side in an annoying way. That is when I'm not daydreaming about strangling him.

I'm tackled by Beckany, the only other female who works here, the moment I walk into Sewn To Death. "Mishka! I missed you! I'm soooo glad you're back!"

She's a bit much sometimes, but she has a good heart. Smiling at her enthusiasm, I walk toward the workshop to put away my bag. "I missed you too, Becks." Her chubby little cheeks are always on the pink side, probably because I've never seen her in a less than stellar mood.

Beckany is scheduled to work the floor with Ryan while I get the peace and quiet of the workshop, filling custom orders. Chase has already made the patterns, so I can get right to sewing. Workshop days are my favorite. I don't have to deal with the headache that can be the general public, and the sound of the sewing machine makes me feel relaxed.

The first order is for a 'dead' purple and blue, two-headed giraffe. I start with purple, threading the bobbin before pushing on the pedal to fill it. After preparing the bobbin case and popping it into the compartment, I finish threading the machine and needle.

I had forgotten how well this keeps my mind from going chaotic, and I wonder had I come back to work sooner, if I would be in this situation with Loch. Even though he can drive me completely insane, it would be bullshit to say I'm not at least partially glad he's here. Learning of the existence of such a being is something most people will never get to experience. Maybe I'm being too hard on him. He can't help what he is and that his kind has a bad reputation. And as he loves to remind me, technically, I did call him. Accident or not.

By the time I have both heads, the legs, and the main body sewn and partially stuffed, half my shift is already over. It isn't until Beckany comes back on her break that I check the clock.

She drinks her energy drink, giggling. "I think we have a ghost."

Normally, I wouldn't think twice about her comment, asking her why to be polite. Today though, I can't stop my thoughts from going to Loch. "What? Why would you say that?"

She seems taken aback by my harsh reaction, gesturing toward the storefront. "I was only kidding. A bunch of the horned teddy bears fell on the floor out of nowhere a while ago."

"Oh." I attempt a casual laugh, but it comes out a little more manic than intended. "That's crazy."

"Do you want anything from the food trucks? I'm gonna go grab something."

I shake my head, forcing a smile. "I'm good, thanks."

The second she's out of the workshop, I whisper with as much volume as I feel comfortable. "Loch? Are you here?"

The question barely leaves my lips when he appears with crossed arms by the supply room. He gestures toward the doors leading to the sales floor. "Whose ass did you have to kiss? The man behind the counter? It's nice. I'd kiss it too."

"I'm sure you would. What are you doing here?"

He scrunches up his face, sniffing the roll of green felt. "I wanted to see what you do for work. Plus, when you're done, I can take you home so you don't have to get a ride."

"You know, you may want to consider getting a hobby."

"I have one." He gives me a wink and smile, a telltale sign he's about to say something inappropriate. "Trying to get in that pussy of yours."

There it is.

11

Powder Pink Panties

LOCH

Her pink tongue sticks out from between her lips while she works, making me imagine all the things she'd be able to do with it. Her coworker almost walked in and caught me, so I've kept up my bransg, concealing me from both their eyes.

It displeases me how she acts differently around these people, a watered-down version of the girl I've spent the last few days with. I do count myself lucky that I enjoy her company, or else this whole thing would be much more inconvenient than it already is.

It was daft on my part to interrupt her this morning. It surely would have been magnificent to watch her make herself come. Especially after the night before. As she slept, erotic whimpering noises slipped from between her lips, and in those moments, I wished more than anything I had the ability to travel through human dreams like my Uncle Leviathan and his descendants. I ended up caving, sending stimulating vibrations to her most sensitive locations, gifting her orgasms whilst she slept.

Making my way to stand behind her, I stare at her bare neck. Her fair hair falls forward around her face as she crouches over her worktable. Without touching her, I allow my lips to hover above the place where the top bone of her spine lifts her pale skin. I suddenly have the consuming urge to kiss her there.

He's close. She stills, dropping the odd toy she's been fiddling with all day. Closing the couple of inches between us, I softly press my lips to her neck. Tiny bumps rise across her flesh, and her breathing becomes jagged, yet she doesn't speak. Maybe she allows me this simply because she can't see me. Regardless of the reason, I slide my hand around her throat, gripping below her jaw as I move my mouth to the place where her pulse beats erratically. Her hair tickles my nose, smelling of her strawberry soap.

I'm worried if I make too sudden of a movement, she'll demand I stop, so I'm careful to barely touch her when I rub my thumb over her lower lip. Fuck, how is this getting me so aroused? With my other hand, I very slowly tug her sleeve down her arm, trailing my mouth across her shoulder.

"Loch." The whisper of my name is so quiet, if I weren't this near to her, I wouldn't have heard it.

I make sure my bransg is extended to her ears so she can't hear me speak. I don't want her to push me away. "You may possibly be the most stunning being I've ever seen." Tracing my fingers down her neck to her breast, I gently rub my thumb over her pebbled nipple. "Your bitchiness makes my cock hard." The quietest little noise slips from her lips while I slide my hand over the spider buttons of her shirt to reach the waist of her jeans. "And you know what else? My desire to fuck you has extended beyond simply wanting to go home."

Just when I'm about to grip the space between her legs, the door beside us opens, revealing her boss with the sexy ass. She jumps below me before fumbling with the deformed toy.

"Hey, Mishka. How's it going?"

"Uh, um…" Her voice comes out rough, so she clears her throat. "It's close to being done. The romper took longer than I thought because of the double neck holes. Once I finish the last few details, it'll be ready to ship."

He looks down at his watch. "It's too late to send out today anyway. Why don't you finish up tomorrow morning?"

"Sure. Thanks again, Ryan. For everything."

Giving her a nod, he backs out the door. A long breath whooshes from her mouth while she carries her project to a cardboard box. Without saying a word, she picks up her bag and walks out of the store.

I follow her outside, expecting her to stop so I can take her home, but she shows no sign of slowing.

After I shigmir behind the closest building and lower my bransg, I adorn my priidzar to catch up to her. "Mishka." I step in front of her, cutting her off. "Where are you going?"

She won't meet my eyes. "I'm just walking off some … stress."

The smell of her arousal fills my senses, the delicate taste on my tongue. She still thinks she can shield her true emotions from me, which is quite darling. Shoving my hands in my pockets, I lower my face to hers, our lips inches from touching.

"You enjoyed that as much as I did."

"I have no idea what you're talking about." She doesn't

even make the effort to sound convincing as she scrunches her eyebrows, her lips in an adorable pout.

"So if I were to slip my hand into those powder pink panties, I wouldn't find you wet?"

Even though she feigns offense with a scoff, there's no sincerity there. "Let's go." Her shoulder bumps against me when she spins around to walk toward the same building I was behind moments ago.

Still refusing eye contact, she wraps her arms around my waist, and I bring my hands to her ass, squeezing her plump cheeks.

I don't cover her in my wings this time, which can minimize disorientation, so once we land in her living room, she takes a second to get her bearings. She wriggles away from me but doesn't chastise me for grabbing her backside.

Turning away from me, she calls for her housemate. "I'm home, are you here?"

Earlier, while we were alone, Leena asked me so many damn questions it was exhausting. At the very least, she promised to do her best to destroy the Ammalok Qew. However, her attempt to catch it on fire was as useless as mine. The pages wouldn't tear either. It must have a weak spot, I just have to find it.

The sound of a door hitting the wall in the hallway signals her presence before Leena squeals her way into the sitting room. "Oh my God, this is the best day ever! First, I find out magical creatures are real, and now this. Look!"

She holds her telephonic communicating device up to Mishka's face, and I read what is supposedly so monumental over her shoulder.

Tim: Hey

Tim: I know I never hit you back after the other night.

I needed to process, and I've had a lot going on. I'm sorry.

Tim: Would you wanna chill with me sometime?

Mishka gasps, her face lighting up with a smile. "See? You just had to give him some time."

"I haven't answered yet. Make him suffer a bit, ya know?" Leena bounces from one foot to the other. "I need to go shopping. I'll get a new coffee table while I'm out too." Spinning on her heel, she burst through the beaded curtains to go back in the hall.

"We're going shopping?" I ask Mishka who widens her hazel eyes with a violent shake of her head.

"Oh, hell no. That girl takes hours to choose anything. Especially when she's this wound-up. I learned years ago to never go on a shopping spree with Leena Harris."

All I heard from that sentence is that Mishka and I are going to be alone for hours. I have to believe she'll eventually give in to what I can smell she wants.

Following her to the cooking quarters, I stare at her ass in those tight jeans, causing my cock to throb. The pain took much longer to make its appearance than it did last time, but now the ache is quickly beginning to creep up around my wings and horns, reminding me it's gaining on two days since my last release.

This woman is going to kill me.

I wouldn't live it down for millennia if anyone at home found out I was reduced to malnourishment all because I couldn't convince a measly human to lay with me.

Me.

The fucking son of Lilith and Asmodeus. It's preposterous at best and ignominious at worst.

Dysfunctional Deities

MISHKA

I groan at the bare refrigerator. We really need to go grocery shopping. There's some eggs and sandwich meat, but nothing that sounds appealing. Leena pops her head into the kitchen waving. "I'm out. See ya." Her keys *jingle* before she returns to add, "If you're gonna let him get it in, please do it in your room. I don't wanna walk in on that."

I whip my head around to glare at her. "Goodbye, Leena."

Her laughing can be heard halfway to the front door, and I curse her under my breath. Facing Loch, I ask, "What do you want to eat for dinner?"

He crosses his arms with a maddening smile as he leans against the kitchen table. "Is your pussy out of the question?"

He's such a pig, so it's complete bullshit that his comment

has me attempting to suppress the jolt between my legs. Giving him my most convincing expression of disgust, I dig my phone out of my purse. "I'll get a pizza."

Loch pushes off the table, walking out of the kitchen still wearing that stupid grin. I fight the urge to flip him the bird while I enter my order into the app.

After what happened at work today, I'm hesitant to be alone with him. I don't know why I let it continue other than I simply didn't want him to stop. It was massively weird to be touched by someone I couldn't see, and I'm sure that's why it was easier to just go with it.

It's ridiculous that I'm hiding from him in my own kitchen. Stalling longer than I can rightfully justify, I grab a bottle of Moscato and two mugs to meet him in the living room. I fall back on the couch next to him, realizing he's holding his head in his hands.

Before I can catch myself, I touch his arm. "Hey, are you okay?"

He jerks at the contact, staring down at my hand then at me, making me pull it back. Since I can't read intentions or whatever it is he can supposedly do, I can't figure out what seems off.

His eyes stay locked on mine for an uncomfortable length of time until I fill my cup up to the brim and down a huge gulp. I scoot the bottle toward him without looking at his face.

I could cry with relief when my phone *pings* with a distraction. That is, until I see who it is. Tossing the phone back on the table, I grumble under my breath. "Not today, not ever, Janet."

He leans back, tilting his head in question. "Who's Janet?"

"The mother of an asshole."

If his raised eyebrow is any indication, he wants to know more. But instead, he shifts the conversation in a surprisingly normal direction. "What is your mother like?"

His question feels genuine, with no innuendo or alternative motive beyond interest. "I have no idea. Apparently, some lady found me inside of a crib displayed at some bougie boutique when I was a baby. My entire adolescence was spent in the system, which is where I met Leena. She's my only family now."

"What's 'The System?'"

Sometimes, even when he appears ordinary like he does right now, he truly seems to be the ancient entity that he is. Then other times, he comes across as almost … innocent? That can't be the right word. "It's where kids who nobody wants to take care of go."

He sucks his teeth while shaking his head. "Mortals abandon their offspring quite easily, don't they?" I can't really confirm or deny that statement, so I shrug. "And Leena? Why was she there?"

Even now, thinking about what her parents put her through has the ability to make my skin itch. At least my parents had the decency to not give me psychological damage before throwing me away. Loch licks his lips, and I shift in my seat, trying not to think about the reality that he can, at least partially, dig into my brain. "Because she was born to pieces of shit who kicked her out when she was barely a teenager."

He leans forward with his elbows on his knees, resting his chin on his folded hands. "Why?"

The string of questions tumbling from his mouth makes him seem somewhat average. Kicking my legs up on the couch, I take a swig of wine. "Because she's trans."

He scrunches his nose in misunderstanding. "What's tranzz?"

The hard Z makes me laugh. Even I can admit that's kind of cute. "She was assigned male at birth."

He jerks his head back as if I have no idea what I'm talking about. "No. She wasn't. Her soul is female. I can sense it." I can't help but let a wide smile curl my lips, knowing how that would make Leena feel. "Souls get put in unmatching skin suits all the time."

Suddenly, I realize he can probably answer so many of the questions humankind has been asking since the beginning of time. "How do you know that?"

"Human souls are pure, raw essence. It has nothing to do with the genetics of their—your physical body. That's simply a casing. Some souls are what you think of as masculine or feminine. Some are neither, some are both."

I wish Leena was here to listen to this. "What about you? Demons, I mean?"

"Divine beings don't have souls. How we appear is a direct manifestation of our essence energy." He pulls up his sleeve, allowing his tattoos to melt into the glowing swirls and lines covering his body. "That's what saziamiin markings are made of."

Ever so softly, I touch over the spots that resemble flowing liquid gold. It moves, tickling my fingertips. "Wow."

"I like your face the best when it's wearing that smile."

I meet his eyes, surprised to see they look pained. Why do I want so badly to kiss it away? That's insane.

Breaking eye contact, I take a drink of wine and switch the topic. "What about your family?"

Lacing his fingers behind his head, he relaxes against the couch. "That's billions of years of dysfunctionality." His eyes glance upward as if he can see past the popcorn ceiling. "Many, many, many years ago, Uncle Lucifer got angry with my grandfather. He had always been the favorite…" His uncle is Lucifer?! Like the devil? Flipping his gaze to mine, he adds, "Until you flesh bags came along. As it *supposedly* goes, Lucifer felt creating you was cruel. Giving you existence without the knowledge of what will become of your souls was setting you up for failure. He confronted Grandfather, who dismissed the notion simply saying, those who were worthy would be fated to be by his side."

I hold up a hand to pause him. "Does He already know who's going to Heaven and who's going to Hell?" He gives no verbal response, but his expression of contempt is answer enough. "Why do you say, 'supposedly?'"

Dropping his voice like we're being listened to, he leans toward me. "If you knew my uncle, you'd know he rarely thinks of anyone besides himself. The idea that he could give a single shit about you is farfetched at best."

"He sounds charming."

"Oh, he is." Even though I was being sarcastic, I don't mention it so he will keep talking. I'll admit, he has me captivated. "It's just much more likely he felt threatened by your race than concerned for it, and at the time, there were only two of you in all existence. My grandfather gave more freedoms and ultimately more compassion to mortals than He did celestials, His own children. Regardless of how it went, I understand where Uncle Lucifer was coming from. He involved my father along with five of my uncles. Together, they recruited eight hundred and twelve lower ranking angels to start a seraphic war." He holds out his hands, insinuating that's the end of the story. "Madriiax would never be the same again."

"Madriiax?"

He rubs his head in the exact spot his horns grow from. "The Silver City. What you call Heaven or Paradise. Humans have a lot of names for it."

I may not be religious, but even I've heard the stories. My voice is barely above a whisper when I ask, "Are they the angels who fell? From Heaven?"

His eyes hold the ever-present mischief that causes them to gleam. "They didn't fall." He gives me that damned smirk which terrifies me yet if I'm honest with myself, turns me on every time. "They jumped." I realize my mouth is hanging open. This is so surreal. "Anyway, they inevitably lost the war and fled, finding the enigmatic shadowland of Madriiax: Maelprog. What you call Hell. It became a home of their own to do whatever they wished without their overbearing father."

Chills slither up my spine from listening to this. "Why do you only speak that way sometimes? You know, in your weird language?"

"Apparently, some Enochian doesn't translate in the mortal world. Usually, when I talk, it comes out in whatever language the person listening speaks, but with certain terms and topics, it doesn't transfer automatically here. Divine places, beings, antiprayers… I've never had that issue at home."

The shrill sound of the doorbell startles me so badly, I nearly spill my wine. Breathless, I tuck my hair behind my ear to answer the door. "Pizza's here."

Without looking back at Loch, I pay the delivery man, taking the pizza boxes to the kitchen and throwing a few slices on a couple plates. Before I go back out there and listen to more information that some people would probably kill for, I get another bottle of wine because I'm going to need it.

Handing him his plate, I sit down to take a big bite. "So your dad and uncles are now…"

"The kings of Maelprog."

I try to word my next question carefully because for once, I don't want to insult him. "Was um, mail-progg already a dark place, or is that what it became?" What I really want to know is if the location turned his uncles evil or vice versa.

"It's always been the opposite of Madriiax and about as far from my grandfather as one could get, so being there stripped them of their holiness, leaving them with only their respective …" he pauses, searching for his next words, "quirks. Thus, your seven deadly sins were born."

"Wait, so who is your dad?"

"Asmodeus."

While the name is familiar, that's the extent of my knowledge. "And his sin is?"

"Lust. Obviously." He gives me a wink that makes it nearly impossible not to smile.

I'll admit, I should have known that. "How does your mom fit into all of this? Is she an angel too?"

He laughs in a way that mildly brightens those dark eyes of his. "No. Absolutely not. She was humanity's first female."

No shit? "Your mom is *Eve?*"

His face falls, eyes widening when he says. "She would gut you and feast on your bowels if she ever heard you say that. My mother is Lilith."

Even though Leena's mentioned her on more than one occasion, I'm pretty sure she's not in the Bible. This is definitely not the story I've heard. "But wasn't it Eve with the apple and Lucifer?"

He shakes his head. "It's amazing how badly you mortals get this wrong. First, Eve and that whole situation came much later. Second, it wasn't my Uncle Lucifer, it was my Uncle Satan. Humans mix them up all the time for some reason. Third, the forbidden fruit wasn't an apple. It was laying with anyone besides each other, or in this case, my uncle."

This is so trippy, it's borderline comical. "Wait, so Eve slept with Satan? I thought Adam tasted the 'fruit' too?"

He nods like it should be obvious. "He did."

"That's hilarious. You know, because of the whole, 'It's Adam and Eve, not Adam and Steve' thing."

Frowning at me, he asks, "Are you not following? There was no Steve. Just Satan."

I snort, taking a bite of pizza and getting back to his story. "Never mind. Then how did your mom end up with your dad?"

His eyebrows relax and he takes a drink of his wine, "She was created for Adam, not the other way around. I personally believe my Uncle Lucifer was infatuated with her from the moment he first laid eyes on her. Adam demanded she lay with him, to which she refused, hiding in the garden. My grandfather sent a murifri down, forcing her to return. When Adam had her back in his possession, he raped her, quite brutally, and Uncle Lucifer stepped in to save her, stealing her away from Eden. From there, Grandfather cursed her with horns, fangs, and the tongue of a serpent to make her ugly. She was banished, destined to spend the rest of her days alone in exile. Only, she wasn't. Uncle Lucifer visited her often, finding her even more desirable wearing the physical proof of her rebellion. After she died, he planned to take her as his bride. Except that's not who my mother is. She will never belong to any man, divine or otherwise." He talks about her with so much love. It makes it easy to forget why I tried so hard to despise him. "She told me that from the moment she entered Maelprog, she desired my father as he did her. Of course, Lucifer turned violent upon learning they were fucking."

I'm still confused. "How does that work? Aren't we little floating balls of our 'essence' when we die?"

He tilts his head back and forth as if he approves of the question, giving me a streak of pride. "Your physical bodies do dissolve into the Earth, yes, but your souls are powerful. Arguably the most powerful energy besides my grandfather. Once outside of this realm, they manifest another exterior. One unable to age or wither, mirroring how the soul sees itself." I must still appear lost because he continues his explanation. "For example, at home, if I was to cut off your head, it would simply replace itself. You would still feel the pain, furthermore, it would be more agonizing than anything your earthly body would be capable of feeling. Hence why it's never-ending torture for the damned."

"Well, that sounds terrifying."

"It's supposed to. That was Grandfather's way of sticking it to my uncles. Leave them in charge of tormenting the vilest products of humanity for all eternity." He grins at me. "Jokes on him, though, because it's fucking fun."

For the ones doing the torturing, maybe. Seeing his pizza, I realize he hasn't taken a single bite. Mostly, he's done nothing more than pick at the pepperoni, making me wonder if food is necessary for him. "Do you even need to eat?"

He tosses his paper plate on the burnt coffee table with a grimace. "Somewhat, only not like you're assuming."

I wait for him to elaborate, but he doesn't. "And what does that mean?"

"What I consume and where my nourishment comes from are two different things. While I can taste the minty flavor of the pleasure you're getting from that peet-za, my nourishment is derived from culmination."

My food goes down the wrong pipe, causing me to cough. "Are you saying you can eat emotions?"

He smiles, and I watch his tongue swipe across his lower lip. "See, you're not so dim after all."

Even though my jaw drops at his insult, I find myself laughing. Heated sensations roll around in my stomach when I playfully shove his arm. "You're such a dick."

Taking my hand away slower than necessary, I watch his eyes travel over my body. I know he's biting back a perverted response. Part of me wishes he wouldn't. I'm starting to welcome his blatantly sexual banter.

Mesmerized by a Mortal

Loch

I don't know what infuriates me more about this human. How much I enjoy her company, or how she can so easily resist me when I'm obviously alluring. She has so many questions, yet I somehow don't tire from answering them. Every time she laughs or tucks her hair behind her ear or even fucking breathes, I wish I could hold her down and sink myself into her body.

"Lucifer was enraged about my parents, making sure everyone in Maelprog suffered for it. My mother was the only one who could calm him. Eventually, she brought both him and my father to her bed, proving her affections were in enough abundance for the both of them, and that her yearning for one didn't diminish her desire for the other. However, it didn't have the effect she was hoping for. To prove her point that she wasn't his to control, she ended up laying with all of my uncles, giving them each offspring, hence how she became known as the 'mother of orseiinak.' After that, he was keener to share her with my father, and truthfully, I think it made him respect her more."

Once I finish explaining the eternal love triangle between my father, mother, and Uncle Lucifer, she's borderline cackling. "I'm not trying to be offensive, but I didn't know Lilith was such a ho."

Now that she's started on the second bottle, she's clearly feeling the effects of her wine. "You say that like it's an insult. My mother is a very powerful and sexual entity. That's one of the many reasons she's revered as queen even though she has no reign over any of the seven kingdoms."

Her eyes glitter when she rests her face in her hand. "So you're Hell royalty. A prince of the lust kingdom."

"Zibiidor Comselh, yes." I take out the pack of cigarettes I stole from the dead fat man and make the end burn with the touch of my fingertip.

Her eyes widen in amazement. "That's cool as shit."

I stare at the smoking stick, flabbergasted at how she could be so incredibly dense. "No. It's hot. That's how it lights."

Her eloquent laugh fills the room again. "I just mean it's a neat trick. Can I have one of those?" She twists her hair around her finger. "I normally throw a fit about smoking inside because of our deposit, so Leena's gonna be so pissed if she finds out I let you do it in here." Our fingers brush together when she takes it from me, and I feel her slight shiver from our touch. I light it for her, and she clears her throat, continuing with her interrogation. "What makes people deserve to go to Ma—Hell? Is it stealing a pair of shoes, or do you have to kill a bunch of people?"

I love the taste and sensation of the smoke moving around on my tongue. "Sin is only sin if it severely hurts another being without their approval and is done so intentionally." She rolls her cigarette between her fingers, staring at it in studious contemplation, so I elaborate. "It takes a lot of sin to get there." After silently finishing her smoking stick, she leans forward to snuff it out in her leftover pizza. I put mine out with my fingers, tossing it on her plate.

Her body has been scooting closer to me over the past several minutes, and her emotions toward me have gone from peppery uncertainty to honeyed fascination. Reaching toward her, I brush my fingers across her wrist. A soft breath makes her lips tremble as she reciprocates, placing her hand on my arm. "You're a misunderstood creature, aren't you?"

"Humans misunderstand most things." She scrunches her nose in offense, and it's so damn darling, I lean forward to kiss it.

It may be her inebriated state, or maybe she's finally allowing herself to warm up to me. Regardless of the reason, once I hear the word, *Kiss*, I know she's going to do it a millisecond before she does. For someone who previously seemed so averse to any sexual activity, her desire has quickly become so heavy that it's compelling. Her hands on my face would have my heart thrashing in my chest if I had one. Her lips crash against mine, yet I can hardly call it a kiss because it's incomparable to the billions prior to it.

My emotions aren't defined the same way mortals' are. What I feel tends to blend together. This kiss, as it deepens, makes it increasingly difficult to keep my priidzar on, but I'm also getting weak. Still, this is not a simple kiss. There's so much more to it, and it's irritating that I can't place why.

Her eyes blink open, separating our lips as her laugh adds a rose tint to her cheeks. "Wow. That was … wow." Her embarrassment is another delectable treat. "I shouldn't be surprised with you being, you know, you."

I want to tell her she has no idea. When she eventually lays with me, which she will, she'll be ruined for any other person after. None of them will have the ability to scratch the surface of the sexual bliss I'll give her. Mentioning that now, though, could set us back, and we're finally making progress.

Rougher than intended, I reciprocate, fisting the hair at her nape with one hand while jerking her onto my lap with the other. She winces slightly, yet from the thick excitement she's feeding me, it's clear she has no objections. Being who I am, I literally want to fuck constantly, but this is more than that. More than my basic physical requirement. It intrigues and annoys me that I don't understand what I'm experiencing.

Her shirt needs to go, and I haven't the patience for buttons. With one rip, it's tossed to the floor.

"Hey!" From what I can taste and smell, her aggravation is trying to peek through, she's just too turned on for it to stick. "That's one of my favorite tops." The sentence is barely completed when her mouth is exploring mine once again.

I don't understand why this is so intense, so different. She's only a human. Even with Semanedai, it's never been so sinfully erotic.

It's impossible for me to hold on anymore. My priidzar falls off, causing her to gasp in surprise, and it pleases me there's not the slightest hint of fear. She scans my form, pushing my sweater up my chest and lifting it over my head. Her fingers are cool to the touch as they softly brush over one of my horns, making me shudder.

Her eyebrow quirks with her question. "Are they tender?"

"You could definitely say that."

My cock is aching in these terrible trousers. They are uncomfortable. I much prefer my necropants. She makes me groan when she wraps her fist around my right horn, slowly caressing it. "Are they like your…" Her eyes lower to my groin that she's currently rocking against.

"They're an erogenous zone. Ejaculate won't squirt from them if that's what you're wondering."

Her laugh is an aphrodisiac all on its own. "Gross." She keeps her steady stroking before doing the same to my left one. My saziamiin glow brighter the longer we kiss.

My tugging on the waistband of her jeans has her hips rolling with anticipation. Right when I'm about to reach inside them, she stops me, and I have to bite my lip in order to keep myself from growling in protest. "What happens if we have sex?"

What kind of question is that? "Uh … orgasms?"

She tilts her head and slits her eyes like it was a stupid answer. What else is she expecting to happen?

"I mean, will you leave?"

I don't know how I possibly forgot about that. I'm much more focused on being with her than completing my task so I can go home. "What exactly did you expect by calling?"

Her nostrils flare. "I don't know, Loch. I was drinking and mostly appeasing Leena."

Now that she brought it up, I don't think I'm ready to go yet. Bringing my hand between her legs, I rub the spot I'm aching for. "There's other things we can do if you want me to stick around."

She glances down to watch me touch her, and the moment our eyes meet again, she wraps her arms around my neck to kiss me with an aggression I've never seen from her. Her tongue slides into my mouth, licking at the space where mine splits. Reaching behind her, I cup her ass and flip her on her back. I lie on top of her to bite her neck and shigmir us to her bed.

It takes her a second to realize where she is, but when she does, I'm rewarded with one of her prettiest smiles. "That's never going to get old."

My finger hooks around her bra strap, lowering it down her arm as my lips follow close behind. The pain is getting stronger and harder to hide. I involuntarily groan at the sharp stab shooting through my head.

"Are you okay?"

"It's been nearly two days since…" I almost mention Leena before realizing that's probably not the smartest idea. From the expression on her face, I didn't need to say it. Shit, I think I pissed her off, and neither her thoughts nor emotions are giving me anything. She shoves on my shoulder to push me away from her. I could scream. I was so close. I prepare to defend myself, remind her she already knew about it, when her hands grip the waist of my pants. I don't move an inch while she trails soft kisses along my stomach. Her small fingers undo the button, and I reach forward to push her bra down the rest of the way so I can cup her impeccable breast.

She lowers the zipper with tedious leisure, and once I'm free, her eyes bulge. I watch her nearly gnaw off half her lip. Grinning, I suck the mix of surprise and fascination off my tongue. There's even a tasty bit of nervousness mixed in. "You okay?"

She swallows, her throat bobbing as she croaks, "You have the glowing tattoos there too, and it's … a lot bigger than I expected." Barely touching them, the pads of her fingers caress the ridges beneath my skin that circle up my shaft from base to tip. "What are these?"

"They're called farzem rings."

She presses her lips together, her cheeks flushing pink. "Wow."

Leaning against the wall, I trace my tongue over my fang.

She crawls toward me, and when she's close enough, I grab the back of her neck, bringing her ear to my mouth. I bite her lobe, whispering, "Are you scared, tin nanba?" Her body tenses, trepidation coating my throat.

Cool breath blows against my shoulder as her demeanor relaxes. "Do you plan on telling me what that means?"

I press the tips of my tongue against her neck, licking where her tendons lift her supple skin. "The closest translation would be 'enchanting thorn.' As in, thorn in my side." When I gave her the name, that's how I felt. Now, though, only half of it remains true.

Her body vibrates with her laugh, and her hand squeezes my waist. "Aren't you one to talk."

She touches me so softly I barely feel it, tracing her fingertips across my abdomen. My cock jerks, the symbols of my home brightening with anticipation from watching her. She takes a deep breath, hesitating for a moment before finally wrapping her cool hand halfway around my erection, making me hiss at the sensation.

Her gaze flicks up to mine, evaporating my last bit of patience when I pump against her palm. Slowly, she strokes me, her thumb running over the tip. "Is it going to do anything weird? Like your tongue?"

I grin at her, continuing to rock into her touch. "It's not going to split down the middle if that's what you mean."

My response is rewarded with a breathy laugh. "Okay." Her tentative conduct is killing me. Suddenly, her tongue darts out, tracing the saziamiin swirling around my shaft. My head hits the wall as I comb my fingers through her flaxen hair, fondling the silver strands at her nape. I grunt at the intensity of her lips wrapping around my tip and watch my cock slowly disappear inside her mouth, one farzem ring at a time.

The hand not in her locks brushes the stray strands from

her face so I can watch her. Her enthusiasm increases every time she lowers her head. I softly touch down her back, caressing the raised scars that are smooth beneath my fingers.

I've mastered control of my stamina, ensuring I and however many sexual partners I'm with reach satisfaction. But for the first time maybe ever, I have to choose between my need to come and my desire to make this last.

It's incredibly difficult not to close my eyes and enjoy what's quite possibly the most pleasurable blow job I've ever had, yet I don't want to miss a second of watching how beautiful she looks doing this.

Her lips glow with the brightening of my markings indicating I'm getting closer to completion. I push down on her head to meet each jerk of my hips, her saliva dripping down my cock. Even though I could easily go longer, I sense the level of discomfort she's feeling. "Unholy fuck. Keep sucking like that, and I'm gonna fill up that gorgeous mouth."

That seems to give her momentum. I consciously control the heat I'm releasing so I don't burn her mouth when my come bursts from my cock, jetting down her throat.

She waits until I'm drained to lift her head, licking her lips before wiping an excess drop of semen from my tip and sucking it off her finger. Pink blushes her cheeks while she massages her jaw.

"You taste ... sweet."

14

Hot and Horned

MISHKA

His white eyes blaze, and as if taken over by his feral nature, his hand flies up to wrap around my neck. He squeezes hard, but just when it becomes painful, he loosens his grip.

"My turn."

A paralyzing grin stretches his face, and in a blink, I'm on the opposite end of my bed, my ass resting right on the edge. Out of instinct, I look over my shoulder at the place we were less than a second ago. I don't know if I'll ever become accustomed to that. His fingers make quick work of my button and zipper, bringing my attention back to him. Yanking my panties and jeans down my legs, his pronged tongue licks his lower lip before he drops to his knees.

My heart thrashes, frantic in my rib cage. His every touch is hot, close to the point of discomfort. Fingers dig into my flesh, shoving my legs open as he lowers his head between my thighs. His horns are perfect for gripping, and I don't hold back my moan when his hot tongue dips inside me, massaging multiple places at once.

"Fuck, Loch," I gasp. My hips rotate on their own, grinding against his devilish mouth. My God, he hasn't even gotten to my clit yet. Taking his time, he tugs on the curled hair between my legs before slowly sliding in a warm finger. He bites the inside of my thigh hard enough to break the skin then licks up the blood that escapes. The shock of it is painful, but somehow feels so damn good it's undoubtedly worth it.

I can't place this familiar feeling I have all over my skin. It gives me the sense of being blissfully weightless. Then I realize it's reminiscent of being high on opium. Everything is perfect, and I'm certain this is the happiest I'll ever be again. Why on earth did I wait so long to allow him to let me experience this? Biting softly, he goes back and forth between my pussy lips, taking them between his teeth all while pumping in a second finger, caressing places inside me that I didn't know could be touched.

I'm panting like a whore, and I don't give a single shit. The vibrations are so transcendent, they bring me to the brink of crying. I stroke his horns in tempo with my thrusting, nearly passing out when his lips wrap around my clit. He sucks on me with mastered pressure while I look down to watch him. If I couldn't see that I am in fact still on my bed, I would question if I was hovering in the air. Drifting.

He sticks out his tongue, pushing back the skin of my hood and giving me the sensation of being licked by two people at the same time. Each hot, muscled tip swirls around the exposed bundle of nerves and pulses in a way that wouldn't be possible for a human. Knowing he has the power to force me to come on command makes his mouth's performance that much more erotic.

I don't want this to end. I want it to last forever, but I'm too weak, and his magic tongue is too proficient. As every molecule of my body separates, the only thing holding me up is my grip on his horns. With each throb of my orgasm, time stands still, draining every bit of vitality I have to give. I don't know how long it lasts, lost in the high of pure, uncut rapture. I have to push away the thought that once he's gone, I'll never feel this again.

I don't know whether he allows me to come down, or my body finally gives out, but every inch of me feels shaky and useless. And that was just foreplay. Can someone overdose on pleasure? If so, I doubt I'll live through having him inside me.

He finally lifts his head, a huge grin revealing his fangs. "Ready?"

I'm barely able to process what he's saying. "For what?"

His mouth latches back on, making me cry real tears. "No … Loch…" The sensitivity is torturous until his tongue resumes its manipulation. My legs tense up, pressing against his ears before he shoves them back open and the tenderness melts into desire. I run my fingers over the short part of his hair, feeling the braids on the side of his head before I tug on his horns for dear life, riding the explosive high that distorts time. Even though I can hear myself, I can't believe it's me making those sounds. The contracting sensation between my legs seems to never stop. When it finally does slow, he shows no indication of doing the same.

"Seriously, Loch, I can't go again."

He doesn't respond, his fingers finding a new place to exploit into bringing me back to the brink. I'm weaving in and out of reality, not knowing when or where I am. After the third or fifth or tenth never-ending flow of euphoria, I'm sure I've been drained of all moisture.

Lifting his head to look at me, he sucks his lip into his mouth and stands to his feet. I whimper in respite, feeling boneless as I lie limp on my bed. He hovers above me, his kisses tender and controlled. At some point, he slides his cock between my lips, but I'm too exhausted to do much performing.

Luckily, he doesn't need me to. His hands clench at my skull, using my mouth however he pleases.

The heated tendrils of markings lining his shaft move against my tongue. The hard rings that are beneath his skin make him even larger in the places they're located, expanding my mouth farther every time one passes my lips. Incredibly, I'm hit with a second wave of vigor, allowing me the zeal to suction around him.

With surprising softness compared to the violent thrusts causing me to gag, he brushes the hair off my face. "You look so amazing like this. Keep going, I'm almost done."

His words of praise give me the fuel to increase my enthusiasm. The tensing of his body has me desperate to finish this with my finest performance. I try my best to move my tongue while his girth stretches my lips. Suddenly without warning, another blissful, overwhelming crash of a supercharged orgasm pushes through my body. My lips are pushed open wider as his dick grows bigger, pulsing in my mouth and emptying his come down my throat.

Every part of me is inoperable. Mind and body. I don't even have the power to sit up, so I use my final drop of energy to close my eyes.

The last thing I process is his hot chest pressing against my back while he covers us with my blanket.

"Sleep well, tin nanba."

My entire body aches. I don't even think I have the ability to get out of bed. The sound of Leena's laughing dances in my ears from behind my bedroom door. Groaning, I roll over to find the other side of my bed empty. I wonder if Loch sleeps. Remembering the night before has me grinning, pulling a soft laugh from my lips.

The vibration of my phone on my nightstand forces me to sit up and grab it. I swipe open the screen to see a message from Ryan.

He wants me to switch my morning shift with Beckany so she can leave early. Sweet, now I don't have to rush.

Falling back against my pillow in relief, I hear Leena laugh again, making it clear I'm not going to be able to go back to sleep. I stand to my feet, groaning in protest of my sore muscles. Bruises sprinkle across my thighs and hips. Simply looking at them leaves a tickle in my stomach. Wrapping my robe around myself, I walk into the living room to see what has Leena so amused this early in the damn morning.

Her and Loch are sitting on the couch as she sips her coffee. "Whatever he's saying can't be that hilarious," I grumble, passing them to go to the kitchen for my own cup.

"Had a rough night, did ya?"

I flip her off when Loch appears in my pathway, causing me to release a yelp.

He gives me a lopsided grin, his hair falling into his dark eyes in an unnaturally hot way. "Hey."

"Hey. No teleporting earlier than nine o'clock."

Clearly unfazed that I'm not a morning person, he follows me to the coffee pot, wrapping his arms around my waist to slip his hand into my robe. Rubbing the pad of his finger over my swollen clit, he bites my ear. There's no point in acting like I don't enjoy his affections after last night. His erection presses into the small of my back, his touch moving farther down until he's dipping his finger in and out of me.

"Are you constantly horny?"

The sound of his laugh in my ear surely has me soaking his hand. "Is that a serious question?"

I turn around to face him, forcing him to remove his fingers. "You gotta at least let me drink my coffee, man."

Without missing a beat, he leans forward, resting his hands on the counter behind me, caging me in. He's in his human form, so his tongue looks normal when he licks his bottom lip. "There's plenty I can do while you drink your disgusting beverage."

It seems a bit pathetic that I feel this giddiness in my stomach after only knowing him a few days. The way he's staring at me right now, it's a wonder I was able to resist him at all. His lips are inches from mine, so I barely have to move to kiss him. Lowering my hand to rub his erection over his pants, I whisper against his cheek, "Once Leena goes to work, I promise."

His face is hard to read as he reaches back between my legs, dipping two fingers into my pussy before sucking them into his mouth. "Then I'll be back soon."

"Where are you—" He vanishes as my hand reaches for the now vacant spot. "Going?" I ask the empty kitchen with a sigh.

Logically, I know it's not good that my heart is flipping around in my chest. His time here is temporary. Right now, though, it's such a wonderful feeling, I manage to push down my worries for another day.

Walking into the living room, I meet Leena grinning on the couch like she's Willem Dafoe in The Smile Man. I act irritated, but I'm honestly excited to tell her everything.

"It's been a long time since I've seen that smile." She crosses her arms, raising a smug eyebrow at me.

I hear myself giggle like I'm twelve, and I don't even care right now. "What did he tell you?"

"The cliff notes." She flicks her tongue out, mimicking cunnilingus.

I shake my head with a laugh. "Gross." After taking a sip of coffee, I set my mug on the cute, baby blue coffee table she bought.

"Well? Do I get your version?"

No matter how hard I try, I can't wipe the smirk off my face. "Did he tell you he can split his tongue down the middle?" For reference, I wiggle my middle and pointer finger.

Her jaw drops, and I must admit, shocking Leena with anything involving sex is a feat in itself. "No way." I nod, laughing at her expression. I can practically see her picturing it in her brain. "That's hot."

"In hindsight, it's a little bit surreal. At one point I felt … high."

She punches her fist against the back of the couch. "I knew I wasn't crazy! I wonder if it has something to do with his demon semen."

My chest compresses at the mention of their time together, and I do my best to ignore it. I know she doesn't mean anything by it. She's obviously happy for me, I just despise being reminded that she was with him first. It's not fair for me to hold that over either of their heads, though.

For the rest of the hour, I give her all the details I can remember, considering I felt out of it half the time. Once finished, she stands up to stretch. "Wow. Now you have me worked up. I'm gonna take a shower and have some me time."

"Jesus." Snorting, I pick up my mug. "Thanks for getting the new coffee table by the way. It's adorable."

She shrugs. "I know. And you're welcome."

I sip on my coffee, turning on the television for mindless noise. While Loch could very well be anywhere right now, if he were here, I'd like to believe he'd tell me. Even thinking about him touching me again has me shifting around in my seat. I have the urge to reach into my panties and rub away the increasing prickles, but after knowing what he can do, I'd hate to waste an orgasm on my own fingers.

I wonder where he goes when he's not here. Even though I have no idea how he would have met anyone else, my deep-seated insecurities still have me wondering if he's been with anyone besides Leena since being here.

Until Harry, I had never been in a serious relationship. Definitely not anything that lasted more than a few months. If I had ever been cheated on prior to him, I never knew about it, and his betrayal has undoubtedly made me much less trusting. The thing is, Loch and I couldn't be committed even if we wanted to. He's not human, and Earth isn't his home. Never mind that he's been around long before me, and he'll be around long after me. Why am I letting myself get attached so quickly?

Is it that he's constantly cheery even when it's maddening, or is it that he's actually a sweet guy under all the perverted comments? Maybe it's because he's so gorgeous it's hypnotic. Not to mention his ability to give sexual pleasure an entirely different meaning. It could simply be because he's a magical being that I never believed in until he showed up in my kitchen.

I blow a stream of air from my lips, causing the hair in my face to flutter off my forehead. Even knowing it's dangerous and stupid, I'm still excited for him to come back. I want to be pretty for him.

Hearing Leena leave the bathroom, I make my way to the

shower, getting last night's residue off my skin. I brush my teeth, apply my moisturizer, and try to determine if putting on makeup for Loch is worth it when he'll likely mess it up. Deciding to keep it simple, I apply blush, mascara, and eyeliner for a somewhat natural look. Leena knocks on the door and peeks her head in, her paint palette earrings matching her colorful striped pantsuit.

"I'm leaving for work. Don't forget, I have my date with Tim tonight, so I'll probably be gone by the time you get home."

Squealing, I clap my hands. "Oooh, have fun! Hopefully I won't see you until tomorrow." She crosses her fingers, and I hold up my pink glitter lip gloss. "Yes or no?"

"No. You're already awhoradorable."

Running my fingers through my damp hair, I toss the gloss back into my makeup bag. "Love you."

"Love you too. Byeee." She backs out of the bathroom, giving me an air kiss.

I stare at my reflection for a moment, grabbing the stupid lip gloss and putting it on. Once I cross the hall to my room, I open the door to find Loch lying on my bed, smoking a cigarette.

"How many times do I have to tell you to do that outside?"

He smirks, putting the smoke out on his tongue. "Better?"

I never would have thought that would have been so hot to watch. My mouth feels dry, so I swallow and clear my throat. "Much. Thank you."

The last word barely leaves my lips when he's off the bed, standing right in front of me. Cupping my face with both hands, he kisses me, his tongue licking the seam of my lips before he slips it into my mouth. His fingers trail down my neck and chest until they wrap around the top of my towel. "Leena's gone."

Now that I've given in to his charms, excitement at feeling his touch again consumes my every thought. I want so badly to sleep with him, but that marks the end. I'm definitely not ready for the end.

His fingers undo the knot in my towel, dropping it on the floor. Reaching around me, he cups my bare ass, picking me up. Wrapping my legs around his waist, my pussy presses against his stomach, and in an unintentional reaction, I rock my hips so my clit slides across his hard abs. I watch his gaze fall to see me grinding on him which only makes me do it more. Fuck. The way he brings that bottom lip between his teeth has my nipples hardening.

Walking backward, he falls onto the bed with me still wrapped around his middle. I hover over him, blonde strands falling in my face that he softly tucks behind my ear. We stare at each other in silence for so long, I wonder if he's waiting for me to say something. His tongue traces his bottom lip, splitting as I watch. Blackness creeps around his eyes like ink while his dark irises are engulfed by solid white.

When the skin of his forehead splits, I place my mouth at the hole, allowing his horn to slide against my tongue as it grows from his head. The smooth texture turns rough when the threading tightens near the base.

He shudders beneath me, his fingers squeezing my waist. "Fuck." Pushing down on my hips, he moves me enough to rub the erection in his jeans against my pussy. His voice deepens, taking on his thickened accent when he says, "Suck on it."

I trace my tongue around the swirls at the bottom, slowly making my way to the pointed top. Stroking the other one with my hand, I bring the tip between my lips, surprised at the subtle malty taste. Since I've obviously never done this before,

I don't go down too quickly or suction too hard. The closer the horn gets to the base, the thicker it gets, so I can't take too much, or the point will stab me in the back of the throat.

He uses his grip on my hips to move my body how he wants, rocking against me. Clawing his fingers up my back, he brings a nipple between his teeth, alternating his licks and bites. Goosebumps rush across my flesh, and with how hot his body is, it's odd that a shiver courses through me.

I continue sucking until his hand presses against my chest, pushing me away from his horn. The sensation of being tickled spreads across my insides when he gives me that mischievous, crooked smile, revealing a bit of fang. "Come here."

Scare and Seek

Loch

I may be young by divine standards, however, I am almost one hundred thousand years old. In all that time, no being has ever made me feel … this. I wish I could eat my own emotions, then I could figure out what they are.

One thing I am sure of, is this isn't natural.

The sounds that come out of her mouth are something I could easily listen to for the rest of eternity. Her cunt hovers over my face, her grip on my horns tightening as if she's attempting to pull them from my skull. I love how she tastes, it's a metallic sweetness that I've never experienced from daemonesses.

Bruises darken the skin on her thighs, and I adore seeing the temporary proof of my touch. Twirling the tips of my tongue around her hard little nub, I suck it between my lips as the little blonde hairs above her pussy brush against my nose. The pace of her breathing fluctuates between slow gasps and fast panting. *Come.* I hear the word right before her arousal flows into my mouth, her clit grinding against my tongue.

"I'm coming, Loch … oh, shit, I'm coming."

Manipulating her orgasm to last a little longer, my fingers explore her clenching pussy. Unholy fuck, I'm desperate to put myself inside of it, yet I'm far from ready to end our time together.

I allow her body to naturally ebb down, her pretty sigh of contentment becoming one of my favorite sounds Grandfather ever created. She lifts her right leg to get off my face, but when she turns around to reach for my cock, I pull her right back.

"Come on, Loch. How about you give me a second to recuperate?"

"How about you give me a second to make you not give a fuck?"

After she momentarily tenses, her hips begin to roll again. I feel her soft fingers on my stomach before hearing the zipper of my heavy blue pants. Her mouth isn't hot like my previous daemonic bedmates, but it's far from cold.

Although she lasts longer this time, I still pull the word, *Hurts*, from her thoughts. Giving her one more orgasm to ease the pain in her jaw, I feed her my come.

Climbing off my body, she licks the residual semen from her lips, curling up next to me to rest her head against my chest. "I can't believe how insane that feels."

She's breathless, her blonde hair covering part of her face. I move it out of the way to kiss her head. This is odd too. We've already done what we're going to do for now, so why do I still want to touch and hold her? I don't understand the point, yet I desire it all the same.

I stare at the scars on her back that are thin and silver.

My fingers brush over their silky texture, and I can't comprehend why it makes me so inexplicably angry that someone could ever harm her bad enough to leave permanent damage.

"What made them hurt you?"

Lifting her head, she rests her chin on her arm to look at me with glossed over eyes. "Hmm? Who?"

"The mortals who gave you these scars."

She traces my saziamiin on my chest with her fingertips, softly kissing them. "It was a long time ago, and I was really young. I don't remember why exactly. I think I didn't eat my food or something. I just remember the whippings. I wasn't the only one she hit either. That kind of thing can be common when you're a foster kid."

Foster kid. That's what the woman called Pygmy last time I saw her. If I ever find out someone is doing that to her, they'll be not only punished for that but what was done to Mishka as well.

While lost in my fantasies of revenge, she grumbles against my chest. "I really don't want to go to work today."

"Then don't." I'd much rather her stay right here.

She shakes her head with a pout that has me wanting to go again. "I just got the job back. I can't call in."

Reaching into the pocket of my undone trousers, I pull out the pack of cigarettes to slide one between my lips. I barely get it lit before Mishka sits up and points to her door. "Outside. I can't let you smoke in here if I'm not going to let Leena."

"Then let Leena."

"Out."

I'm not sure why I let her order me around or why I kind of like it. Meeting her determined gaze, I take a deep inhale then shigmir to her front porch to release the smoke.

I sit in the little chair next to the ashtray, shivering from the chilled, wet air as I watch the vehicles driving back and forth in front of her house until one unexpectedly pulls into her driveway. A man steps out with a scowl, his heavy anger wafting off him in waves.

"Who in the hell are you?"

I take a long drag off the cigarette, already jaded by whoever this asshole is. "How'd you know where I was from?" His confusion is the perfect post orgasm snack. Chuckling at his foolish expression, I have half a mind to take off my priidzar and really freak him out.

Taking a small paper bag out of his hideous brown jacket, he steps out of the rain and onto the porch. "Is Mishka here?"

Now it's my turn to be caught off guard. I'm not good with human ages, but with his graying hair and boring clothes, I assume he's quite a bit older than her. Since I know for certain he's not her father, I'm not thrilled with the possibilities of what the alternative could be.

I inhale more smoke, thinking of the most colorful way to tell him to fuck off when Mishka opens her front door. "Harry?" Her suffocating anxiety along with how hard her heart is beating at the sight of this dull human lifts me to my feet. "What are you doing here?"

His eyes flash to mine while he closes in on her. "You wouldn't answer my texts."

Stabbing the butt into the tray, I cross my arms. "Yet you're still too dimwitted to figure out she clearly doesn't want to talk to you."

Mishka glares at me. *Quiet.*

The unwelcome parasite lifts his lip in a snarl before raising his voice to her. Not a smart move on his part.

"Is this guy your boyfriend or something? Didn't take you long, now did it?"

Her mouth falls open, rage consuming every other emotion she was previously feeling. I grin at him. "I'm far from a boy, and the fact that I can still taste her pussy on my tongue suggests we're much more than friends."

Pink dances across her cheeks, her head snapping in my direction. "Loch!" She jabs a finger toward her front door. "Go inside."

Doing what she says, I smirk at the seething man on her porch. Of course, I'm not going to actually wait inside. Once I pull up my bransg, I slip on my sweater that was draped over the couch and shigmir back outside, refusing to miss a word of their exchange.

"You really have the balls to be opinionated on what I'm doing after you stuck your dick in someone else while we were still together?"

Unholy fuck, her anger is exquisite. He reaches out to touch her, pleasing me when she turns away in revolt. "If you would have talked to me, I would have told you it was an inebriated mistake. I would have apologized."

Her head tilts, causing her blonde hair to fall off her shoulder. "Oh really?" she croons sweetly. "Golly, that changes everything."

I gape at her regardless of being hidden. She can't be that easily manipulated.

"Watch the attitude, Mishka. Sarcasm isn't attractive on anyone." Ah, sarcasm. That's a human quirk that always throws me. "And are you high right now? You look blitzed out of your mind."

She crosses her arms with a scoff. "Not that it's any of your business, but no, I'm not."

"Whatever. We need to talk about the baby." He holds up the bag he's carrying. "You left these."

The what now? My head snaps back and forth between them, realizing there's so much I don't know about her. Not that we've had an eternity together to talk about our pasts.

She smacks her lips, jerking the bag from his hand. "Fine. The baby's dead, just like this relationship. You flaming. Piece. Of. Shit. Good talk."

I'm torn between being rock hard from her feistiness and being caught off guard by the mention of their deceased offspring.

He leans forward, nostrils flaring. I'm not above hanging him from the tree in her yard if he comes a step closer to her. "Mishka, come on. I screwed up, okay? Let me fix this. You can't throw away three years over something so stupid."

His hand reaches up to her face, cupping her cheek, and she doesn't stop him. I have the sensation of something snapping inside my chest, and it hurts. She closes her eyes, leaving her emotions so muddled nothing is coming through clearly. When she opens them, her cinnamon ire gushes down my throat.

"I didn't. You did. Getting your dick wet meant more to you than I did. I don't care how damn drunk you were."

I watch his hand snake around her waist, making it incredibly difficult to not break his legs. "I love you, baby. Please forgive me. I'm begging you."

For whatever unfathomable reason, he takes her tense stance as an invitation to kiss her jaw. The same moment I'm about to grab him by the neck and slam him into the concrete, she shoves her hands against his chest. "Stop. Get off me, Harry."

Instead of listening to her extremely clear request, he pushes his body flush to hers, trapping her between him and the door. Still kissing her, his hand reaches into her robe. Is she allowing this? I can't describe how watching this is making me feel, but I do know I despise it.

"Let me show you how sorry I am. I'll make you forget all about that punk kid inside."

No.

132

The moment the taste of her fear hits my tongue, I reach for the back of his jacket at the exact moment she grunts, thrusting her arms in front of her to get him away. "I said get off me! I don't ever want to see you again. Leave me alone."

Seeing the tears in her eyes brings back the stabbing sensation in my chest. Her heartbreak is choking me. How could he hurt her? How could he purposefully cause her an ounce of pain?

When she goes inside and slams the door, I shigmir to the back seat of his car. She may not plan on making him suffer. I, on the other hand, have every intention of doing just that.

Storming back to his vehicle, he grumbles to himself. "Bitch."

My first thought is to simply kill him. Then I think better of it, because even though Mishka obviously hates this guy, she still cares enough to cry for him. She's not the one I want to torment.

I wait until he stops in front of a large home. As he turns off the engine, I reveal my true self for a moment, allowing him to catch a glimpse in his mirror. "What th—"

He spins around to look in his backseat where, of course, he sees nothing but the black bag next to me. Shaking his head, he exits the vehicle and walks up the pathway.

For the first hour after he's inside, I'm subtle in my taunting. Touching him, dropping my bransg quickly enough to appear in his periphery or any mirrors he may pass, waiting until his jumpiness morphs into panic.

Ghost.

I've only ever used this particular trick for those who've been sentenced to eternity in Pashbab, but this is a special case. Using a mirage, I create a blood trail leading him to his bedchamber. His heart is pounding so fast, I worry he'll overwork himself too soon, and I won't get my fill.

Slowly following the imagined spots of red, he stops at

the bed where ruby liquid drips from the mattress to a pool on the floor. With shaky hands, he pulls back the blanket, revealing what he thinks is a mutilated newborn baby. His scream is a much higher pitch than I would have guessed possible. He walks backward, desperate to get away from the bed before I let him run into me. When he spins around, I drop my bransg long enough to bare my fangs.

He sprints from the room, locking himself in the lavatory where his heavy breathing echoes in the otherwise silent home. Uncovering his ears from my bransg, I devour his terror, flapping my wings so he knows he still isn't alone.

"Stay away from her." My voice is loud in this small room, causing his head to roll around on his neck while he searches for the source.

He slides down the wall and curls himself up in the corner, his urine leaking across the floor. "I will! I swear!" He's full-on sobbing now. "I'll never talk to her again."

Staring at him in silence for several long moments, I give him a false sense of security. I decide this prick needs a permanent reminder. Just in case he ever decides this was all in his head.

I keep picturing him touching her even though he knew she had no interest in his advances. Crouching beside him, I'm quick about it, so he doesn't have time to react or realize what's happening until it's done. When I yank his hand off the floor and bring his fingers into my mouth, my teeth easily tear through his fragile flesh, his weak bones crunching with the force of my bite.

His agonizing wails mixed with the horror flooding my senses has me taking a moment to relish in it before spitting the three detached digits onto the floor by his feet. It's quite comical to see him hold up his hand in front of his face, realizing what's happened. I lick his blood off my fingers, enjoying the sound of his continuous screaming.

They're gone.

For now, I'll leave it at this, unless he's stupid enough to come anywhere near her again. For one last parting gift, I smash his washroom mirror, watching the shards rain down on him. After I stop off in his cooking quarters to wash his blood from my hands and face, I return to Mishka.

The thread of our attachment leads me to her room where she's pulling on a flared pink skirt sprinkled with kittens over her black, holey stockings. Standing behind her, I inhale her scent, enjoying the realization that a hint of her previous arousal remains. I press my lips to her neck, making her jump. "Jesus Christ, Loch. Can't you ever walk through a damn door?"

I brush her hair over her shoulder, wanting nothing more than to lift that skirt and pull her back onto my face. "No." When she turns around to face me, I kiss her.

"Where did you go?" she asks.

It's hard to know how she'd react, and I won't lie, so I opt for evasion. "You look lovely, tin nanba."

Her painted lashes flutter as her cheeks brighten with her smile. "Thank you." She smooths out her short sleeved, black blouse that shows off her every curve. I trace my finger where a strip of her pale stomach peeks out above the waistband of her skirt.

Grabbing the neck of my sweater, she pulls it closer for inspection. "Is this blood?"

Shit.

Quickly kissing her cheek, I say, "I'll see you when you're done working."

"Loch!" she calls right before I pull up my bransg.

Sensual Sky

Mishka

Obviously, there's something he's keeping from me. Considering he disappeared immediately after Harry left, I'd be stupid to not at least make sure he didn't do anything to him. Tying up my black boots with the bows, I pick up my phone, letting my finger hover over Harry's number. I told him not even a few hours ago I didn't ever want to speak to him again. And I definitely don't want to give him the wrong idea if he's fine. With only a few minutes until my Uber gets here, I text Leena.

> **Me: Will you call Harry and make sure he's alright?**

Seconds later, my phone *pings*.

> **Leena: Why the shit would I do that?**

Me: Because I think Loch might have done something to him.

Tossing my keys in my bag, I go outside to wait. I really ~~ed~~ to get a car soon.

Leena: We could only be so lucky.

I consider telling her about the blood on Loch's shirt until I decide to explain that part in person. If he would have told me what happened, I wouldn't be so anxious right now. At least I know Leena will do what I ask no matter how much she hates Harry.

At about a block away from work, I hear my phone going off in my purse.

Leena: He sent me to VM, but he answered my text saying he was fine and to leave him alone.

I'm not sure if that makes me feel better or worse.

Me: Thanks. I owe you. Have fun tonight.

All day at work I keep glancing over my shoulder for signs of Loch being here. I'm embarrassed for myself that I miss him after only a few hours. I mess up an order and double charge a client because my head isn't here. Ryan gives me a few curious looks, though he never says anything, probably chalking it up to what went down a couple weeks ago.

My disappointment is hard to hide when my shift ends and still no Loch. After closing out the drawer, I go to the back room to get my phone and set up a ride.

"Did you make this?"

His unexpected voice makes my heart leap into my throat. One of the custom dolls appears on the table before Loch materializes with a smirk. My skin feels hot, and my stomach flip-flops from simply laying eyes on him. Part of me wishes

I could go back to hating him, or at least, thinking I did. It's uncomfortable knowing he has this power over me.

Zipping my phone back into my bag, I throw the strap over my head. "No, Ryan finished that this morning."

He walks toward me, eyes traveling down my body. "Happy to see me?"

Pushing my shoulders back, I attempt nonchalance. "Just wondering where you've been all day since you vanished with blood on your clothes."

Wrapping his hand around the waistband of my skirt, he tugs on it to pull me against his body. His lips fall on mine, tingles sprinkling across my skin like I'm overdosing on endorphins, no longer caring where the blood came from at this point.

His teeth bite my lip before he asks, "Are you ready to go?"

I can't help fantasizing about having the night to ourselves and how far things could progress. It sucks so badly I can't sleep with him without losing him.

Snapping me out of my thoughts, his wings release from his back, reaching almost all the way across the room. When they curl around me, it's as though I drank a concentrated shot of warmth and solace. I close my eyes, resting my head against his chest and inhaling his spiced scent until I feel him tremble beneath me.

The sound of rushing water is in my ears when he says, "We're here."

Since I was expecting to be in my house, I cover my mouth in shock to see we're standing on a bridge. Peering over the edge, I watch a waterfall crash into the creek. The sun is setting, creating a pastel sky. I've never been here this late in the day.

"We're at Multnomah Falls. How did you know about this place?"

"I saw it in a book with shiny pages at your house." His

arms hold my waist, his hot breath warming my cheek. "Don't let go."

After hearing the loud flap of his wings, my body becomes weightless, the drop in my stomach causing me to dig my fingers into his back. Looking over my shoulder, I scream at the sensation of him shooting downward, dropping so far I think he's going to dive right into the water. He straightens at the last minute, flying parallel with the stream before soaring above the bridge. Water droplets splash against my skin as the waterfall roars in my ears, making me instinctively close my eyes.

Gusts of air whip violently at my legs, and I no longer hear the rush of water, so I crack open my eyelids to see a bird flying behind us. It's difficult to speak with the wind slapping my hair around my face. Or maybe it's that I'm scared shitless.

I make the mistake of glancing down which has me trying to swing my legs around his waist. "Shit, shit, shit." We are so much higher than I thought.

His laugh is the only thing keeping me from passing out. He spins, flipping the world on its axis. "I got you. Promise."

My purse keeps hitting my back, and I oddly think how grateful I am that I zipped it. If I wasn't so terrified of plummeting to my death, I may be able to appreciate how captivating he is this way. It's almost too surreal to accept that I'm doing this.

The same moment I think I could become accustomed to being so far above the ground, his wings beat down, propelling us higher. It's freezing up here, but his heat keeps me from being too uncomfortable. If I'm cold, though, he must be frigid. I realize we're up in the clouds. No sooner than the thought crosses my mind, he bursts through one, surrounding us in solid white. It's almost otherworldly up here. His hand lowers to squeeze my ass, and I can't even enjoy it because he suddenly dips, flipping me upside down, spiraling us back toward the ground. My heart is going to beat right out of my chest at this rate. Right when I've convinced myself that this is the end of my life, he levels out.

"Trust me, tin nanba. You're safe."

I dig my fingers a little deeper into his flesh, yet I also take a deep breath, truly appreciating the way the world is presented from the heavens. His lips press against my forehead as he flies me across the Oregon skyline. I can't believe this is really happening. The way this feels, the way everything looks from up here, it's the literal definition of magical. If I wasn't already falling for him, this would have done it.

Now I'm completely screwed.

By the time our feet land on solid ground, I spin around, a little wobbly and laughing from exhilaration. "That was hands down the craziest thing I've ever experienced!" He brought us to the coast, the ocean's waves crashing beside us. It's amazing how quickly you can get somewhere by flying. The sky is dark now, the only light coming from the moon and stars.

Yanking my bag over my head, I drop it onto the sandy beach before running up to him and hugging my arms around his neck to crash my mouth against his.

His hot hands press into my waist, picking me up just to lower both of us to the sand, never once breaking our kiss. The warm sensation of his touch moves up my thigh until he rips my fishnet leggings and reaches into my panties. Slowly pumping his fingers, he kisses my neck, the sharpness of his teeth scraping my skin. "I have something to tell you."

The words are a bit ominous, but his hands are making it hard to care. My response is muffled against his shoulder. "Okay." I unfasten his pants, reaching inside. The sound he makes the moment I touch him has me clenching around his fingers. It's an amazing feeling to know I have such an effect on him, especially since he has such a big one on me.

"I don't ... I don't know what I'm feeling." His markings tickle the pads of my fingers, the hard rings causing my hand to stutter. "I want you so fucking bad, tin nanba, yet somehow, I don't want to leave you even more." I don't want him to leave either. I want to experience all of him while I have the chance because I know there will come a time when I'll miss his frustrating quirks. "Why did you summon me? Truly?"

I can feel the burning tears threatening to make an appearance. "I don't know. I wasn't taking it seriously."

He tugs my panties to the side, rubbing his solid cock against my folds as his rings tap against my clit. Groaning under his breath, his face twists up in pain. "Fuck, I don't know what to do."

He doesn't strike me as the type of person to require comforting, but in this moment, I know in the deepest part of me that's what he needs. "There's absolutely no possibility you could come back?"

Biting his lip with his fang, he rests his forehead to mine. "There are only three ways to leave Maelprog. Two of them are not within my power, and the third may as well be the same."

Holding his face in my hands, my fingers rub over the braids twisted on the side of his head. I want to ask him what the ways are, but he pretty much just told me none of them are possible. Wishing I knew what to say, I whisper, "Loch…"

And just like that, the universe gives me the finger when my phone screams from my purse. What's worse is it's Leena's ringtone, and considering she's with Tim, she wouldn't be calling me right now if it wasn't urgent.

"I'm sorry, I have to get that."

He drops his head, pushing off his arms to let me get up. For the first time since I've known him, he looks … sad.

Marvelous Massacre

Loch

E ven though I'm grateful for the interruption, I'm also
irritated by it. The conversation was heading into unfamiliar territory. Her touch as well as her mere presence is becoming compulsive. What's happening between us
is dangerous, yet the alternative is miserable to think about.

Mishka digs the device out of her satchel. Her tone from
her initial greeting snaps from gleeful to panicked in less than
a second.

Hurt.

Her hand shakes as she holds the phone to her ear.
"Where are you right now?" I stand up to adjust myself, curious what could have so easily distressed her. "And you're
alone?" The terror seeping from her pores coats my throat
when her shiny eyes meet mine, confirming what she's feeling.

"Don't leave that spot. Loch and I will be there soon. I love you, okay?"

Once she ends the call, her panic tastes bitter following the palate of arousal and sadness she served me moments ago. "What's wrong with Leena?"

She yanks her fingers through her hair. "I'm not completely sure, I just know it's bad. Come on." Wrapping her arms around my waist, she rests her head against my chest. "Let's go."

"I need to know where we're going."

Her head jerks as she flounders for her phone. "Right." After pushing a few buttons, she shows me the map on her screen. "Take us to the dot."

The location is roughly one hundred and forty kilometers from here. Tightly hugging her against me, I cocoon my wings around her, carrying our bodies through what mortals consider space and time.

In a single breath, we're standing in a darkened corner of a residential area. Mishka's head whips around, searching for her friend.

"Leena?! Where are you?"

Scared. A voice that sounds nothing like the lively girl we came for chokes behind us. "I'm here."

She crawls out from a bush, limping on bare feet. Her makeup is smeared, and her clothes torn, but the closer she gets, it's clear she's been severely beaten. From her taste and smell, it's apparent her pain is not only physical. Her soul has also been tattered.

The streetlights illuminate the heartbreak on Mishka's face when she runs to her. "Oh, baby girl, what did he do to you?"

"I–It all happened so fast." Leena's voice breaks as if it's hard to take in air. "He was acting weird, so I thought he was nervous. Then another guy came over. He seemed fine at first, until he started asking me all these horrible questions—" Sobs choke her before she can continue. "The next thing I know, Tim was holding my arms back and his friend ... he undid my shorts. They started laughing, calling me all these slurs." Her desolation gets stuck in my throat. There's so much of it. *Why?* She can barely stand up, her shakiness becoming tremors. Cries transform into screams the more she speaks, and her strained words are ammunition for my unholy rage when she explains what she's suffered at the hands of malevolent men. "They cut my hair. I tried to fight them..." Leena falls against Mishka, nearly knocking her off her feet. "They took fucking turns, Mishka!"

Raped. Every word she speaks both in her thoughts and verbally is inspiration for my fantasies of the atrocities I will perform. I'll make them plead for their agonizing deaths, and only then will I send their polluted souls to Zibiidor Comselh.

It hurts. Her shoulders vibrate when she wails into Mishka's shoulder. "They kept hitting me, punching ... kicking. I can still hear them laughing! It's bouncing around my brain!" Finally, her words fall to a whisper as she struggles to breathe. "I think I need to go to the hospital."

Normally, I would enjoy this feast of emotions I'm currently consuming, yet in this moment, all I can think about is the agony I'm going to cause in her name, and how much I'll enjoy every fucking second of it.

"Loch, can you bring us?" Mishka asks. I saw an infirmary the day I found Pygmy, so I wrap my arms around both of them, bringing us to a medical facility.

Before Leena can find her bearings, I ask, "Where are these men?"

She looks around us, her gravelly gasp interrupting her cries. "How did—"

144

While trying to be gentle and still get her to focus, I grab her arms. "Leena. Where are they?"

She squeezes her eyes closed. "Uh—um, a blue house about three doors down from the place we just came from." My priidzar has been shed, and when her eyes shift up to meet mine, it sobers her a bit. "It has a brown door, and a, um basketball hoop in front of the garage."

"What are you going to do?" Mishka asks, but I have the feeling she already knows the answer.

Kissing her on the head feels appropriate. "Get Leena taken care of."

I don't give her a chance to respond, my boots landing right in front of the basketball hoop Leena spoke of. Even in the yard, I can hear the gleeful laughs that will momentarily become wails.

Landing inside reveals the two men enjoying the last few breaths they'll ever release from their lungs.

"Which one of you is called 'Tim?'"

One of the men gazes toward the other who stares at me in shock, giving me my answer. I groan at how delicious their terror tastes. Neither of them could dream of being quick enough to escape their fate of reciprocation.

Piece of shit number one attempts to run when I grab his hair, sinking my teeth into his throat, swallowing his lifeblood. I drink the warm liquid while watching the one named 'Tim' slowly back up against the wall. Using my power to distort the world around him, I make it appear as if metal bars have raised from the floor, trapping him where he sits.

When the flow of blood pouring into my mouth slows to a trickle, I toss the first sinner to the floor, reaching for an asymmetrical, triangle shaped, glass sculpture. Tim gapes at me from behind the mirage of his cage, his mouth open in a muted scream. He stares with bulging eyes as I tear down the first man's jeans, shoving the sculpture into his rectum until I feel a puncturing sensation. After rolling him onto his back, I grip his cock in my fist, burning it from his pubic region, force-feeding him the crisp remains. Before his soul takes its leave, I pierce his stomach with my horn, slicing up to his throat. His entrails fall from his gut, and I reach down to cup his blood in my hand, drinking it while his muddy brown soul escapes his body.

I lick my fingers, my saziamiin markings burning bright beneath the scarlet. Stalking toward Tim, I smile at him cowering in his imagined prison, unable to move courtesy of his paralyzing terror and perception of entrapment. His trousers are soaked with his own urine when he holds his hands out to cover his face.

Devil. "Please. Please, I'll do anything! I'll sell you my soul, I'll do whatever you want, just don't do this. *Please!*"

To him it appears that the bars pass through my body, allowing me inside his cell. I crouch down to his level, squeezing my fist around his neck, releasing enough heat to make it incredibly painful but not enough to disintegrate his flesh. "Your rancid soul is already mine. I want you to know, the agony you will endure for all of eternity, is so much worse than your miniscule brain can comprehend." I jam my finger against his temple, gulping down every ounce of his horror. "Cacrg dae uls a capimao aai efr mefgraoek tilaba omaoas."

"Wh-what?" He is barely capable of asking the question with his limited airflow.

"Until the end of time, you will remember her name." His eyes widen with a furious shake of his head. Flipping him to his stomach, I rip off his soiled pants to spread his legs. The level of heat I release from my body is completely in my control, and my cock is no exception.

I rip the flesh of his anus as I force myself into his body, just as he forced his into Leena's. The louder he screams and cries, the faster I thrust into him, slowly melting away his rectum. When his innards begin to boil and his shredded soul has long since left this plain, I remove myself from his smoking corpse. Lifting my trousers, I don't allow myself to finish.

I'm not sure how competent the watchmen are these days, however, I can't have this glorious scene of justice leading back to Leena, or Mishka for that matter. After I clean myself in the washroom and find some fresh clothing in one of the bedchambers, I purify the home with flames hotter than anything residing on earth.

Two Times the Trouble

MISHKA

It wasn't long ago that Leena was on this side of a hospital bed watching over me. Her poor face is beginning to bruise, and some of the deeper cuts have already been stitched. Since I'm not related to her, the doctor won't tell me the extensiveness of her injuries, I just know she's doped up on so many painkillers that she's passed out.

She refused to answer any of their questions, even the police officers who showed up to interrogate her. Part of me is grateful she kept silent because I can pretty much guarantee Loch is doing more than any correctional system could. Seeing her lying here, appearing lifeless, flashes me back to the first time we met ten years ago. It was in a shit hole of a foster home right after she had gotten out of juvie. It was messed up because that's where they sent us older kids when there wasn't room for us.

She wasn't always full of the vibrant energy she's grown in to. At the time, she wasn't going by Leena yet and wasn't on hormone therapy. She was constantly tormented by not only the other children in the home, but also the foster parents themselves. I remember this undeniable need to protect her, and how I ended up losing an entire day's worth of food because I bloodied one of the crueler boy's nose. She didn't want anything to do with me, even yelling at me to mind my own damn business. *I don't need the pity of a white bitch with a God complex*, she'd said. Even though it hurt my feelings, overlooking bullies has never been my strong suit.

One night, I woke up because I had to pee so badly my stomach hurt, and when I got to the bathroom, I found her lying in her own vomit on the floor next to an empty bottle of *Tofranil*. She had taken the entire thing. It was her final 'fuck you' to the world that had caused her nothing besides suffering. I thought for sure she was dead. I'll never forget how I screamed so long and so loud my throat hurt for days. I didn't see her again for a week after that. The day she came back, she marched up to me and I swear, I thought she was going to hit me. Instead, she gave me one of the only hugs I'd ever had.

From that day on, we were best friends. We got separated once we left that home, but never went more than a couple days without talking on the phone. The day we were old enough with money saved up to live on our own, we rented our first apartment. It was a studio infested with cockroaches and smelled of mold, but we loved it. It's been the two of us ever since.

While I believe she'll physically be able to recover from this, I'm more worried about how this will set her back mentally and emotionally. She's constantly happy, putting on a carefree front, but I know there are still dark shadows of her mind she has to keep at bay daily. Even though time has improved things, there are still so many negative influences saying she's an abomination. That she, as a person, is wrong. I would die for her, and I'll forever have her back. Still, there's no way for me to comprehend what it feels like to be her. Where hate is violent, love is subdued, so it makes sense for the screams to overpower the whispers.

I keep remembering what Loch said about her soul being female. It's so unfair, and I wish I could change the narrative society has put on people like her. Regardless of how she will cope with this, I'll be whatever she needs me to be, just as she's always been for me.

Leaning over her sleeping body, I kiss her head, whispering, "I love you so much, Leena."

"Mishka." Jolting upright, I nearly fall out of the hospital chair I must have passed out in. I find Loch's gaze fixed on me, his brows narrowed. "You have to go. I wanted to let you sleep, but the lady in the pajamas says it's too late for visitors."

I fist the arms of the chair, shaking my head. "I'm not leaving her. They'll have to drag me out of here."

He sighs, and before I know it, we're standing in my living room. He's scared me, pissed me off, and frustrated me to the point of losing my mind, yet this is the first time he's truly made me furious. I slam my hands against his chest, knowing he probably can't feel it.

"Why would you do that?! What if she wakes up, and I'm not there? What if she's all alone?!" He doesn't stop me from punching him. Instead, he stands there until I wear myself out, falling against his chest in tears. "How could he hurt her like that?" I sob into his shirt.

Tucking his arm under my legs, he picks me up, carrying me to my room. He lies me on my bed, covering me with the blankets.

"She won't be alone." His finger pushes up my chin to make me look at him. "And the men who hurt her? They paid for their sins."

Wiping my runny nose, I ask the question I likely already know the answer to. "What do you mean?"

"I'll stay with her. If she wakes up, I can drop my bransg for her. The humans in the infirmary won't know I'm there. I'll return for you once you're allowed back in, okay?"

I nod my head, hardly believing that just a few days ago, I thought I hated him. "How are you this way? Aren't demons supposed to be evil?"

Even amidst the horrific events of the night, his smile manages to comfort me. "I guess that depends on your definition of evil. From where I stand, only humans possess that characteristic."

He bends over, kissing my head, and I grab his face to press my lips against his.

When he stands upright, I know he's about to vanish, so I ask, "What happened? To Tim and his friend?"

His finger traces from between my eyebrows to the tip of my nose, the soothing warmth of his touch spreading through my entire body. "They suffered. Tremendously."

I open my mouth to ask him to elaborate, but he's gone.

Heat spreads to my toes when soft touches pepper down my neck. I crack my eyes open, realizing the sun is still rising, and

Loch is lying next to me in bed, kissing me. A few days ago, this affection would have earned him a punch in the throat regardless of the uselessness of it. Today, his touch is comforting and welcome.

"Leena's awake. Her doctor said she can come home today." His words bring back the events of the previous evening, causing me to shoot upright. I'm counting every single one of my lucky stars that today is my day off. "She told me to tell you not to worry."

Tossing off the blankets, I slip into my flats while trying to tame my hair. "She can tell me herself. Let's go." I must admit, I could really get used to this instant travel thing.

I hold my arms around his waist, and before I can exhale, we're in her hospital room. The doctor is speaking to her, forcing us to wait until he leaves to show her we're here. Leena's sitting up on the bed wearing different clothes than the ones she had on last night, making me assume Loch came back to our house to get them for her.

As soon as the doctor leaves, I don't waste a second, rushing to my closest friend and squeezing her so tight I make her groan. "Shit, sorry. I'm so happy to see you up."

Even though she's smiling with her mouth, her eyes don't light up like they normally do. "I'm fine. Just sore." The slow-motion way she's moving pulverizes my heart. "And ready to get out of here."

Right on cue, a nurse walks in, carrying a clipboard. "I have your discharge paperwork, Liam. We just need you to sign it, then you're free to go."

Leena's face falls, her fingers clenching at her blanket. "I've asked you not to call me that."

The defeat in her voice immediately has me lunging at the nurse. I feel Loch's hand on my wrist, but I'm already so close to her face that she takes a step backward. "Her name is *Leena*."

I yank the clipboard from her hand, turning my back on her while listening to her footsteps leave the room. At least that gets me a small smile from the girl who's been my lifeline for close to half my life.

Opening the little closet, I take out the plastic bag that has Leena's things in it. I start to empty it when she shakes her head. "I really don't want to ever see those clothes again. Will you get my handbag, and make sure my phone's in there?" As I do what she asks, she gasps. "Hold on. Turn up the TV."

Watching the screen makes my stomach feel like it's trying to eat itself. Police cars and fire trucks fill up the very same street we met Leena at last night. I turn the volume up enough to hear the news reporter speaking of the phenomenon that neither the fire nor the police chief can explain.

The scene behind me baffles investigators. A single home seems to have disintegrated overnight, leaving not one piece of rubble or debris. All that remains of the residence is the charred lot it once sat upon. What's even more inconceivable is none of the surrounding homes were impacted by what can only be assumed was a fire.

I don't need to ask to know this was Loch. Who else would have the capability to do this? And I'm pretty sure this isn't the first time. He hinted as much when speaking of saving Pygmy. I've been so consumed by his magnetism and the way he makes me feel—both physically and emotionally—it's easy to forget what he truly is.

Staring at him, I let out a short breath, praying I'm wrong. "Loch…"

He gives me an expression that's almost innocent. "What?"

Leena's head flicks back and forth between us when it dawns on her. I'm surprised that her face doesn't hold fear, but awe. "Did you do that?" She gestures toward the television. "Did you kill them?" she whispers.

"Yes. I." He waves his finger like the conductor of a symphony, bopping her on the nose with the last word. "Did." Oblivious to the depravity of his actions, he sits in a chair and holds his hands behind his head.

To save myself from cardiac arrest, I put an end to this conversation. "Let's wait until we get back home to talk anymore, okay?"

It's not long until the nurse I snapped at earlier returns with a wheelchair, staying silent while Leena sits down and hands over her signed paperwork. Loch and I follow behind until the nurse stops outside of the main entrance.

"Is there a car I can take her to?"

Lying through my teeth, I tell her we're getting an Uber. Loch waits until the nurse is back inside before picking up Leena and carrying her to the side of the hospital. I hold onto his waist long enough for him to transport us back to our house.

Bringing us to Leena's room, Loch lays her on the bed where Shittles *meows* for attention.

"Get some rest for the next few days, okay?" She nods, already about to fall back asleep when I cover her with her pink and blue comforter. "Can I get you tea or anything?"

She keeps staring at Loch as if she's seeing him for the first time. "Was he scared? Tim?"

He quirks up one side of his mouth, his eyes sparkling. "Immensely."

Rolling over, she turns her back to us. "Good."

Once we're in the living room and far enough away from Leena to not disturb her, I spin around to face Loch. All the anger I feel toward myself for being so damn stupid spews out all over him. "You're a fucking murderer!" I'm trying to

154

whisper, but honestly, I'm scared and confused. He's a demon for Christ's sake. How dense could I be? Letting myself become comfortable enough to actually start falling for a creature from Hell? I'm absolutely pathetic. "You killed two human beings, and according to you, brutally. You even act like you're proud of it!"

His head snaps back as if I punched him in the face. "They hurt Leena. Your friend. Your family. I thought you'd be happy." He throws his hand toward the hallway. "She is."

"Leena is not in her right mind right now! Do you not get this? And I don't even know what you did to Harry or whoever you took Pygmy from." His head tilts when he opens his mouth to say something, but only air comes out. "How many people have you hurt since being here?!"

Instantly, he's nose to nose with me, his wings fully extended. I wish I could sense emotions the way he can because I can't tell if he's angry or … hurt. "I am orseiinak!" He's never yelled at me until now. Baring his fangs, he literally growls at me. "I punish sinners. That's what I do." I've never seen him this terrifying. His eyes burn so bright, I'm surprised they don't sear a hole in my head. "Those men, along with the asshole you call Harry, deserved everything they got."

I knew he did something to Harry.

"This isn't Hell, Loch! You can't torture living people."

His nostrils flair, the tattoos on his neck illuminating orange before his hand clasps around my throat, causing panic to pulse through my veins. "I did all of that to protect innocent humans who had endured pain by their hands, yet here you are, suffocating me with your fear!" His voice echoes around me as his grip tightens.

I stand up on my toes to get close to his face, my breath shaky as the adrenaline forces my heart to pump faster. Consumed by my anger and fear, I allow it to dictate my words. "I was wrong. You are evil." The moment I say it, I wish I could swallow the statement back. The sheer agony on his face strangles my heart in a vice grip. Releasing my neck, he backs away from me. "Loch. I…"

He scoffs with an expression twisted in disgust, and before I can apologize, he vanishes. I reach up to where his hand was, still hot from his touch. Leaning against the back of the couch, I steady my breathing.

I don't know if I've ever been so conflicted with my own emotions. There're so many of them contradicting each other. What he did was terrible, but what about what they did? He took their lives because they destroyed Leena's. If I could agree with what I'm feeling deep, deep down, I'd believe they got exactly what they deserved.

Not knowing what else to do, I decide to calm my nerves with some tea. While in the kitchen preparing water, I must black out because in what feels like seconds, the scream of the kettle rips me back into the present. Quickly removing it from the stove so I don't bother Leena, I scoop two spoonsful of sugar into my mug, pouring the steaming water over my raspberry tea bag.

I have no idea if Leena heard the yelling earlier, so I leave the tea to steep and check on my friend. Peeking in the door, I see she's fast asleep with Shittles curled up in the bend of her legs. If I wasn't worried about waking her, I'd kiss her on the cheek. I'm so grateful she's going to be okay. At the very least, her body will be anyway.

I bring my tea in the living room, sitting on the couch, staring at the table that replaced the one he ruined. I feel so shitty for what I said to him. The truth is, he isn't human. It's unfair for me to expect him to act like one. I've always had a preconceived idea in my head of what demons were, yet he obliterates everything I thought I knew. I think that makes me forget that he has spent lifetimes making the worst of my species suffer for their choices. In his world, killing those men was valiant. Of course, by my standards, what he did was far from good. If I see it from his perspective, in a way, it was chivalrous. His brand of chivalry anyway. I think beneath all my morals and humanity, there is a part of me that's grateful he did what he did. That's terrifying.

If he is still here with me, I want him to know, I don't believe what I said. I should really put myself in his shoes and attempt to see things from his perspective. It's what I'd want him to do for me.

"Loch, if you can hear me, I'm sorry."

My phone *pings* with an email notification, waking me from the sleep I apparently fell into. It's been a couple of hours since Loch left. Selfishly, I'm glad he's stuck here and will have to come back eventually. I'm grateful there's a time limit for how long he can be away from me.

Stopping by Leena's room to check on her, I find her still passed out. I'm groggy from my cat nap, so after taking a shower, I start some afternoon coffee, desperately needing the caffeine.

With my steaming beverage in hand, I lean over the counter to search for some answers online. I click the internet icon, typing, *interactions with demons* in the search bar.

One of the top results reads: *The belief that demons have sex with humans runs deep.*

I sip on my java while I skim the article. It's nothing besides speculation. No proof of anything, and the image used couldn't be further from what incubi truly look like. At least not according to my experience. Everything I find is opinion and theories. There are a few stories I find about possession, but none that are remotely close to my situation.

"Humans are so full of shit."

I knock over my coffee, wetting my phone and yelping in surprise. "Fuck, Loch!" He backs up when I slam the now empty mug on the counter, yanking open a drawer for a dish towel. "You really have to stop doing that shit." Looking at him standing there in human form, my brain tears itself between wanting him to hold me, feeling guilty, and questioning if I can trust him at all. "Where did you go?"

"To visit Pygmy."

His fascination with her is somewhat sweet if not a bit weird. "How is she?"

"Asleep now."

"What's your deal with the kid, anyway?"

He shrugs. "Human children don't come to Maelprog. They're peculiar."

His voice has softened as though he's trying not to piss me off. Once I dry my phone and clean the spilt drink, I toss the rag on the counter to see him staring at me.

"What?" I snap harsher than intended. I've gone through a lot of feelings around him, but it's never been awkward like this.

It's so out of character for him, the way he hesitantly moves closer to me. If I didn't know any better, I'd think he was nervous. "I utterly despise how you looked at me earlier." He briefly closes his eyes. "Please don't—You don't need to be frightened of me. I'm not a monster."

"I shouldn't have said that." I close the space between us so he doesn't have to. "You're not evil."

He softly brushes my cheek with tentative fingers. "I would never do anything to harm you. I need to know you know that."

Undoubtedly, I do know that. Even so, learning he's capable of such dark violence to the point of homicide is jarring. I'm still struggling to wrap my head around it. "Can you promise me you won't 'punish' anyone else while you're here?"

Gripping his hand around the back of my neck much gentler than he ever has before, he kisses me, sending vibrating sensations across my flesh. When our eyes meet, he gives me a small smile. "I promise I will do my best."

It's hard to comprehend how a simple touch can cause me to waver so quickly, making me wonder if he has me under some kind of Hell magic. Although, if that were the case, we most likely would have had sex by now. "Loch…"

His hot lips kiss across my shoulder to my neck. "It's who I am, tin nanba. It's who I've always been, and who I'll always be."

I feel his fingers slowly sliding beneath my shirt, and I lift my arms so he can take it off. "Isn't there a rule about interfering with humans or something?"

He licks his lips, lowering my bra strap down my shoulder, his erection pressing against my stomach. "That's a Madriiaxian decree."

Trailing my hands down his chest, I drop to my knees. A long, slow breath leaves his lips when I lift the hem of his sweater and undo his jeans, lowering them halfway down his thighs. His cock jumps from being freed, the symbols burning brightly. I swirl my tongue around the tip, staring up at him in his now natural form.

I'm slow with my licks, mentally preparing myself for the exertion that comes with demonic blowjobs. While it's fun, it can also be incredibly exhausting. Apparently, he's not in the mood for patience because his hand pushes on my head as he thrusts himself between my lips. He's violent with it, such an extreme change from his tenderness seconds ago.

"Fuck. You're so good at this." He moans out his words of praise until he suddenly stills, shaking his head. "Mishka," he breathes out, swallowing before he orders, "Stop. We need to talk." The way he says it causes my heart to flip. What could be so important to talk about now?

"Well, that's going to have to wait."

The unknown voice startles me so badly, I shriek like a banshee. "Jesus Christ!"

Standing across the kitchen is the owner of the voice in full demon mode. Wings, horns, glowing tattoos and all. Curly blond hair frames a face as devastating as Loch's. "Not even close."

My brain is currently unable to process what's happening while Loch pulls up his pants and tilts his head at the creature. "Vilum? What the fuck are you doing here?"

Inspecting his reflection in the mirror magnet on the refrigerator, the demon, who Loch is clearly acquainted with, responds like he's never been more uninterested. "I'm here as messenger."

I refuse to believe this is happening. Again.

"Will somebody please tell me why demons keep appearing in my goddamn kitchen?!"

7СЄЄ
19

Fanatical Formurifri

Loch

If I were able, I would kill him. Could he have picked a worse time? I need to tell her that we have to finish this. My insides are still raw from the way she revered me as the villain when she said I was evil. She has no idea what I'm capable of. All she's seen is the side I've shown her. If she ever knew the truth, she'd never look at me with gentle eyes again.

Vilum obviously wouldn't be here if his message wasn't important, but still, I'll make him regret this at some point. Instead of punching him in the dick like I want to, I introduce them. "Mishka, this is my brother cousin, Vilum."

She shakes her pretty head, the mix of shock and irritation rolling off her is delightful on my tongue. "Your brother-cousin? What are you? Backwoods demons?" I'm not sure what she means, but her face looks adorably comical when she suddenly remembers she's half naked. Scrambling for her clothes, she huffs while yanking her top over her gorgeous breasts. "Are there any more of you I should be expecting?"

Disregarding her question, Vilum adjusts a stray curl in the mirror. Similar to all of my Uncle Lucifer's children, Vilum is only interested in Vilum. However, him being here has to be pretty detrimental, so his presence in the conversation shouldn't be too much to ask. Clapping my hands in his direction, I snap, "Vilum! Can you tear your attention away from yourself for five seconds, and tell me what's going on?"

He removes a gohed from around his neck, and I immediately recognize it as Uncle Lucifer's. Divine Maelprog energy rolls off it in gusts, making me homesick. "My orders are to give you this. It'll take you back home immediately, breaking all bonds you have to the half-breed."

I blink between him and Mishka. He can't be talking about her. I would have sensed it immediately. "Half-breed? She's not—"

"All I know is Uncle Michael is pissssssed." He glances back at his reflection, running his tongue over the tip of his fang.

My confusion over his half-breed comment is consumed by my astonishment at the mention of my uncle in Maelprog. Considering how long ago I was born into existence, not much surprises me anymore. But right now, I'm gaping at him. To my knowledge, murifri in Maelprog is impossible, and he isn't speaking of a lower level either. Uncle Michael is a *formurifri*.

An archangel.

I've never met any of my family that stayed behind, and I'd be lying if I said I wasn't a little disappointed I missed it. Mishka's eyes dart back and forth between us while my thoughts struggle to stay still. "I'm not understanding. What was he doing in Maelprog? What could he possibly want?"

Tossing the gohed at me, he lowers his wings. "You away from her." He nods toward Mishka. "She's his offspring." His words hit us at the same time, unifying our response.

"What?!"

"What?!"

Mishka's heartbeat picks up so fast I can hear it, her excitement and panic tangling together to the point she's shaking. "Are you talking about *the* Michael? 'Leader of the heavenly army' Michael?!"

Her voice rises with each of her questions. Vilum clicks his tongue and points a finger at her. "You aren't as dull-witted as you appear."

If I wasn't so overwhelmed with information right now, her mouth falling open in offense would make me laugh. I shake my head at Vilum. "How is that possible?"

His shoulders sag as though this entire conversation is boring him to oblivion. "From what I heard, there was a female human." He returns his attention back to the mirror and his hair. "Uncle Michael became infatuated, broke a few rules, and bam," his fingers spread apart, mimicking an explosion, "half murifri baby."

Mishka rushes to him, her excitement spicy on my tongue. "Do you know who my mother is? Is she in Portland?"

He holds up his hand to shut her up. "No, Grandfather killed her off in childbirth. Your birth. Apparently to punish Uncle Michael for fucking a human … or something like that."

All emotions fall dormant from her face, making her almost statuesque. A gust of breath whooshes from her lips when she sways in disbelief. I want to kiss her, hold her and comfort her, but I'm hesitant to make my affections apparent to Vilum.

"I still don't understand. She's completely human. I would be able to tell if she was celestial."

Smoothing his hair, he shifts around impatiently. "I have no idea. Does she have an emetgis?"

Realization beats me over the head. I can't believe I didn't recognize them on her back. It was simply too impossible to comprehend.

"Halo scars. The piece of shit cut off her wings with his halo." Though I say it more to myself, they both hear it clearly.

Wings?! The word blares in my brain.

Vilum groans in annoyance, wiping nonexistent filth from his trousers. "Don't care. I did what I was ordered to. You do whatever you want." He closes his eyes to recite the antiprayer. "Lkantum blans noan forskl."

I turn to Mishka who is staring at the empty space where Vilum was standing. She mumbles to herself, her conflicting emotions leaving a mildewed taste on my tongue.

As if a bucket of sorrow was dumped over her, she sobs so hard she can barely catch her breath. "I—I…"

Of all the human sentiments, this is the one I despise smelling on her. I hate seeing her cry. Her being angry is one thing, it's actually sexy, but her heartbreak is rancid in my mouth. I wrap my hand around the nape of her neck to press her against my chest, using the other to rub her back. "Shhh. It's okay. This is Vilum's effect on mortal emotions. He has the ability to amplify whatever it is you're feeling. Breathe, it'll pass."

I hold her tight, letting her tears wet my sweater. Wrapping my fingers around hers, I wait until the oak flavor of her sadness becomes nothing more than a subtle aftertaste. She backs away from my embrace, and I realize the last few minutes have made her look different somehow. "Take off your clothes. All of them. We need to find it."

Snapping out of her trance, she stares up at me with shiny, tear-filled eyes. "Find what?"

"The emetgis. A divine seal. Michael had to have suppressed your celestiality with one." As if on autopilot, she strips down nude, waiting for me to inspect her. And I do. Every single inch. It's nowhere to be found. "This doesn't make sense."

Her mind is so chaotic, I can't pick out a singular thought of intent. Sliding down her cabinets, she allows herself to fall to the floor, and that's when I see it. On the heel of her right foot is the pale outline of a murifric emetgis.

While I am Maelprog born, I'm still technically half murifri myself. My fingers brush over the mark before I cup her foot with my palm, meeting her gaze. "I'm going to remove it, and it's going to hurt. Horribly."

Her cool fingers grip my forearm. "Wait. What will that do?"

If only I knew. "My best guess? You'll transform into your natural, murifri form."

She yanks her foot from my grasp, shaking her head so violently her hair whips against her face. "No. I need ... I need to process this."

I do understand, but my skin itches in anticipation to see her true appearance. I sit beside her on the floor, resting my head against her cabinets.

We stay silent for many moments while I spin the gohed, Uncle Lucifer's sigil glowing from within. All I would have to do is slip this around my neck, say the antiprayer, and I would be back in Maelprog. However, that thought is no longer appealing like it once was.

So suddenly that it surprises even me, she snatches the gohed out of my hand, slamming it on the floor over and over. *Fuck you!*

"No! Mishka, stop!" I grab her wrist, her raging fury caus-ing her chest to rise and fall. "This is one of fourteen gohed in all of creation. If you destroy this, my uncle will destroy me."

Never taking her eyes away from mine, she throws it across the floor, climbing on my lap to straddle me.

"My *father*," she says the word with so much delicious disdain, I find myself sucking the sweet, earthy flavor from my lower lip, "doesn't want you near me, right?" She gives me a mischievous smile I've never seen on her beautiful face. Bringing her lips next to my ear, she whispers, "Imagine how he would feel if you were inside me."

Fucking antichrist. Knowing what she is makes this bor-derline sacrilegious, and I don't think there's anything in ex-istence that could turn me on more. I mean, technically, I'm always aroused, but this is entirely different. The saziamiin across my skin glow as she presses our lips together, dipping her tongue into my mouth.

Her hands move down my chest, gripping the fabric of my shirt in her fists. When our eyes meet, she presses her forehead against mine, just below the horns. I've never not known what I want. I can't stay with her, yet I can't stand the thought of our time being over.

Instead of voicing my confliction, I bring us to her room.

Death by Demon Dick

Mishka

Before I can ask him to take us to my bed, we're standing next to it. I lift my Pretty Cult tee over my head, watching his dark eyes move down my body. He does the same with his sweater, revealing his glowing symbol tattoos swirling across his chest and abs. Undoing the button of his jeans, he releases his wings. I reach out to touch his feathers. They are so soft and silken, yet they have a secure firmness to them.

When his pants fall to the floor, I take in his full natural form. His long, black lashes blend in with the darkness around his snowy eyes while the raven strands of his hair fall between his alabaster horns. I trace my fingers along the muscles of his stomach, feeling him tense beneath my touch. He reaches his arms around to unclasp my bra, slowly lowering it down my arms.

Is this really it?

My stomach flips and my heart pounds as he lowers me onto my soft comforter, biting the skin of my neck and shoulder. He yanks my shorts and panties down my legs, not wasting time by earning my orgasm with his tongue. Instead, he simply forces it out of me. It's so powerful that my vision shifts, small black dots appearing on my ceiling while I cry out his name in between obscenities.

It's incredible that I somehow feel him across every inch of my body, including the parts he isn't even touching. My legs fall open for him, my pussy yearning for what is sure to be reality shattering euphoria. Reaching between us, he pushes two fingers inside me, spreading them apart as if to stretch and prepare me.

"Are you sure this is what you want?"

It's such a heavy question. Every single part of me wants to feel our bodies together, yet the idea of him leaving is heart crushing. I just can't stay in this limbo anymore. If what Vilum said is true, then my father—even thinking that feels impossible—wants to take Loch away from me. I can't stand the idea of that happening without us being together this way. And now with the necklace, Loch has the means to go whenever he wants.

I fight the urge to cry, unable to tear my eyes away from his solid white ones. "I want to feel you, and we can't put this off forever." He shuts his eyes for a moment, only responding with a barely perceivable nod. I wrap my fingers around his thick shaft, my knuckles bumping over the lifted rings beneath his skin. I adore the feeling of the markings under my palm, even if I'm a little worried about it hurting. "Will it burn me?"

He takes out his fingers, his black hair falling over his

grinning face. Grabbing my wrist, he yanks my hand from his erection to hold it over my head. "I'll be careful."

It feels like his gaze is reaching into my soul, and for all I know, it is. The hot tip of his cock slides between my folds, wetting it with my arousal. I can't believe we're finally doing this. The muscles in his shoulders move beneath his flesh when his body jerks above mine. The very second the first ring pushes past my entrance, I worry I won't be able to accommodate him. I don't think I can stretch much farther, and he's nowhere close to being all the way in yet.

He presses his lips together, the sound of his guttural moan making me tense around his shaft. My free hand grabs his hip, digging my fingers into his skin. Somehow, it's not hurting. Every single cell in my entire body is buzzing.

His fingers brush the hair from my face before sliding down my jaw to reach my neck. With another push, he slides in deeper, and once I relax, I'm able to adjust to the next ring.

He gives me a smirk, leaning down to bite my ear. "Are you ready?"

I take a slow breath and nod. His body goes taut just before his hips lurch, forcing the rest of his length inside of me. I suck in the air, gasping as my hand flies up to grip his arm. Heat blooms deep inside, his cock getting warmer by the second.

"Fuck, you're really tight," he says on a heavy exhale.

He starts slow, allowing me to adjust to the repetitive contracting his rings cause. The pressure they put on the walls of my pussy has me arching my back, pushing my body harder against his.

His teeth nip at my chin before his soft lips are on my mouth. He picks up his speed, the space between each of his rings ensuring that their penetration is unmistakable. My head slightly spins when the softness of my bed is replaced with a cool hardness. Without slowing his pace, he's teleported us across my room where he rams me against the wall. I open my eyes to watch the tips of his tongue swirl around my nipple. Every slight movement is magnified yet in slow motion, which is odd considering how hard he's pounding into me, making me whimper each time.

The moment he lets go of my wrist, I grab his shoulders as he rocks my body upwards with each of his thrusts. I'd probably be embarrassed to hear the sounds I'm making outside of this moment, but I can't help it. It's almost too much. Almost.

"I'm gonna fuck the holiness right out of this pussy." His blasphemous words intensify the flood of the hot wetness dripping down my legs. Although his size is considerably much bigger than anyone I've ever been with, there's still no way he should be able to hit the spots he's hitting. Warm tendrils seem to move around inside me, working with the rings to massage multiple places at once. I feel so close to coming, but for some incomprehensible reason, I can't. I use his shoulders to lift and lower my body onto him, chasing the ache that's beginning to consume me.

I focus on the feeling of his hot skin against mine, the sensation of the markings moving across my skin. I try to memorize the sweet, spicy hot scent he gives off, begging my brain to imprint the memory of his sharp jaw, high cheekbones, and the way he looks biting that full bottom lip. I'm scared that when he's gone, I'll forget what he looks, smells and feels like.

In a dizzying moment of disorientation, my breasts are suddenly pressed against my sewing table, his hot hands gripping my hips as he impales me from behind. He leans against my back, moving the hair off my neck to bite my shoulder and kiss my scars. His warmth is crawling through my insides, and

I cry out at the insane mixture of the pain from his teeth and the nirvana coursing through me.

"Celestial cunt is officially my favorite."

Shit. I keep thinking my orgasm will crash over me, but it continues to stop abruptly. I grunt in frustration, pushing faster against him.

He chuckles in my ear before I'm flipped around, my back pressing against my comforter once again as he returns us to my bed. He holds my thighs open, watching himself dipping in and out. The lips of my pussy glow from his markings, his smirk causing the muscles deep inside my stomach to twitch.

"You come when I want you to, tin nanba."

He's controlling it? I know I should be furious, but I can't embrace it while being torn in this war between pleasure and torment. His heated hand wraps around my throat, his tempo slowing to a tedious pace. Kissing me as if he's angry, his split tongue tangles with mine, a maddening contradiction to his unhurried strokes.

He brings me to the brink once again only to yank away my release. Tears roll down my cheeks, my fingers scraping across the flesh I know I can't make bleed.

"Damn it, Loch. Please ... let me come. I can't take this."

His fangs show with his smile. "Beg me again."

He could turn a nun homicidal. "You fucking asshole, let me come!"

I don't want this to end, but I don't know if I have the physical energy to take much more. Although this would be an incredible way to go.

Death by demon dick.

Moving his hand from my throat, he brings it to my face. All traces of playfulness fall from his expression. "My life will never be the same without you. I'll miss you, Mishka."

It's impossible to react how I want to when an eruption

of paralyzing ecstasy shoots through every vein and nerve ending. I blink in and out of delirium, an intoxicating fire pulses through my body for an immeasurable amount of time.

Using the only remaining self-control I possess, I hold him tight against me, hoping he can't leave while he's in my embrace.

"Loch…"

His entire body is illuminated, from the blinding white of his eyes to the burning images across his skin. The sensation of freefalling consumes every mental and physical part of my being, my mind somehow comprehending that this is it.

He grows larger inside of me, making me feel impossibly full. The very second he comes, my eyes fly open. People talk about being able to feel it when a guy finishes inside them, but I never really could tell that much. Right now, though, I can feel every burning gush pumping into my body.

"I'm an angel," I whisper into his shoulder. "Take me with you."

The flood of liquid heat slows, and he finally locks his gaze to mine. "You're a half angel with an emetgis. You don't belong there." There's truth in what he's saying, regardless, it still feels like a slap in the face. He kisses me hard, whispering against my lips, "Goodbye, tin nanba."

Cousin Coitus

LOCH

The last thing I want to do is separate our bodies, but I can't stay inside her forever. Her arousal sparkles over the luminosity of my saziamiin markings, and as I slide myself out of her for the last time, she jolts with each farzem ring I remove. I scoot off her bed as she squeezes her eyes closed, waiting for me to be flung back to the depths of home.

I wait too, but it doesn't happen. I'm still here, in her room. I had assumed it would be instantaneous. From what I was told, the moment the purpose of summoning is fulfilled, we are immediately ripped from this world.

Yet I'm still in the mortal realm.

Walking to the side of her bed, I kneel on the floor, licking the glittering tears streaming down her flawless face. It's surprising how fascinating they are. Her eyes spring open, widening at the sight of me.

She lurches toward me, wrapping her arms so tightly around my neck that if I required oxygen, I'd be suffocating.

"I guess you're stuck with me a bit longer."

Laughing in a contagious way, she leans back to hold my face in her hands, looking so happy it's impossible not to kiss her. "What does this mean?"

"It means there's something you wanted from me when you called that I haven't provided yet." It's clear from how she's biting the inside of her mouth, she's trying to pick apart her brain, attempting to retrieve what that could be. Truthfully though, I'm glad she doesn't know. "What now, cousin?"

As if being pulled back by an invisible hook, she gapes at me in horror. "What?!"

I snort at her gaping expression. Did she really not put that together? "Your father is my uncle. Remember?"

Both of her hands fly up to cover her mouth. "Oh my God."

"You mean Grandfather," I tease her.

"This isn't funny! It's…" she drops her voice to a whisper, "incest."

I laugh, jumping back on the bed with her. "We're divine." Moving a stray hair from her eyes, I hold her chin to look at me. "We're all related in one way or another. It's not the same as it is with humans."

Her eyes dart around in her skull, attempting to process what I'm saying. "I mean… I guess that would be a side effect of immortality?" Her scrunched up nose is too cute not to kiss. "It still sounds sick."

She climbs off the bed to get her robe draped over the

back of her vanity chair. I shigmir into the cooking quarters for one of Leena's cigarettes, returning before she turns around.

I barely get it lit when she's screeching at me. "Are demons as deaf as they are infuriating? Do that outside! How many times do I have to say it?"

I almost mention that she was just talking about coming to Maelprog with me a few minutes ago, and if she has a problem with smoke, she would've had a really hard time, but since I'm in such a good mood, I let it slide.

By the time I finish and meet her back in her room, she's thrown on a pair of short trousers and a lavender top that says, *You Deserve To Be Fingered By Edward Scissorhands* in mint colored script. With her hair still in sexy disarray, she buckles up a pair of blue and white sandals.

"I'm starving. I'm gonna take Leena's car down to the pod for some sandwiches and stop at the pharmacy. I'll be back in a bit," she sing-songs, spinning in a circle. I love seeing the intoxication from my seed evident in her eyes. Swaying a bit, she drapes her satchel over her shoulder, kissing my cheek. Before I can suggest coming with her, she adds, "Stay here in case Leena wakes up. I don't want her to be alone."

I watch her ass when she walks out the door in disbelief that I'm still here. Now, though, I don't have any idea what will take me away from her, leaving me waiting for what will at some unknown time cause the inevitable.

With nothing else to do, I go into the living room and fall on the couch. Picking up the small black rectangle with buttons, I turn on the tele-vision. Everything I'm able to get on the screen seems to make the time go by even slower, so I keep clicking until I finally find something worth watching.

I assume by human standards, both men on the screen have decent sized cocks, and one of them is extremely attractive. At least this will help keep me busy until Mishka gets back. Propping my feet up on the coffee table, I light a cigarette. That's one upside of her not being here, she can't complain about me smoking inside.

I hear footsteps behind me, so I turn around to see Leena walking out of the hallway. "Hey, lovely. How are you feeling?"

She runs her fingers over the uneven, thick ropes of hair on her head, still appearing half asleep. "Uh … I don't know. I could use a Lortab." Shifting her gaze to the tele-vision, a small smile lifts her lips. "Are you watching gay porn?"

I take a drag off the smoke and scoot over for her. "I guess. I'm fond of how the blond one uses his mouth."

Sitting next to me on the couch, she reaches for the pill bottle on the table. Now that she's awake and I have company, I push the button that makes the screen go black.

"Considering what went down between us, I'm guess-ing you're pan?"

Fucking mortals and their forever changing languages. "I don't have any idea what that means."

She shifts uncomfortably, pain evident in her frown. I reach out for her arm, but she flinches away from me, which confirms what I did to Tim and his rapist counterpart was more than justified.

"What genders are you sexually attracted to?"

It's not something I ever really thought about. "I don't know. All of them?"

A laugh with very little heart leaves her lips. Turning to look behind us, she narrows her bright green eyebrows. "Where's Mishka?"

I point to the door. "She asked me to stay here with you while she went to get some food."

"Hmm." Reaching for one of the cigarettes, she lights one. I raise a brow because Mishka has made it clear she doesn't like it. "You were already doing it, so when Mishka bitches about it, I'll blame it on you."

I rest my head on the back of the couch, smirking at her. "Fair enough."

She stares at the smoke rising from her cigarette and asks, "Do you want something a little stronger? I've been saving it, and now seems as good a time as any."

"Sure."

Moments later, she returns with a small glass pipe, burning whatever's inside with her lighter. Coughing so hard I wonder if she'll throw up, she hands the marijuana to me. It won't affect me the same as it does humans, but I enjoy the taste.

She clicks her nails on the pipe. "Do you know…" Shaking her head, she spits out the rest of her question as if she's running out of time to ask. "Is Tim in hell?"

There's not a fraction of doubt in my mind. "Yes. I am a little disappointed I couldn't be there to welcome him and his friend, though. Too bad I didn't feel right about doing the same to the furry guy."

She yanks her head back with a cough. "The 'furry' guy?" Curling her lips up into a genuine grin, she releases a whimsical laugh. "Holy shit, do you mean Harry?"

"Right. That was it."

Her laugh trails off, and she falls somber, blowing out a long breath. "Will I go too?"

I can't imagine why she would think that, however, I've learned more often than not, humans keep their darkest secrets locked away tight. "I don't know. What have you done?"

She frowns at me. "What do you think?" Her hand waves up and down her body. "I'm … this."

"What? Sexy?"

She tries to hide her smile and remain serious. "No, dumbass. Trans."

"Why would you think that would earn you eternal torture?"

Her body falls against the couch as though all the relief she's releasing was physically weighing her down. "Let's just say, I've been told so a few times."

"Maelp—Hell isn't a catch all. You have to be a truly malevolent person to end up there."

She inhales the smoke of her pipe. "I owe you, Loch."

The comment makes me feel like I missed something. "For what?" *Tim.* She meets my eyes with her watery ones, suddenly making it clear. "Oh, no, lovely. It was quite the pleasure. If you ever want the details, all you have to do is ask."

Nodding, she says, "Maybe someday."

Divine Douche

MISHKA

With the bag of food in one hand, I use the other to open the door. I'm finally coming down from my high since having sex with Loch earlier. I carry everything to the kitchen where the sight of Leena cutting her hair in front of two makeup table mirrors has me dropping everything on the counter, rushing over to her. "How are you feeling?"

Checking her locs for evenness, she doesn't meet my eyes. "I'm fine."

She's obviously not. I feel like I'm seeing the Leena I met all those years ago, the Leena drained of her true spirit. Logically, I know this is going to take time, and I can't begin to fathom what she's feeling, in every sense. I also know I'm being selfish for missing my friend. Mostly, though, I don't want her to suffer anymore.

"Your hair is looking pretty. Do you want some tea?"

She shakes her head, laying her shears on the counter. "Do we still have some of that vodka?"

I swallow because I don't want to mother her, but I couldn't bare it if she hurt herself even more. "Aren't you on pain meds?"

She spins away from me toward the cabinet. "I'll check myself."

I grasp her hand. "Leena—"

"What, Mishka?! Are you going to stand in the way of the only thing that will possibly numb the fucking…" her finger slams against her temple, "horror film on repeat in my brain?"

Ever since the day she hugged me for the first time, she's never once raised her voice to me this way. Instead of fighting her or letting her outburst bother me, I wrap my arms around her. "I love you. Please, tell me what I can do to help you."

Unraveling herself from my embrace, she speaks in a voice so cold, it doesn't even sound like her. "You can let me get fucking drunk."

I stare to the floor, the tears wanting so badly to fall. She's ripping my heart apart, and yet, it's not a fraction of what she's probably feeling right now. I wish I had a magic wand to take this pain from her, or at the very least, knew the right words to say.

She sighs loudly, and when I lift my head, she won't look at me. "I'll stop taking the meds, okay? The liquor will do more anyway."

Reaching into the cabinet, she carries the bottle out of the kitchen to go back to her room without a single word. Leaning against the counter, I drop my face in my hands with a groan, having the desire to scream at the top of my lungs.

In the past week, I've been stalked by and started to fall for an actual demon from Hell, found out my father is a fucking archangel, and now I have to helplessly stand by as my best friend spirals right in front of me. And those are just the highlights. Not to mention, where is Loch?

I grab the broom to sweep up the hair, finding the magical necklace that Loch's cousin … our cousin—God, that's weird—gave him sitting in the dust bin. I pick it up and toss it into the junk drawer, bringing my sandwich back to my room to eat alone.

Once my food is gone, I slide on my headphones, lie back on my bed, and allow the music to lull me in and out of sleep.

Mishka. A voice I've never heard echoes around me, bouncing off the vast emptiness of my dream. At least, I think I'm dreaming. *Awaken, child.*

My eyes open, the spinning fan on the ceiling is the only thing I see. Taking off my headphones, I sit up and my scream falls silent. I'm physically unable to move my gaze from the white eyes staring at me. Gigantic, milky wings span nearly the length of my bedroom. A cool breeze flutters through my veins as I watch the crystal images on his skin moving like water. The opaque pants and robe-style shirt he's wearing fit him to perfection while his hair, which appears translucent, falls to his broad shoulders. Somehow, I know who he is before it's spoken audibly in my mind.

I am Michael.

Opposite of Loch's chaotic aura, his is calming, allowing my chest to rise and lower with steady breathing.

"What have you done, Daughter?"

If it weren't for his lips moving, I wouldn't have been able to tell the difference between him speaking in my head and him talking out loud. It takes a moment to register he asked a question. "What? What do you mean?"

"The son of my fallen brother. You gave him your virtue." Regardless of the aggressive nature of his statement, his demeanor remains utterly passive. At least it snaps me out of whatever trance he had me in.

Chortling in offense, I cross my arms. "You must not have been paying attention because I gave my virtue to Bryson Lawrence in his basement when I was thirteen."

I could swear his white eyes flash brighter. "I gave clear and explicit orders that the child of Maelprog was to return to the depths without defiling you."

Are all immortals assholes? "Oh? You mean the same way you 'defiled' my mother and got her killed?"

"You do not know of what you speak." His features have barely twitched. How is he so emotionless? Even though Loch, and Vilum for that matter, are both maddening, they're also incredibly vibrant. Michael is just detached. Is that an angel thing?

"Are you gonna clear it up for me then, *Dad*?"

"Your mother was well aware of the dangers surrounding our coitus." Wow. He even makes sex sound dull.

"You're saying she willingly died for some angel dick?"

It could be my imagination, but I think his wings spasm. "Your anger is not unwarranted. However, vulgarity is not necessary."

He may be able to stay calm and collected, but I, on the other hand, have about had it with angels and demons alike. I stand on my bed, mostly because it makes me taller, and I feel less intimidated beneath his gaze. "Okay. What about abandoning and mutilating me? Was that necessary?"

"Yes. However, you weren't abandoned." His eyes quickly blink to the wall behind me. "I've watched over you and put Leena Harris in your path not only as a companion, but also to satisfy your murifric need to protect."

I almost retort that he did a sucky job of watching over me when his words fully sink in. Suddenly, I feel sick. Meeting Leena wasn't chance. It was premeditated. Doubt shadows my thoughts, having me question how much of my life has been out of my control. "Are you seriously saying you gave me my best friend so I could be her literal fucking guardian angel?" He doesn't answer which has me laughing in pure rage. "I didn't ask to be a part of any of this! Is my love for her even real?!"

"I simply chose someone who would defend you with the same fierceness that you would defend her. It's not within my desire or power to mold your emotions."

I don't know how I haven't lost my mind with the amount of information I've acquired over the last few days. I still have so many questions, and now that Vilum told me about my mom, my curiosities about her are at the front of my mind. "What about my mother? What was her name?"

"Polina. Your appearance is akin to hers." When he lowers his wings, the crystal designs across his arms vivify.

The next question I want to ask has been in the back of my mind since Vilum told me about her, but I'm scared for the answer. Although, if I don't ask now, I may never know. "Did she go to, you know, Heaven?"

With the slightest tilt of the head, he allows me to release the breath stuck in my chest. "Her soul will spend eternity in Madriiax, yes. Although, I am forbidden from seeing her, so any questions you may have following her death I am unable to answer."

Considering he has the emotional range of a cumquat, it's hard to say, but I would assume that would make him sad. "Wow. God's a bit of a—"

"Please do not finish that sentence."

I narrow my eyes at him. "Can you read my 'intentions' the way Loch can?"

"No. I can speak to your mind, not retrieve anything from it. That is a gift only Asmodeus and his offspring possess."

That's mildly comforting, I suppose. I step off the bed to walk closer to him, imagining how many of his traits I have hidden beneath his seal. "Why didn't you ever show yourself to me? Tell me what I was?"

"You were still in her womb the day Polina chose your name, deciding she wanted you to live a mortal life for as long as was feasible. The least I could do was honor her wishes."

She named me. For whatever reason that makes me smile. My eye catches the glint of something peeking out from beneath his flowy top, and I point to it. "What's that?"

Looking downward, he reaches his hand inside his clothes, pulling out a large, blindingly bright ring. Wait… "Is that a halo?" Once again, his only reply is a nod. I want so badly to touch it. "That's what you used to cut off my wings." I don't need him to verify, I already know. "Why do that if you were going to hide me beneath a seal?"

"Wings can be difficult to manage. They've been known to break through an emetgis on occasion. I couldn't risk it."

"You seem like you suck at picking and choosing what you think is worth the risk."

His jaw clenches ever so slightly, and he somehow appears taller. "Even angels are fallible."

"Yeah, no shit." I always thought if I ever met my birth parents I would be ecstatic, showering them with questions, but I'm angry with him and honestly, his mere presence is a bit draining. "Why exactly are you here, Michael?"

"To inform you that you are forbidden to associate with the son of Asmodeus, and if you continue to defy these orders, I will be forced to take action myself."

"Are you seriously threatening me?"

"I'm warning you."

The last word barely escapes his mouth when he vanishes, the billowing curtains the only evidence he was here at all.

I'm frozen in place, incapable of moving for several moments. Finally, I'm able to sprint out of my room and down the hall. I pound on Leena's door, frantic to tell her what happened. Right before she answers, I question if I should. She doesn't need this shit right now with everything she's been through.

I'm taken aback when she greets me with a huge grin. "Oooh, are you here to drink away the bullshit with me?"

I take the bottle from her and flop down on her bed, taking a swig of the burning liquid. "My dad just showed up."

For a second, she appears completely sober when her jaw falls open. "I'm sorry, what?!"

23

Daemonic Daycare

Loch

The moment my bond with Pygmy allowed me to realize she was going somewhere new, I felt I needed to scope it out. Not to mention, it was apparent Leena wanted to be alone. Luckily, I'm not far enough from Mishka for it to be uncomfortable.

I smile at Pygmy who squeals at my arrival. I keep putting on my priidzar then taking it off again because it's one of her favorite games. Picking her up is out of the question, since mortals tend to have issues with children randomly disappearing right in front of their eyes, so I tickle her into a laughing fit.

The only other person here with her is a man who I'm guessing is fairly young. He's a bit on the twitchy side; his anxiety has been thick since I arrived. Currently, he's on the phone, pacing as he glances at Pygmy every few seconds.

"Lilac will be fine. What was I supposed to do? Leave her there? She's my niece and your granddaughter." He rubs his head in frustration, taking a long drink from a glass bottle. "I remember, Mom, but Kelsey's choices are not her fault."

She was alone.

Is the Lilac he's speaking of supposed to be Pygmy?

The man holds the phone away from his ear while his face appears to scream, yet no sound comes out. Holding the phone to his forehead, he takes a deep breath before returning it to his ear. "I'll figure it out. I'm thirty, not eighteen. You and Dad cannot possibly take on a toddler, and you need to deal with Kelsey's funeral. I can do this." Closing his eyes, he huffs. "Yes, I'll call you in the morning. Good night, Mom."

He tosses the phone on the counter before bending over the pen he has Pygmy in. He reaches down for her, causing me to flinch until he gently touches his fingers down her cheek.

"You're gonna learn real quick, your gran is a nutcase." Picking her up, he bounces her on his hip. "Sorry, Lilac. I think you're gonna have to sleep in the Pac-n-Play tonight, just until I can get you a bed. Is that okay?" Her mumblings are incoherent, though he laughs at her all the same. "Are you hungry? Let's see what Uncle Philip has for you to eat."

Pygmy reaches for me when he carries her away. I do wish I could hold her, but, at least on the surface, this human seems to desire her safety, so I decide to take my leave and come check on her tomorrow. "Bye, Pygmy. I'll be back later."

Arriving at Mishka's house, I find her in Leena's bedchamber, both of them two thirds deep into a bottle of liquor. Leena squeals once she sees me, her spirits synthetically lifted by her inebriation. "Loch! Loch's back!" She holds up her arm, showing off a blue bracelet with a copper token tied in the middle. "Look, Mishka made you one too!"

Mishka falls on the floor when she tries to climb off the bed, laughing as she rolls on her back. "Where've you bleen?" Hiccupping with her slur, she points at me. "I tol' you to slay with Leeena."

Leena crawls across the bed to hang off the edge and shake her head at Mishka. "No, no, no, don't get mad at him, okay? I told him I dinnit need a sabybitter."

Mishka attempts to sit up, increasing her hysteria. "Sabybitter. Thas what you said."

They repeat their gibberish three times. Both of them are completely wrecked. I light a cigarette because I doubt Mishka is going to give a shit about me smoking in here right now.

Leena sits up, wobbly on her knees while she takes another swig from the bottle. "Ohmygosh, Loch! Guess what happen—"

Mishka brings a finger to her mouth. "Noooo! Shhhhh. Shut up, shut up."

Of course, now I'm curious, but I don't know how much I'd be able to follow if they told me now anyway, and I can't pick up a single thing from their floating brains.

Leena covers her mouth with her hands, consumed by another fit of laughter, falling back on the bed. By the time I'm done with my smoke, Leena's passed out, and Mishka's not far behind. Covering Leena with the bedspread, I lean down to pick up Mishka.

I carry her to her room, putting her in her bed. When I climb beneath the blankets with her, she slides something over my hand. Similar to the one Leena boasted of earlier, it's a bracelet made of black cording, the silver token has letters stamped into it that reads, *An angel's demon.*

I can't put into words how that makes me feel. I've never gotten a gift from anyone … ever.

She flops her arm up to show me. "I made a," she hiccups, "matching one for me too." I hold her hand still enough to read it.

A demon's angel.

"Mishka…" I don't know how to finish the sentence, but I don't have to because she reaches between us, trying to stroke my cock. I'm half tempted to let her, but she can't even talk. There's no way she's in any position to fuck. "Go to sleep, tin nanba."

She whines yet doesn't even finish her protest before she's snoring next to me. It's still difficult for me to visualize her as divine. I want so badly to see her true appearance. Wrapping my arms around her, I fall asleep with her head on my chest.

Mishka's grumbling is so loud, it wakes me up. "Oh, God. I feel like shit. And I have to work in…" she lifts her head up to see her clock, "two hours."

If she would let me remove her emetgis, she would no longer be able to get drunk, never mind sick from it. Throwing off the blankets, she drags her feet to her robe. "I need coffee."

Leena's sitting at the table in the cooking quarters and doesn't seem much better. "There's aspirin in the cupboard above the stove." She rests her head on the table. "Is there anywhere that makes burgers this early? I really need some grease."

"I don't know," Mishka groans. "I need to take a shower and get ready for work."

"Sucks to be you. I get the day off. I told my boss I had a virus."

Mishka throws back her pills with her coffee before walking over to her friend and kissing her on the head. "Take all the time you need, okay?"

As Mishka shuffles out of the room, I drop down in the chair across from Leena, tapping the table with my fingers. "What happened last night?"

"Can you please not do that?" She presses a hand to her head for a moment then points at her satchel. "Go get me something to eat, and I might tell you."

After she writes down what she wants, I shigmir to the address she gave me to order her food. By the time I get back, Mishka's dressed, still looking worse for wear. "Can you take me to work? I really don't want to ride in a car right now."

I'm starting to get antsy at all the secrecy, but it'll only take a second, so I do what she asks, bringing her to the back of the doll shop. With a half-hearted kiss, she leaves me to go inside.

Causing Leena to squeal, I land back in the chair I was sitting in prior. "Okay. Tell me."

Her burger's partly gone, and she seems a little more alive. Getting some food in her stomach must have done her some good. She wipes her mouth with a napkin. "Well, you already know the part where Mishka's an angel, and apparently, her dad is the archangel, Michael. I'm still having a hard time processing that part. Anyway, last night while you were gone, he showed up."

My priidzar falls off, the saziamiin on my arms burning in a complicated concoction of anger and nervousness. "Uncle Michael was here? In this house?"

Biting off a piece of her potato stick, she stares at my change of form. "That's what Mishka said." She takes a swig of her fizzy drink then belches. "Sounds like he really hates your guts."

I realize I'm fidgeting with the bracelet Mishka made me. I still can't figure out why it puts me in this unfamiliar mood simply by looking at it. "The feeling is beginning to be mutual. What exactly did he say?"

She wipes her shiny, greasy fingers on her napkin. Standing up to get her cigarettes off the counter, she leads me outside. "She was pretty freaked out when she told me, and I was already drunk, but something about him making sure you two aren't a thing." I take my own cigarette out of her pack without asking. "Dude, Mishka is going to have to start buying you your own if you keep smoking all of mine."

Sluffing off her comment about the smokes, I rest my head on my hand. "How does he plan on doing that?"

She shrugs, "How the hell am I supposed to know?" Her eyes squint at me as she takes a drag. "Where did you fly off to last night anyway?"

"I was checking up on Pygmy."

Her confusion is salty in my mouth. "What the shit is a Pygmy?"

I'm a little surprised Mishka never told her. "She's a child. I brought her here after ridding her of her vile father."

She widens her eyes, the brown irises appearing lighter in the sunlight. "And by 'ridding' do you mean like you did with Tim and his friend?" At this point, there's no use in denying it, so I nod. "Christ, you're a real vigilante. So what, you just kidnapped the kid?"

"I prefer the term 'saved,' but that's semantics."

She whistles. "Wow. And what are the semantics of what happened to Harry?"

"I simply scared him. Among other things."

Blowing out smoke, she snorts. "It's the 'other things' I'm curious about."

191

I'm on edge when I go see Pygmy. I'm sure my uncle's visit was his way of securing Mishka's entrance into Madriiax at the end of her human life, and I know that's where she belongs. It doesn't change that I loathe the idea of her becoming the side of my family that turned their back on mine.

Lilac.

I watch Pygmy's uncle frantically click away on his computer machine, tearing his fingers through his hair. Pygmy holds her hands up, wanting to be held, and I almost give in when his back is turned.

"I'm sorry, Lilac. Uncle Philip has to find you a daycare he can afford. I'll play with you in a bit, okay?"

The idea streaks across my mind like a lightning bolt. I wink at Pygmy and shigmir back to the house. Leena is in the living room, reading a book called *Spiritual Healing.* "What's your phone number?"

She jumps in surprise, glaring at me. "Goddammit, Loch. Why do you need my—"

"I'll explain later, just write it down."

"Okay, okay, sheesh."

I snatch the paper from her hand and return to Pygmy. Luckily the tele-vision is already playing, so I turn the volume up and use an illusion to create what appears to be an advertisement for affordable childcare. I add Leena's face, phone number, and address.

Pygmy's uncle takes the bait, turning toward the imaginary ad. Grabbing his phone, he taps in the number, so I wink at Pygmy then return to Leena so I'm there when she answers his call.

"Hello?" Her forehead creases while she shakes her head. "I think y—" With wide eyes, her voice turns a bit squeaky.

"Wait, how much?" Shifting her gaze to me, she glowers. "And you got my number from the TV?" I don't speak, using my mouth to form the words, *Say yes.* "Uh … no website, but yeah, I'm totally qualified." She sticks up her middle finger before grabbing a writing utensil out of her satchel and writing something on her hand. "Awesome. See you then." Once she hangs up, she crosses her arms, popping her lips. "What the hell did you do?"

"Pygmy needed someone to watch her. I don't like her continuously being passed around to strangers."

I reach for one of her cigarettes, and she rips it out of my hand. "I don't know anything about kids!"

I'm definitely going to need to get my own pack. "Then why did you say yes?"

"You told me to! Plus, it's four hundred extra bucks a week, and he sounded desperate."

If I'm being honest with myself, I'm not sure why I have such an attachment to the child. Yes, I find little humans intriguing, but I also have a sense of responsibility for her. It will also be a comfort to know she's safe and taken care of when I go home.

"I can help you as long as I'm here."

She jams the cigarette between her lips. "Oh, yes you will." Shaking her head, she walks past me, mumbling, "I can't believe I let you talk me into running a motherfuckin' daycare with a demon."

ลฦๅๅ
24

Losing Loch

MISHKA

Thankfully, I was scheduled in the back again today. Customers are not something I think I could have dealt with this morning. At least I don't feel like I'm dying anymore. Beckany went on a food run that saved my life.

The bad thing about being back here is I'm alone with my thoughts. I can't stop thinking of what Michael said about taking care of things himself. What does that mean? Part of me wonders if he's bluffing to scare me, while the other part is reminded this is an actual angel who probably has more power than I can imagine.

It also pisses me the hell off. He mutilates, abandons, and turns a blind eye to me for my entire life. Now, because I'm hooking up with a supernatural bad boy, he wants to play the overbearing father role.

I know I'm going to have to talk to Loch about this. I'm just scared he'll take the necklace sitting in my kitchen drawer and leave me forever. Of course, I could hide it, but do I really want him to stay if he doesn't one hundred percent want to? Now that he didn't evaporate into thin air when we did the one thing we thought would cause him to, I'll spend every moment wondering what it is that will send him back. The worst of it is, there's a part deep inside hoping he's here to stay for the rest of my life, and I know how dangerous that is for my heart.

Knowing there's an afterlife changes things, and even though Loch said I can't go to Hell with him, I don't understand why. He's part angel too, and his mother was human once. Heaven is supposed to be this ultimate goal, yet the idea of going there for eternity with my asshole father doesn't sound like a good time. If I'm not there to be a torturer or torturee, would Hell be so bad?

Hand stitching the rib cage onto the outside of the skele-kitten I'm making, I poke myself with the needle from the sensation of my legs being forced open beneath the table. My skirt appears to move up my legs on its own before my panties are tugged to the side. His invisible fingers slide into me, and I drop the doll.

"Loch."

I feel the tips of his tongue licking at my clit, forcing me to bite my lip in an attempt to contain my moan. My hands grip the table as I roll my hips onto his invisible mouth. This order needs to be finished, and I'm so close to being done, but there's no way I can work with an unseen demon eating me out.

My head drops back with the shocks of ecstasy tingling

up my spine. The door to the backroom flies open, making me jump in my seat. His grip on my legs keeps me in place regardless of my effort to pull away.

Beckany tilts her head at me. "Are you okay?" I don't trust my voice right now, so I nod. "I have to tell you about the customer who was just in here."

He doesn't let up with his tongue or his fingers, and I'm so scared she's going to hear the wet sounds my pussy is making as she tells me about the hot guy she thinks was flirting with her. It's impossible to sit still when I know at any moment, I'm going to come undone.

"Are you sure you're alright?"

Even though my voice is shaky, I'm able to speak without panting. "Yeah. I had a long couple of days, and I'm … tired."

She arches a skeptical brow. "Oh, okay. Well, I'll close up so we can go."

"Mmhmm."

The moment she shuts the door, he shows himself, still working his fingers, he ceases the assault of his tongue long enough to smirk up at me. My hands grip his moving head while I keep glancing at the door to watch for Beckany.

"She's gonna be back soon, Loch." Finally, he allows me my release. He reaches up to cover my mouth, the endless pulsing between my legs threatening to make me cry out. My thighs tremble against the chair, my whispered words muffled beneath his hand. "Shit, Loch. Oh, fuck."

As my chest heaves and my skin is still tingling with the afterglow, he crawls up my body to kiss me. I can taste myself on his tongue. Before he breaks our kiss, he goes invisible again, leaving me breathless.

196

After closing up the shop with Beckany, I make my way past the alley. A hand grabs my arm, pulling me against a hard chest. "Don't be mad." That phrase can't mean anything good. When I open my mouth to ask him what the hell he did, he squeezes my shoulders, kissing me to cut off my question. I pull back from him to find us standing in my living room where Leena walks in from the kitchen.

"Did you tell her the shit you pulled today?" Crossing my arms, I wait for one of them to tell me what's going on. "Apparently, we're a daycare now." I look between them because even though I know what the words mean, I have no idea how they apply.

Loch gives me these pathetic eyes that I've never seen from him. "Pygmy's uncle needs someone to watch her while he works. It would give me peace of mind to know when I can't be here, she's being taken care of by someone I trust."

The way he talks about leaving sounds like he's going to die, and I guess that's how it would feel. Even as the thought flits across my mind, my stomach knots with dread. My only option is to force myself not to think about it.

I still don't understand his fascination with the kid, but I do wish someone would have cared that much about me at that age.

"And does her uncle know we're two twenty-five-year-olds who don't know shit about childcare?"

"Oh, no," Leena pipes up. "That's the best part. He thinks we, or rather I, am certified because someone," she frowns at Loch, "gave him that impression. And we start tomorrow morning, so we're going to have to arrange our schedules around that."

I drop my head back with a groan. "Why does this feel illegal?" Tossing my hands up, I ask Leena, "Do you really want to do this?"

She shrugs. "She's not even two. It can't be that hard. Plus, it's an extra four hundred a week, and I can move my shifts to later in the day. It's Monday through Friday, eight to six."

"That's only like eight dollars an hour!"

"Yeah, to hang out here." I'm starting to think this is more appealing to her than she's letting on.

Deep down, I know Loch's motive for this was sweet, so it makes it hard to be too mad at him. Nonetheless, this is going to be incredibly inconvenient. "We can give it a shot, but I swear, we better not go to jail for fraud." The grin on Loch's face is mildly contagious. "Well, apparently, we need to go shopping for some kid shit."

Since I have no idea what a child that age needs, I decide to figure it out tomorrow. Some toys, snacks, and kid safe dishes will have to be sufficient for now.

I should have just sent Loch with the money because he picks out everything anyway.

When we get home, I see Leena has used some poster board and wire to make a sign for the lawn. It's covered in rainbows and says, *Leena's Little Ones*.

She's definitely put some thought into this.

After dropping the bags in the kitchen, I pour myself some wine and Loch kisses my neck. "It's kind of you to agree to this, but you do have murifri blood. Protection is in your nature."

I give him the side eye then fill up my glass up to the brim. "Speaking of, we need to talk about Michael."

His hand flattens against my stomach, sliding in my skirt. "Leena told me. I'm not worried about my uncle."

I take a big drink before setting the glass on the counter. My knees weaken as his fingers move inside me. "He didn't sound like he was messing around."

Next thing I know, I'm in my room bent over my bed, my skirt flipped up to my waist. "I say we call his bluff."

It's impossible to not rock back on his hand while he fingers me, his free hand snaking up my shirt to cup my breast. The heat of his erection presses against my ass, his markings tickle as they move across my skin. Without preparation, he forces himself into my pussy, my body jerking forward from impact accompanied by his hiss of approval. It's the oddest sensation to be stretched so far so quickly without pain. Still, I release a yell from the mere shock of it. The tempo of his thighs slamming against my backside doesn't slow as he pushes my shirt over my head and unclasps my bra. Even though I can't see from this position, I can feel his horns scraping down the curves of my back. His hot lips kiss at what I now know are my wing amputation scars.

"Have you thought anymore about letting me remove your emetgis?"

I've tried not to think about it because it's terrifying. Not even Loch knows exactly what it will do to me. While Leena hasn't expressed it, I know her well enough to know she's feeling inadequate. She's the one who's always been into the magical stuff, yet I'm the one who's supernatural.

He yanks himself out of me, only to bring us to the center of my bed with me straddling him. Pulling me down onto his erection, he thrusts up, bottoming out immediately. The tips of his tongue circle my nipples, feeling so amazing I arch my back. His hands holding my waist gives him the ability to use my body, lifting and lowering me to his discretion.

"I'm scared. I don't want to be an angel." I hold onto his horns, using them as handles as I rotate my hips.

"I'll be right here … for as long as I can be." I know what he really means. He could vanish at any time. "You don't have to be scared." His hands hold my face gently as he kisses me. "Whenever you're ready."

The truth is, I don't know if I'll ever be ready. I also wonder, what if I die with the seal still intact? Will I die human or immediately transform into a divine being? Mortality is scary, but I think not knowing who or what exactly I'll become is even scarier.

He slows his pace, each thrust becoming more languid. The rings of his cock pull out a moan every time he lowers my body onto his. It's odd how it can feel like forever and an instant all at the same time. He erupts inside of me, sending a comforting, bubbling heat to consume me, calming an anxiety I didn't know I had.

Kissing my shoulder, he lifts me off him before standing up to pull on his jeans. Once he fastens them, he leans over to press his lips to mine as a sudden gust of wind blows my hair across my face. Trinkets and makeup products fly off my shelves when a high-pitched ringing sound *screeches* in my ears. With a flash of light and a *crack*, an illuminated ring lands in the wall right above Loch's head.

My stomach and heart intertwine at the sight of Michael's furious glowing eyes staring at us from the foot of my bed. In less time than it takes to open my mouth, he's standing next to Loch, the grip he has on his arm clearly causing him pain.

"Stop!"

Michael doesn't acknowledge that I spoke. He doesn't look at me at all, his gaze is a raging inferno glaring at Loch. "I made my instructions clear. You were to return to the flames from whence you came. Instead, you rebelled just as the fallen before you, violating my daughter with your abhorrent touch."

Loch's eyes glow equally bright. Baring his fangs, he stands chest to chest with Michael, challenging him. "I violated her with my abhorrent tongue too, you prick. And trust me when I say she fucking loved it."

I could kill him for choosing this moment to be a smartass. Grabbing his arm to keep him anchored to me, I realize I'm still completely naked, and I use my free hand to yank the blankets over me. Michael rips the halo from the wall, his growl sending ice through my veins.

For a split second, my eye catches the illuminated symbol in his necklace. Suddenly, my vision sees only solid white, and the snapping sound of wings is all I can hear. By the time I'm able to focus, my hands are empty, and they're both gone.

Home in a Handbasket

Loch

Michael. Formurifri a balit. Archangel of virtue.

His presence has an effect on me that's hard to discern. I'm partially intrigued, partially nauseous, and partially terrified. Being scared is not an emotion that I'm accustomed to. Regardless, it's not fear for my well-being that I'm experiencing, it's the dread of knowing I've lost her. Mere seconds ago, she was in my arms, and now I'm facing eternity without her.

The icy grip around my arm ignites a pain I've never experienced in all my one hundred thousand years of existence.

Though his expression gives little away, his touch is draining me. His eyes are white like mine, and his wings pearly, similar to my father's. He pulls them back, leaving no doubt in my mind what's coming. Orseiinak are no match for pure murifri, especially one of his stature.

With a swoop of his wings, I feel the exact second my bond to Mishka snaps. The colors of Drilpa Nalvage circle around us, closing in until he tosses me against the gates of Maelprog. They open beneath our feet, revealing the seven kingdoms as both of us spiral around the fire rise down to the streets of Zibiidor Comselh.

Michael climbs off me, allowing me to my feet. I'm barely able to shake out my wings before he's at my throat with his halo. *Go near her again, and I will end her mortal life, bringing her home to where she belongs. I will not start another war over an insignificant child of Maelprog.* His lips stay pressed together, yet I hear his voice perfectly clear.

"Get your deplorable murifric hands off of my son." My mother's voice booms from behind me, her black eyes wishing death upon Michael. "You are not welcome in my home."

My father falls from above us, landing between my mother and uncle. "What is the meaning of this, Brother?"

"I do not wish to be here any more than you desire my presence." He digs the halo into my neck, searing the flesh of my throat. It's a pain I've never encountered, yet it's nothing in comparison to what I'm feeling in my chest. "He laid his hands upon my daughter, soiling her. I will not stand by for that." He finally releases me, turning to my father. "Out of respect, I came to Lucifer, ordering he retrieve the boy, yet my demands have been disregarded."

"You no longer have dominion over us. He is my son. Why not come to me?"

Michael's lips raise in what some might call a smile, but it's much more sinister. "You and I both know Lucifer was generous in giving you this kingdom, but he is the true king of Maelprog."

My mother lurches for him with a shriek, baring her fangs when my father grabs her wrist, yanking her back to stop her. "Never return to this place, Brother. Next time, I will send throngs of lower orseiinak to tear you apart."

While he remains stoic, I still see his wings twitch as his posture stiffens. "Orseiinak cannot kill formurifri, no matter how many there are. You know this."

Lifting his head, my father's smirk is clearly a warning. "Perhaps. However, they can cause you great agony."

Using the force of his wings to propel him in the air, Michael glares down at us. "Keep him away from her, Brother." He gives me a final glance. "Remember what I said, child of Maelprog."

The moment he's flown past the gates, they close, once again becoming a flaming sky. My mother hurries to me, inspecting my neck. "Are you alright, my wickedling?"

Thankfully, she's referring to my physical state because I don't know how to express my emotional one. "Yes, Mother. I'm fine."

Her touch is gentle against my face, the jewels of her horns *jangling* with the jerk of her head. "We were told you were summoned. How in all that's unholy did you end up intermingled with the daughter of Madriiax filth?"

My father's face remains cold, though he's still here, so he must be curious. "She called me. Her emetgis hid her celestiality. I didn't realize she was more than human. Uncle Lucifer never told you about her?"

When my mother smiles how she is now, it's not going to be pleasant for anyone. "He will come to regret that."

Her long, black nails scrape across my jaw before she whistles for Ors. When he arrives, she climbs onto the back of the monstrous cronug, likely to have words with my uncle, leaving me alone with my father. His black suit is pristine besides the ash falling on his shoulders. "Were you aware Michael wanted you away from the girl?"

Wiping my hand over my mouth, I nod. "He sent Vilum." Shit. The gohed. "But I didn't want to leave. I enjoyed her company as she did mine, so I decided to let the summoning run its course."

Holding his hands behind his back, he steps close enough to speak into my ear. "If it's not already clear, I agree with my brother on this. You are forbidden from ever seeing the daughter of Madriiax again."

Obviously done with this conversation, his form evaporates, leaving me alone in the street. I look above me to the closed gates. I'll never see her again, and now I'm meant to go back to meaningless orgies and torturing the damned as if nothing has changed when everything has.

I shigmir back to my room in the castle before word gets around that I've returned. The pull in my chest guiding me to her is gone, something else that I don't understand taking its place. How do I get this torturous mix of rage, sorrow, and emptiness out from beneath my skin? Pacing my floor, I rip my hands through my hair. I try to yell it away, shatter it away by slamming a chair into a mirror, breaking the headboard of my bed, ripping the fabric of my pillows, and stabbing holes into the wall with my dagger. Nothing helps.

I'm left heaving in my destroyed room. There are only three ways I'd be able to get back to Earth. Mishka can't summon me twice, but I suppose Leena could. Even if she did, I would be tied to Leena, not her, and I could never risk Michael taking her mortal life. The very idea of him keeping her trapped in Madriiax forever is desolating. I could be a messenger if there ever was a reason in her lifetime and I was the one chosen to go. Regardless, the same issue remains. Each of my uncles have a gohed, which are impossible to steal. They must be given to you by whoever's sigil it possesses, making that the least probable option of all.

As I rub my thumb over the token of the bracelet Mishka made for me, I realize there is a soul in Maelprog who can connect me to her on some distant level, and it's all I can think of to fill the abyss she left behind.

Arriving at the Pashbab cells, I find his folder, reading through his lifetime of cruelty. Although he had his own share of abuse early in his life, who he became and the humans he hurt were his choices alone.

I slowly open his cell door to find him hanging from his neck, choking and yearning for breath. When our eyes meet, he attempts to scream, but considering his position, it's impossible.

"It's good to see you remember me, Tim."

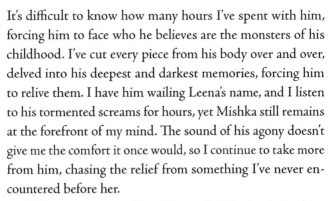

It's difficult to know how many hours I've spent with him, forcing him to face who he believes are the monsters of his childhood. I've cut every piece from his body over and over, delved into his deepest and darkest memories, forcing him to relive them. I have him wailing Leena's name, and I listen to his tormented screams for hours, yet Mishka still remains at the forefront of my mind. The sound of his agony doesn't give me the comfort it once would, so I continue to take more from him, chasing the relief from something I've never encountered before her.

There are so many things I yearn for. Her laugh, her kiss, her snark, her kindness, her smile, her anger, her joy, her … presence. I'll never feel the same way that I did around her, and because of that, I get the sensation that there are pieces of myself I left back in the mortal realm.

"Loch." My mother takes the spider device from my hand to drop it on the floor, her voice gentle. "You've been in here all night." I wonder how long she's been standing there witnessing me fall apart.

My shoulders heave as I watch the blood splatter to the floor as it drips from Tim's feet. "How did you know I was here?"

She walks up to Tim, twirling her finger in the blood on his chest before bringing it into her mouth. While the blood of the damned appears to be the same as that of the living, it's a completely different substance. It's not nearly as delicious, but it's not bad. "The night is silent, wickedling. His screams can be heard all across Zibiidor Comselh." Returning to me, she tilts her head. "My exquisite boy. I've sensed a change in you since your return."

While I might have done it as an extremely young orsei-inak, I have no memory of ever producing tears, yet with my mind constantly reminding me I'll never see her again, I'm getting choked up. I don't want to look my mother in the eyes for fear she'll see my torment.

She holds my chin, her long nails scraping my skin, forcing me to meet her gaze. "The murifri girl. She's special to you."

My breath is jagged as I work my jaw. "Yes." I jerk my face from her touch. "She is."

Walking past her, I leave her in the cell to walk the streets of Zibiidor Comselh alone. Normally, I'd enjoy watching the performance orgies or stop in one of the shops to get my cock sucked, but now the thought of being touched by someone else has taken on a grimy layer of displeasure and lost the appeal that was previously an integral part of who I am. I'm not made for this. I was born for lust, not whatever is poisoning my mind. My mother, my father, any of my siblings, none of them could possibly understand. I don't even fucking understand. Though, there may be one person in all of Maelprog who might.

On the highest floor of the tallest castle, my Uncle Lucifer's quarters reside. The fire of his sigil burns, so I know he's inside. As I bring up my fist to knock, the doors open before I can touch the marble.

He stands at the opposite end of the room, his back to me while he watches over his kingdom with the fire rise burning in the distance. "I was wondering when you'd come to see me." Turning in my direction, he beckons me to join him.

I walk across the skin rug made from Adam's post-death hide. He and my father still argue over who should have it. Since Adam was humanity's first rapist, my father believes it should be his. However, Uncle Lucifer loathes him with a raging passion for what he did to my mother, making him desire it as a prize. My mother convinced them to share it, switching off every thousand years or so.

I feel like I should mention his divine pendant, even knowing he is fully aware of its location. "I apologize for not using the gohed, seeing as you sent Vilum for that very reason."

His white curls are pristinely coiffed around his statuesque features and pursed lips. "Hmm. Do you? I assume if you were truly remorseful, you wouldn't have had to have been forcefully dragged here, by Michael of all beings."

I lean against the obsidian pillars lining his balcony. "When did you know you loved my mother?"

The smallest of smiles lifts his lips as he sips from his goblet. "I used to say it was the first time I saw her, an ebony beauty dancing in the garden. Now I know it was the moment she refused Adam. Refused to be anyone other than who she was." He stares out in front of him, the flaming sky stretching across all seven kingdoms. "She may not be an easy creature to love, yet it's her stubbornness that makes her all the more delectable." His pet cronug flies to meet him, lying submissive at his feet. "The daughter of Madriiax. Do you love her?"

I scoff. "Don't be ridiculous, Uncle." The moment the words are released, I realize the expansive falseness of the statement.

Almost a lie. Something I've never done.

With a subtle tilt of the head, his lip quirks. "Of course. However, if you did, I would tell you to not let anyone, not even the creator himself, keep you from her."

I would never be so disrespectful, but I want to scream at him that it isn't that easy. "What can I do? Uncle Michael said if I went anywhere near her again, he'd take her mortal life and bring her to Madriiax. Then she really would be unreachable."

"You're a clever boy. You are my nephew after all. I suggest you ponder on it. One thing I will tell you is there is nothing in this realm or the next that could keep me from your mother. Regardless, it's you that must make the choice." I watch the ashes fall from the sky. Even though he may understand what I'm feeling better than I do, he still can't help me. "Don't worry about the gohed. I'll send Vilum to fetch it."

He's given me something to think about, because he's right. She's what matters. She's all that matters, and I have to find a way to either return to her or bring her to me.

I've always been told he was stripped of his holiness. The part of him that was the murifri Samael is dead, yet when he speaks like this I can't help wondering if that's true. He was the murifri a olpirt. Angel of light. His ability to bring hopefulness to this situation makes me believe that light still remains. And that it always has.

I turn to take my leave. "As always, your intelligence cannot be surpassed. Good night, Uncle."

"Loch."

His commanding voice forces me to stop. "Yes, Uncle?"

"What you're feeling will not fade. The divine are not like humans. The agony of her loss is certain to not only remain intact for all eternity but will increase as the time passes."

AZAZEL
26

Torturous Transformation

MISHKA

"Loch! Loch!" I scream for him, knowing he can't hear me. Jumping off the bed, I throw my clothes on before I rush to the kitchen, pulling open drawers, not remembering which one I put it in. I'm high from Loch coming in me, and I can't think straight. "Shit. Where is it?"

"Whoa. Are you okay, what's going on?" Leena asks behind me.

"He's gone." Once I say it, the barrier holding back my tears cracks, allowing them to flow freely. "Michael took him." I'm crying, but it's as if there's a film over my emotions, not allowing me to experience them properly. "I'm never going to see him again."

Taking me by the hand, she pulls me against her to hold me. "Oh, Mimi. You knew this had to happen at some point." She combs her fingers through my hair shushing me. "He's a demon. You're an angel. How was that really supposed to work?"

Shoving her away from me, I continue ripping apart the drawers. "I have to say goodbye. I have to tell him…" I shake my head because I've never even admitted it to myself, and now it's too late.

Finally, I find it. My fingers wrap around the necklace, the flaming symbol flickering inside.

"Mishka…"

"I have to, Leena."

"And what if you can't come back?" She presses her hands against her temples before jabbing them in my direction. "Don't be stupid!"

"I'll figure out a way. I won't leave you. It just can't end like this." I throw the pendant over my head, feeling its weight against my neck as I close my eyes.

"Mishka!"

Nothing changes, nothing happens. When I lift my eyelids, I'm still in my kitchen, right in front of Leena. "Shit! Why isn't it working?!"

Her relief is apparent with the fall of her shoulders. "Maybe it's because technically you're still human."

Shit! Why didn't I let him take off the stupid seal while I had the chance? I toss the useless piece of jewelry back into the drawer, seeing the knife caddy on the counter. Reaching out to grab the handle of the biggest knife, I hold it out to her. "Cut it out of me."

She jerks back, her mouth open in repulsion. "Cut what out of you?"

I use the knife to gesture toward my feet. "The seal. Cut it out of my foot."

Holding her hands up, she steps away from me. "Yeah, fuck you. That's not happening."

While I may understand why she wouldn't be up for doing this, it doesn't make my frustration any less potent. "Fine. I'll do it myself."

Stomping over to the kitchen chair, I rest my ankle on my knee. I can barely see it. My stomach lurches in anticipation the moment the tip of the blade gets close to my skin. Leena covers her mouth with both hands, watching me with wide eyes. Maybe I can break it by slicing through it?

Closing my eyes, I press the tip of the knife to where the arch in my foot meets my heel. *One, two, three.* Using as much force as I can, I rip the blade across the thick flesh, sucking in air.

"Oh my God." Leena's words are muffled behind her hands that remain over her mouth.

I take a deep breath, wanting to scream when I see that what should have been one long cut is actually multiple short cuts in a line. The parts covered by the seal remain perfectly intact with no sign of damage. "Fuck!"

I drop the knife, and it *clatters* while I stare at my wound. The cuts are pretty deep, blood beginning to run down my foot in rivulets. Since I'm still buzzing from being with Loch, the pain is bearable. Leena hurries to get a dishcloth from one of the drawers, instantly using it to put pressure on the gashes.

She shakes her head. "You crazy bitch. Hold this here while I go get some tape and gauze."

Damn it. I do as she says, considering if I have the balls to turn on the stove and try to melt it off. I'm fairly certain Loch was planning on burning it. I should probably at least allow the cut to heal a bit before trying.

Leena returns as I keep my gaze on the stove, begging my brain to come up with a better solution. Suddenly, it hits me. "Wait. The book! You were never able to destroy it, were you?" She told me she tried everything she could think of, but the thing was indestructible. "We can resummon him. We did it once, we can do it again."

Her eyes narrow with a huff. "Shouldn't we have tried that first?" She tilts her head, and I despise the look of pity she's giving me right now. "And if that's all it took, don't you think he would have told you that?"

I know she's right, but I can't do nothing. "We have to try."

Sighing, she finishes wrapping my foot. "Okay. I'll get the stuff."

While she gets set up, I limp around, doing everything I can remember to recreate the first time, right down to putting on the same clothes I wore. I get a bottle of wine and the coffee mug I used. It makes me nervous to not have the miscarriage blood, but we cut my hand since it's the only option we have. Leena makes a remark about me being 'more sliced up than a loaf of bread,' but the floaty sensation is still all over my body, so I don't even register the sting. When it comes time to make my list, I try to remember the exact qualities I wrote down the first time, including Leena's additions.

Speaking the enchantment, I stare at the book, plucking out every memory from my brain. I loved the way his jet-black hair would fall into his equally dark eyes. His living tattoos felt like they were breathing beneath my fingers, and his damn smirk used to irk the shit out of me. He had the ability to be terrifying yet somehow one of the sweetest people I've ever met. Rarely was anything worth him taking seriously, and he was horny all the damn time. The sound of his laugh could get me wet, and his kisses could be anywhere from violent to gentle. I'll never know anyone like him, even if my lifetime is infinite.

"Mishka." Leena takes my hand, kissing my knuckles. I open my eyes to realize I'm crying.

She hands me a tissue, and I take a deep breath. "Now we wait."

We drink wine and watch television. The high from sleeping with Loch is wearing off, causing me to understand how selfish I've been. I've been so worried about Loch and my dad, I haven't properly checked in on her.

"How are you doing? You know, with everything?"

She turns off the TV, calling Shittles up to her lap. "I'm honestly not sure. Knowing Tim is gone and suffered during his last breath is comforting. Sometimes, I feel fine, then others, I remember it so vividly. It hurts so bad. I'd do anything to take the pain away."

I take her hand and squeeze it. Her reaction to all of this makes me realize I was an enormous baby over the whole Harry thing. She went through such a horrific ordeal, and she hasn't been wallowing in bed for days.

"You're the strongest person I know, but don't think you need to be, okay?"

She gives me a smile, kissing my cheek before she stands up with Shittles. "I'm gonna crash. Philip's gonna be here early to drop off Lilac."

"Lilac? Are you talking about Pygmy?"

"Lilac's her real name." Kissing Shittles wrinkly head, she backs toward the hall. "Sweet dreams, Mimi."

"Yeah." I stare at the cut across my palm. "Sweet dreams."

I don't move from the couch. I find myself continuously glancing over my shoulder, hoping he'll be standing there with his ornery grin. He never is. Walking to the kitchen, I make some coffee to help me stay awake. I listen to music and do some Pilates. Anything so I don't fall asleep and miss him in case the spell worked.

Eventually, I must have passed out because the next thing I know the sun is up, and Leena is shaking me on the couch.

"Get up. He's here."

My heart twirls in my chest. I jump to my feet, instantly feeling the throbbing sting of the cut across my heel. I search for him until it hits me that she was talking about Pygmy's uncle. The disappointment causes my eye sockets to burn, but I smooth out my clothes and attempt to tame my hair with my fingers. My hand is so sore I can't close it. Between my hand and foot, I welcome the outward pain. It's much more preferable to what I'm feeling inside.

Leena swings open the door, smiling at the handsome man on our porch. Even from here, I can see his eyes light up as they travel down her body. He adjusts Pygmy on his hip, holding out his hand while trying to keep her diaper bag on his shoulder.

"Hi. You must be Leena. I'm Philip."

"Hi! Yes, it's nice to meet you. Come on in."

Her voice is higher than normal, an obvious indicator that she's nervous. Philip evaluates our house with a frown. "Where are the other kids?"

She glances at me with a nervous laugh. "Well, right now, Lilac is our only child."

"And the toys?" Leena points to our sad little pile of plastic games and dolls still in the bags. He nods to the coffee table. "Is that a wine bottle?"

I grab it to hide behind my back. "It was mine from last night. Sorry."

Tilting his head, he looks between us. "I don't mean to be rude, but this doesn't seem to be a very kid friendly daycare."

He's struggling to keep the little girl still, so I reach my arms out. "Here, let me hold her and take your bag." Hesitantly, he passes her over. "Hey, Pygmy. Wanna go play?"

"What did you call her?" Leena's eyes widen with her glare, and Philip looks like he just saw a dead body. "That's the only word I've ever heard her say."

I clear my throat, wishing I had Loch's ability to disappear. "Um…"

"Okay, something is definitely weird here. I don't know if this is a good idea."

Panicking, I blurt out the first lie I can think of. "Why? Because we're trying to build our business, and I called her a common baby nickname? We have to start somewhere. How will we ever succeed if nobody gives us a chance? And the name is simply a term of endearment, it's what my mother used to call me."

Leena's green brows shoot up, her eyes going back and forth between me and Philip. Now it's his turn to release an awkward laugh. "Shit. I'm sorry. I'm new to this guardianship thing. It was sprung on me, and I'm worried about Lilac, but you're right. Everyone deserves a break."

Jumping in, Leena adds, "Well, since she's currently our only kid, she'll get all the attention, and I can send you photo updates throughout the day if it would make you more comfortable?"

His hand rubs the stubble on his face as he nods. "Thank you. I would appreciate that. I'll be back at six." Ruffling Pygmy's brown hair, he kisses her head. "I'll see you later. Be a good girl."

Leena opens the door to let him out, waving at him for a moment before shutting it and sliding down it to the floor. "Jesus, that was close."

I sit Pygmy on the ground, needing coffee. Especially after

a shit night's sleep. "Well, have fun. I'm already late. And if you didn't notice, the spell didn't work."

She crawls on the floor to the kid, making her smile and pulling her onto her lap. "I know. We'll keep trying stuff, okay? I'll do some research and see if I can find any other rituals."

"Okay," I say even though I don't truly believe any of it will work. Last time was a fluke. A lifechanging fluke.

After my coffee and a shower, I get dressed, finding Leena and 'Lilac' playing with her new toys on the floor. "See ya. Good luck, today."

Leena stands up, hugging me. "I'm still here, you know."

Now I feel horrible. My heart may be crushed, but she just went through a heavy trauma. It's not her job to nurse me through a supernatural break up right now. I have to deal with this alone. It isn't fair to put this on her. Pushing my shoulders back, I kiss her cheek and hug her tighter. "I know, and I'm lucky as hell for it."

Work seems to last weeks instead of hours, and everyone keeps asking me what's wrong. I can't even work alone in the sewing room because of my hand. Halfway through the day, my eyes get so heavy, I almost tape them open to keep them from falling.

As desperately as I want my bed, by the time I get home, Leena has to get to the salon, so I have to watch Pygmy until her uncle picks her up. At least it's an easy gig.

Once she's gone, I immediately go to my room and open my drawer. Loch had left his weird patchwork pants in the bathroom a few days ago, so I put them in here for safekeeping. Bringing them to my nose pulls tears from my eyes when I get a hint of his sweet, spicy smell. I hold them against my chest as I crawl beneath my sheets without bothering to change out of my clothes.

His fangs bite my shoulder in between kisses, his gentle fingers trailing down my back. "I'll always be with you, tin nanba."

The tears wetting my face smear against his cheek when I pull him closer. "But you're gone."

"Hey." A hard jab hits me in between my shoulder blades, pulling me from my dreams. Dreams of Loch. "Wake up, half-breed."

There's only one being who's ever called me that. My eyes snap open before I shoot up into a sitting position. "Vilum!" He's crouched beside me, holding my curling iron which I can safely assume is what was poking me. I reach out to him, ready to hug him for being the best sight I've seen since Loch was taken.

He jumps off the bed with a grimace, holding his hand up to stop me. "I'm here for the gohed." Taking a deep breath, he inspects his nails, speaking in monotone. "And I'm meant to tell you Loch wants to come back. Something about Uncle Michael killing your mortal side … I don't know."

"Wait, what? Why would he do that?"

Straightening out his clothes, he adjusts a stray curl. "I honestly wasn't paying attention."

I don't understand. He's actually willing to take my life to keep me from Loch? Father of the fucking year, that guy. I assumed he couldn't interfere like that. Or at least that he wouldn't. This takes strict parenting to an entirely different level.

Vilum clears his throat as he admires his ass in my vanity mirror. "The gohed, half-breed. I know it's here somewhere."

If Loch could take off my seal, then it would make sense Vilum could too. Then there would be no reason I couldn't go to Hell. That would keep Michael from knowing I was even with Loch.

Getting out of bed, I stand behind him. "Take off my seal."

His lip raises enough to reveal a fang when he laughs. "No, I will not be doing that."

I am so sick and fucking tired of these supernatural dickheads doing as they please without giving a damn about how it affects my life. Walking close enough to him that he has nowhere to go unless he teleports, I jab my finger into his hard chest. "Listen to me, you self-absorbed piece of shit. Here's what's going to happen. You are going to do whatever Loch was going to do to remove this goddamn seal and then you are going to fly me down to Hell so I can talk to him myself. Got it?"

He gives me a smirk that reminds me of Loch. "Now I'm seeing why you got his dick so hard." Running his tongue across his teeth, he sighs. "Fine, but let me see the gohed."

I lead him to the kitchen, taking the pendant out of the drawer. "Here." With the force of it being yanked from my grasp, it flies across the room, landing right in his open palm. "Whoa! You have telekinesis powers?"

"Sure." I'm pretty positive he doesn't know what I meant by that, but I'm also thinking he doesn't care enough to ask.

Sitting in one of the chairs at the table, I lift my right foot and point to the seal. He drapes the pendant around his neck before kneeling in front of me and placing my heel on his knee. "This is going to hurt a lot, isn't it?"

"Oh, enormously." With rolling eyes, he sighs. "Your fear is disgusting. Use this." He brings the leather band on his wrist to his mouth, undoing it with his teeth. "Bite down."

I take it from him, doing what he says then nod for him to go ahead. His hand cups my heel, giving off a comforting warmth. It doesn't take long for it to start burning, so I bite down on the leather, trying not to scream. My resilience doesn't last. If I wasn't watching him, I would swear he was melting my skin into mush.

His bracelet falls out of my mouth when I cry out, watching the orange glow beneath his palm get brighter. The agony transcends as the flesh of my back tears apart. I can hear it ripping as I imagine blood pouring down my spine in rivers of ruby. I've never had a seizure, so I don't know what it means that my body's convulsing. All I can do is dig my nails into the table and hang onto the back of the chair. My yells are loud yet distant in my ears. Logically, I know Leena is calling my name, but I can't open my eyes to see her. My hair whips around my face like I'm in a wind tunnel.

With the abruptness of a lever being pulled, my entire body ceases feeling any pain. To the contrary, suddenly I don't feel anything at all. I'm perfectly weightless, made of air, thin streams of water flowing across my skin.

Finally able to inhale, I open my eyes. The world that was here moments ago is gone. This is so much greater, so much more. I hold up my arm, gazing at the silvery-blue symbols shimmering on my skin. Even my heart tattoo glows. Air tickles my palm, moving faster until I can feel it on my face. I've always thought of air and wind as being invisible, yet somehow, I'm looking at a ball of it spinning in my hand. I laugh with overstimulating jubilation. This is surreal.

Leena stares at me with her brown eyes that have little golden chips floating in them I never noticed before. Somehow, I know she's terrified. It tastes … vinegary? Everything is beyond vibrant, breathing and alive.

"Don't be scared, Leena. This is exhilarating." Even my voice is different. I walk toward her, and she doesn't move, though, her uncertainty that tastes of pepper, is still very much present. "It's like living in a world of pencil drawings only to wake up and find it's really animation drenched in colors you never knew existed."

With a shaky hand, she reaches out to touch me. "Your hair. It's clear. And your eyes," she trails her fingers down my arm, touching the crystal lines moving across my skin, "You don't have irises." My skin has become sensitive to her touch, and it's odd to partially understand the things Loch could feel. She circles around to my back, her horror, which has a distinct fruity aroma, is apparent. "Mishka. Your wings…"

Vilum whistles next to us. "Damn. Uncle Michael hacked the shit out of those things, didn't he?"

The closest mirror is in the hallway. The moment I picture it, I'm standing in front of it, Leena calling my name in the kitchen. Solid white eyes stare back at someone I have no memory of. "I'm here." Turning around to see my back, the grotesque reflection of featherless, sawed-off bones stick out like skeletal hands from my shoulder blades.

Leena turns the corner with Vilum right behind her. The hate I have for my father seems to engorge itself every time I think about him. He stole my mother, my wings, and my choice. I refuse to let him take anything else from me, and I will never, ever stand by him. In Heaven or elsewhere.

"How do I hide them?"

For once, Vilum seems to search for words. "Um … practice, I guess? I don't have previous experience with breaking a birth-given emetgis."

"What's an emmett-giss?" Leena asks, breathless.

"A seal. It's what's kept me human all these years." The truth is, I'm humiliated for Loch to see my tattered, broken wings, yet I know in my heart he won't care. Taking Leena's hands, I pull her against me in a hug. "I promise I'll be back, okay? Take care of Shittles and Pygmy until I return."

The woodsy taste of her sorrow floods out of her, pouring down my throat. She falls to her knees, shaking her head and sobbing so hard she's struggling to breathe. "Don't leave me! I can't do this alone, I can't!"

I drop to the floor with her, wrapping her tight. "I love you. I could never ever leave you behind." If my father can go to Hell and back, so can I. Pressing our tattoos together I kiss her head. "I swear to you. I will be back." I don't want to leave her this way, but I can't go without Vilum, and Vilum is the reason her emotions are so amped up.

He holds out his hand, and I take it. "Come on half-breed. I have a party to get ready for."

Blowing Leena a kiss, I smile at Shittles poking her head into the hall. Vilum wraps his fingers around the pendant. "Zacam oi gohed de casarm te as oln."

Even though I'm aware he is talking in the Enochian language Loch spoke, I somehow understand exactly what he said.

Return this divine jewel to whom it was forged.

In a blur of colors and textures, sounds and smells, I'm spinning, falling and flying until my bare feet land on heated stone. The air is hot and thick, causing me to deeply inhale, smelling the scent of something I can't place, I just know it's burning.

"This is unexpected, Vilum."

My eyes look toward the voice that floats into my ears like intricate music I've never heard, meeting the white eyes of the most painfully perfect creature I have ever laid eyes on. A black crown sits among his snow-white curls that highlight pale skin, and I'm surprised he has the same crystalized markings I do, only tinted with gray. His large wings are white, with the tips appearing to have been singed, darkening them.

Vilum shrugs, taking the necklace off and handing it to the angel. "She's pushy."

A stunning woman with jewel laden horns walks slowly toward us. Her purple gown matches the gems in her crown and is gorgeous against her dark skin, trailing the ground behind her. Her solid black eyes home in on me, and I unintentionally swallow in intimidation. Long talon nails, growing from her fingers covered in diamond rings, scrape across Vilum's jaw as she brings her red lips to his cheek.

"You're a good boy. Now go, get dressed. You have a handsome orseiinak waiting for you in the ballroom."

She doesn't have wings, though through her smile I can see she's fanged like Loch and Vilum. Is this Lilith?

As Vilum releases his wings to fly out of the massive open doors, I'm left alone with the man and woman staring at me as if I would be a delicious roast. We're standing in a lavish room where everything is black, from the shiny floors to the roughly textured walls lined in paintings of what I assume is the celestial war Loch told me of.

"You're the murifri who's had my wickedling in such a sour mood." I clear my throat because I'm pretty sure that wasn't a question, but I need to be ready to speak if it is. "Will you put those mangled wings away, dear. They're quite unpleasing."

"Lilith," the glamorous angel warns. "She's a welcome guest in our kingdom. Don't be brazen." His hand slides across her stomach, reaching into her plunging neckline. Her eyelids fall slack when his shoulder jerks, and I attempt to stop staring at his hand moving beneath the fabric.

"There's nothing to be embarrassed about, child," Lilith mewls.

"Go enjoy the ball." Lucifer bites the skin of her cheek.

"I'll get the murifri girl a gown and join you shortly. There's no need to miss the festivities, temptress."

Scratching her nails up his arm, she removes his hand from her gown, swaying her hips as she leaves the room, never giving me another glance.

The angel tastes his fingers before gently bowing his head at me with a smile. "While exquisite, my queen can be a bit unabashed. Welcome to Maelprog, daughter of Madriiax. I am Lucifer, King of Rorvors Comselh." Bending his elbow, he holds it out to me.

I take it, though, I want no connection to the place my father dwells. "With all due respect, Your Highness, if I am the daughter of anything, it's Earth."

His white eyes flash. "Of course. Come. My nephew will be greatly pleased by your arrival. But first, we must find you a gown fit for the Decennial celebration." He grimaces as his eyes scan my jeans and rainbow striped top. "We can't very well have you seen in … that."

ลางวาล

27

Waltzes and Wings

Loch

Semanedai's gloved hands slides over the shoulder of
my black brocade frock coat. Her teeth nip at my neck
before I shrug her off for the hundredth time tonight.
She doesn't understand, which I can relate to because I can't
either. All I know is that even though she's still the alluring
Aldonitas orseiinak that I couldn't keep myself out of a few
weeks ago, I'm not the same anymore.

Taking her hand off my shoulder, I spin around to face
her which she takes as an opportunity to rub my dick over
my formal trousers, tormenting me further. I'd be lying if I
said I wasn't in pain, and it's not helping that half the attend-
ees around us are partaking in sexual activities. Not three
feet from us, one of my brothers has his face in between the

thighs of one of Belphegor's daughters, his crown still resting on his head.

I sigh, prying her touch off me yet again. It's not in my nature to turn away from sexual pleasure, especially when I'm this starved for it. It's so physically agonizing to refrain, but I will see Mishka again, and I'm determined to be able to say I waited for her.

"Let's go dance, shall we?"

She pouts, still allowing me to lead her to the dance floor where we waltz amongst the royal orseiinak of the seven kingdoms. I don't know if I'll have the strength to make it through the entire night. Not to mention, the competition between my father and uncles that will come later in the evening. My body feels heavier with each passing hour. It's worse here than it was on Earth. The symptoms are much more potent.

At the end of the melody, slaves pass through the crowd, their chains *clank* as they carry trays of blood-filled chalices. I've never met an orseiinak who didn't love blood of any kind. It's just not the easiest commodity to come by, so it's reserved specifically for occasions like this.

I wave one over, and he informs us of our choices. "If you would prefer ram, I'll need to go fetch it. I have goat and pig's blood in abundance if that would be satisfactory."

Taking two chalices of goat's blood, I lead Semanedai to an alcove of Lucifer's castle that has a great view of the fire rise and is quieter than the main ballroom.

The music is faint in the background which is better for my agonizing headache. As we sip our blood, she leans up against me, and I allow her hand to roam until she tugs on the string of my trousers.

Grabbing her wrist, I grit my teeth because she is making this so much more excruciating than it already was. "I told you, I can't do this to Mishka."

Her face twists in disgust. "What happened to you in the mortal realm, Loch? You are Zibiidor orseiinak. It's preposterous and wrong for her, a murifri of all beings, to expect your monogamy. If she truly cared for you, she would understand. Look at you! Your wings are wilting, and your eyes are dimming right along with your saziamiin. Can you even fly?" She isn't wrong. I feel dreadful. The chalice *clinks* against the glass of the banister before her hand slides down the front of my pants. I bite my lip, hating myself for throbbing in her palm. "I'll only use my mouth."

My breathing gets harder once she falls to her knees, watching the jewels on her crown glitter from the light of the sconced flames. Fuck, I can't do this! I just need to so badly. Her fingers untie the cords keeping my erection contained, and I shake my head. Imagining Mishka's face if I ever had to tell her my discomfort was more important than breaking her heart is enough to have me gripping Semanedai's shoulders.

I open my mouth to tell her to get up, that this has to stop, when a very angry voice yells in my head, *Motherfucker!*

My shoes fuse to the floor, and I intake a sharp breath at the sight that swells up my throat. The girl glaring at me is not the one I left behind in the mortal realm. My mind and body are stunned in place, seeing her this way for the first time. Her hair is longer now and bordering translucent. Her white, bright eyes are furious, her pale blue saziamiin markings flickering in the candlelight. If her features didn't make her stand out like a beacon, her ivory gown overlayed with pastel gray lace definitely does. White ropes crisscross her chest that rises with her inhale, but as she exhales, her body tremors with rage.

"Mishka, I swear to you, I was not going to let this happen." Glancing down at Semanedai still on her knees, I whisper through clenched teeth. "Get up."

"I literally came to Hell for you, asshole!" Her eyes shift to the ceiling, and now that I can't taste what she's feeling, it's hard to tell if she's going to cry in anguish or laugh in incredulity. "I can't believe this is happening again."

I am nothing like the disgusting human I assume she's comparing me to. She must know that. While it doesn't seem to be the best time to tie up my trousers, it's probably better than leaving them open as I walk to her. "I won't lie to you, I've proved that, so you have to believe me when I say I wasn't going to allow this to go any further."

"This is ridiculous." Semanedai spouts behind me, finally getting to her feet. I scowl at her over my shoulder, but she's not one to be easily deterred. "You've been denying me and who you are, making yourself sick. For her? A fucking murifri! For decades, I have spent mostly every night in your bed, and now after a week on Earth, you're going to be controlled by this bitch?"

"That's enough, Semanedai!" Regardless of our friendship, I refuse to allow her to disrespect Mishka right in front of me. "You're right, I'm not the same orseiinak I was before. And you know what? Good. For thousands of years, I have done the same thing, fuck and torture over and over and over, and it didn't mean anything!" I meet Mishka's softened gaze. "She does."

"Fine, Loch." Semanedai stabs her finger in my chest. "Destroy yourself for all I give a shit."

Lifting her skirts, she storms off. Although I know she has no real love for me, her essence of greed never mixes well with rejection. I do understand her anger as well as her inability to comprehend how I could feel this way. At the proper time, I will attempt to make amends with her, but right now, I can't take my eyes off Mishka.

"I'm sorry you're in pain, I—"

I can't wait a moment longer. I grip the back of her neck, cutting off her words to crash my mouth to hers. Our energies, born from opposite sides of Drilpa Nalvage, tangle together and create a strangely neutral sensation. No heat or cold, no dark or light, only … peace.

I use the remaining energy I have to shigmir the both of us out of Lucifer's castle, not breaking our kiss until we're standing in my bedchamber. She looks around, covering her mouth. Her lips aren't the bright pink shade they once were, and while I do adore her in this form, part of me longs to see human Mishka. "Holy shit. Your room is bigger than my entire house."

Thankfully the slaves have finished replacing and mending the things I destroyed, returning the room to its previous state. I would have hated her seeing it that way.

I'm going to show her everything in Maelprog. I'll hold her hand as we walk down the streets of every kingdom. Kissing her again, my hands run up her back until my fingers hit bone.

Her wings.

Our lips part as she takes a step away from me, staring at her reflection in the floor. "I don't know how to hide them. They're hideous."

I think I understand how Uncle Lucifer felt when he saw what Grandfather had done to my mother. There's nothing about her that could ever be hideous. I remove my crown to place it on my nightstand. Lifting her chin, I nip at the tip of her nose. "Don't ever hide a single part of yourself from me. Please?"

Her lips raise into the smallest of smiles. "Your manners are getting better, orseiinak." Hearing her speak in our divine tongue has my cock straining more than it already was.

Flipping her gaze downward, she grabs my obvious erection over my trousers. "Let's get you feeling better."

Both hands dig into her waist, spinning her around to bend her over my bed. I kiss up her spine, until a soft flutter at the base of her wing bones catches my eye.

I can't believe it. The smallest pale pink feather sprouts from the destruction her father caused. They're healing. Her feathers aren't pure white just like her hair isn't perfectly clear, because she's Earthborn.

Pushing her skirts over her waist, I tear away her panties, my fingers gliding through her slickness to touch her clit. I grin at the movement of her saziamiin now present across her pussy. "How did this happen?" I push two fingers inside. "Your transformation? You being here?"

She rolls her hips, the softest moan falling from her mouth. "Vilum removed my seal, and … oh, fuck, Loch." I take away my hand to shigmir on the bed, standing in front of her mouth before I untie the strings of my pants. "He used Lucifer's necklace to bring us here." When the last word leaves her pale lips, I slide between them, markedly unprepared for the new sensation of her mouth. Tendrils of pleasure swirl around my shaft as she takes all of me down her throat.

This is already relieving the pressure in my head and the strain on my wings, but I want to be one hundred percent for this. I have no intention of being outside of her body for the rest of the night. Pushing her head down so her lips kiss my pelvis, I hold her there, coating her throat with my come, shuddering with relief as my vitality replenishes.

I want you to fuck me.

Her voice is loud in my ears, but there's no way she could speak with my cock in her mouth, and I've never been able to pick up thoughts anywhere near that precise. The only time that's ever happened was with … Michael.

Unholy shit. She's doing that.

I almost tell her it's considered rude to use certain abilities on other orseiinak, however, she's not a daemoness, and besides, I like it. Sliding out of her mouth, I lean down to kiss her. "Go stand in front of the mirror. I want to show you something." Disappearing off my bed, she materializes by the mirrored wall on the other side of my room. Grinning, I shigmir right in front of her. "Now it's my turn to get used to that." The dress she's wearing has so many buttons and clasps that it would take a combination to get her out of it. Since I'm fairly certain she's much more resilient now, I focus my heat on the fabric, scorching it off her body fast enough to not singe her skin.

"Whoa! I barely felt that."

I stand back to take in her nude body, so immaculate with the iridescent swirls marking her porcelain flesh. Falling to my knees, I drape her leg over my shoulder running the tips of my tongue along each side of her hard little button. She wraps her hands around my horns, riding my face until she pushes down on my head. I don't realize what she's doing until she guides my right horn into her entrance, her pussy clenching around the sensitive appendage. Fucking antichrist. I've wanted to do that since the first time I saw her, but I was too scared of hurting her. I bite her thigh, no longer expecting red blood, so it's a lovely treat when the crimson liquid falls onto my tongue. Not even that tastes the same. It's sharper, sweeter, maybe thicker.

Moaning, she thrusts her body up to the tip before sliding back down again. I can feel the saziamiin inside her pussy swirling around my horn. My cock twitches between my legs from the sound of her arousal. I can't stop staring at the reflection of her face painted in desire while she watches herself.

In between kisses on her soft thigh, I tell her, "Bend over with your palms against the mirror."

With a sharp intake of breath, she lifts herself off my horn to do what I say. I shigmir to grab the hand mirror off my armoire and reappear behind her, pressing my hardness between her ass cheeks while fondling the single feather on her wing. Rubbing my tip along her folds, I hold the hand mirror at the right angle for her to see.

"Look," I whisper. The moment her eyes lift to see what I'm showing her, I force our bodies together.

Her fingernails scrape against the glass. "What is that?"

"Your wings. They're growing back." Our eyes meet, then I drop the mirror on the floor, watching the perfect combination of our divine bodies together. "This is what we are. Murifri od orseiinak."

She pushes off the mirror, her wings pressed against my chest as she reaches around to grasp the back of my neck. "Angel and demon."

I wake up to the sound of Mishka's snoring, making me smile before I open my eyes. Now that she's here, our dynamic is bound to change. I really wish she would have thought to bring the Ammalok Qew. It makes me uncomfortable to know it's still in the mortal world. If it were to fall in the wrong hands, there's a chance I could be summoned away from her. Leena will keep it safe for the time being, but what about in fifty years? A hundred? A thousand?

I'm supposed to go to work today. I didn't realize until I went to go see Tim the other night that I can't continue being a guard at Pashbab. Even though being with the prisoners sexually is a form of torture and not pleasure, she won't ever understand that. While I have every intention of being transferred to sorting, she still has the right to know. The truth is I have no desire to stick my cock into anyone besides her regardless of the setting.

Even with her murifri side being released, she's still half mortal, so I'm not sure if she's retained her need for food. Careful to not wake her, I get out of bed to pull the cord attached to a bell in the slave's quarters to call for Murkus. Once he arrives, I send him to retrieve a cake from Uncle Beelzebub's kingdom.

She's still sleeping upon his return but awakens as he's setting up the table. I smack him across the head. "You woke her up. You're lucky I'm in a good mood or I'd flog the shit out of you for that."

He bows. "My apologies, Prince Loch."

Mishka's jaw drops, obviously appalled. "Did you just threaten to whip him?!"

"Yeah, so?" I jerk my head toward the door so Murkus will leave. "He's my slave. I can do whatever I want." I pull out her chair. "Come eat. I got you some cake."

She throws off my hide bedcover and does not seem pleased. It was so much easier when I could taste what she was feeling. Pointing to Murkus who's nearly out the door, she snaps, "Apologize to him." I scoff because she must be joking. "I'm serious. And you having a slave? That's a whole other conversation."

"Mishka—"

"Do it. He didn't do anything wrong."

While she's absolutely right, we definitely need to have a talk, for the sake of this moment's peace, I grumble, "My apologies, Murkus."

He blinks between us, clearly having no idea what

response is expected of him. "Thank you, my prince. Miss." He bows, and I've never seen him leave a room so fast.

Her hands are on her hips with raised brows. "Are you going to explain why you treated him that way?"

I sit at the table without any idea of why she's so upset. "He's a slave. It's what he was born for. I'm not any different than any other royal in Maelprog."

"That's horrible." She finally sits. "Why does he deserve less respect than you?"

We're going in circles. I'm not sure what she isn't grasping. "Because ... he's a slave."

With a huff, she crosses her arms. "Well, I'm not fucking the other royals, so I'd prefer it if you not beat him and treat him like a normal demon." Her gaze travels over the elaborate cake on the table. "What's this for?"

Thank antichrist, she's changing the subject. "It's breakfast. Are you hungry?"

Picking up the fork, she stabs it into the cake. When she tastes the first bite, the sound of her moan has me between her legs with my tongue in her pussy before she can swallow. She jumps in surprise, her mouth still full. *Really? Now? I'm eating.*

I pump my fingers, curling them inside her. "So am I."

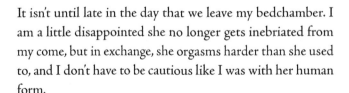

It isn't until late in the day that we leave my bedchamber. I am a little disappointed she no longer gets inebriated from my come, but in exchange, she orgasms harder than she used to, and I don't have to be cautious like I was with her human form.

Since the garments she wore here are still at my uncle's castle and the gown he gave her is now ash, she's wearing my clothes. Even though they hang off her, and the trousers need to be tied up with rope to stay on, I think she looks adorable. We still make the first stop of our Maelprog tour at the shops of Rorvors Comselh to get her some clothes. She picks out a long, loose-fitting orange dress with roping tied around the waist that exposes her back and wings. Since we're here, we also get our hair done, hers curled and pinned up on the sides while mine is re-braided above my left ear. By the time we make our way to Levithmong Comselh for some food, she appears like a legitimate Maelprog native.

As we pass the ice cream and candy shops, she asks, "You don't need to eat, yet you have an entire kingdom centering around food?"

"We don't need to eat. It doesn't mean it can't be pleasurable."

"Is there anything here that isn't junk food?"

"What would the point in that be?"

Crossing over into Unphic Comselh, my Uncle Satan's kingdom, we pass Corlbin, who I've been avoiding since my return. His gaze immediately drops down to my hand laced with Mishka's. He's always had a jealous streak I could keep in check in the past by giving him adequate attention. Now that isn't possible.

"Loch. When did you get back?"

I scratch my eyebrow, wishing I would have had the foresight to have had this conversation with him earlier. "A couple days ago."

He gives Mishka a quick glance before grabbing the back of my neck and pressing his lips to mine. My fingers are being crushed in Mishka's grasp as I place my hand on Corlbin's chest to gently push him back. The skin between his eyebrows squishes together in confusion. "Do you want to see me tonight?"

This is something I've never had to do since monogamy is

mostly nonexistent in Maelprog. Even though we've never had the outright discussion, I know Mishka isn't comfortable with me being with anyone else, and the very idea of someone other than me touching her has my saziamiin glowing with rage.

"I uh, I'm with Mishka now." I hold up our entwined hands.

He glances between us. "And?" I know he understands what I'm getting at, but he's clearly going to make me be blunt.

"I'm *only* with Mishka now."

His lips rise into a grin, laughing so hard, he throws his head back. "You? I've never seen you with one bedmate at a time much less what you're attempting to suggest." Walking past us, he softly swipes his fingers over the front of my trousers. "You know where to find me when you're ready."

There's truth to everything he said, but what he doesn't get, what I don't even get, is as long as I have Mishka, everyone else is irrelevant. I bring her hand to my lips to make her look at me while we cross into the Land of Anger. The expression on her pretty face makes me once again hate that I can't taste or smell what she's feeling.

I'll be inadequate.

I don't know if I took that from her or if she gave it. Either way, there couldn't be a bigger falsehood. She speaks before I can open my mouth to tell her so.

"Will I be enough for you, Loch? Just me? Because I—"

Those words coming out of her mouth have me stepping in front of her, wrapping my hand around her throat so she's sure to fucking hear exactly what I have to say. "I want you to listen very carefully. I have lived for thousands of years, been with thousands of orseiinak, and nothing has or will ever compare to you. If there is anything you can be sure of, it's that." I release her neck, deciding on a whim to tell her everything. From this day forward, I will never keep anything from her again. Moving a strand of hair from her face, I look into those solid white eyes, glistening from the burning sky. "I punish the damned, turning their sins back on them. Raping the rapists, molesting the molesters. It's my job, and it has been since I was two thousand years old. I can't even do that anymore because of you. For the first time in ninety-eight thousand years, I am going to leave my guard position at Pashbab because you are all I want. Do you understand?"

She gives me a blank stare, standing up on her toes to kiss me. Her hand caresses my cheek, whispering, "You just said some really dark shit, and somehow, it was the sweetest thing I've ever heard." Her breath stutters against my lips. "You're really gonna quit torturing souls for me?" I nod, and she releases a shaky laugh. "Good."

We arrive at the arena to watch the fights that are a continuous affair in Unphic Comselh. Since fighting to the death isn't an option, I suppose they can get fairly brutal by human standards, and there are a few times I think she's going to throw up her deep-fried licorice cake. She covers her eyes when the face of one of the fighters gets shredded to the bone across the grated wall. To get her to relax, I tug her dress up her thighs, sliding my hand between her legs.

She grabs my wrist. "What are you doing? There are people everywhere."

Pulling free of her grasp, I slip my fingers into her wet pussy, biting her shoulder. "They're not people, and believe me, none of them care." It takes her a moment to relax, then she eventually realizes all eyes are focused on the fight instead of us.

The evening is quickly coming upon us, so showing her around Aldonitas, Invigil, and Zibiidor Comselhs will need to be reserved for another day because there's one last place I think she'll enjoy, and it's the perfect time of evening for it.

The Zodinu River flows through all of Maelprog, but this specific part is contained to Otiopag Comselh. We cross a bridge made of manganite to reach where the zildar tiantas float in a restricted area.

She reads the sign, tilting her head. "Wandering beds? That sounds interesting."

At the bottom of the pathway, the massive beds carved of black jet and lined with padding, pillows, and blankets come into view. Her face is wearing my favorite smile. She giggles at how it wobbles, but once we're both seated it doesn't rock too much.

"This is the most insane thing I've seen so far, and this entire place is out of a fairy tale. Or a nightmare depending on your point of view. Is this a river of lava?"

I lay back, wrapping my arm around her to hold her against my chest. "Not exactly. It's a liquified form of fire. Ialpr." As we let the zildar tiantas carry us down the river, we pass by the bottom of the fire rise.

She tilts her head back to watch it pouring into the burning sky, mouth gaping in awe. "Is it falling upward?" I can't help grinning. None of this stuff has ever been special to me until today, watching her fascinated eyes take it all in.

When a slave floats by offering us drinks, I notice a few more of her wing feathers have already come in, and the bones are beginning to get longer. After bringing the glass to her lips, she squeezes her eyes shut, her mouth creating a small O. "What on earth is this? It's sour and spicy at the same time."

I swallow my own large gulp, but I drink it all the time. "It doesn't exist on Earth. It's teloc juice. It's made from teloc berries."

She sets her glass in the holder, rolling onto her stomach. Resting her chin on her hands, she lets out a heavy breath. "What are we gonna do?"

I tuck her glassy hair behind her ear. "Besides fuck each other all night?'

Disappointment tints her features while she bites her lip. "I can't stay here, Loch. I have to go back to Leena."

I shoot upright, forcing her to do the same. "What are you talking about? If you go back, we'll never see each other again. If Michael finds out you were here or catches us together, he'll kill you and imprison you in Madriiax."

"That's why I'm asking what we're going to do." She takes my hand, sitting up to crawl onto my lap. She traces the saziamiin on my fingers, her soft kisses trailing up my neck. "We can't be apart for too long or you'll get sick." Her hand moves to stroke over my erection, but for once in my entire life, sex is not what I'm worried about. "Do you think your uncle would let me use his necklace to go home?"

She can't do this. I don't think I can let her go a second time. Kissing her forehead, I close my eyes. "I don't want to let you go."

I hate the sadness of her smile. "I know, I just can't leave Leena, not right now."

Wrapping my arms around her, I wish I could force her to stay, even though I would never force her to do anything. I shigmir us back to my bedchamber, and our feet barely touch my floor before a hand is around my throat, flying me across the room and slamming me against the mirror. Shards of glass burst around me, and all I see is my father's blinding, rage-filled eyes.

"I gave you a fucking order!"

Watching over his shoulder, I see Mishka's hand over her mouth, her eyes glowing brighter. I don't need to taste it to see her fear, and I hate she's feeling it here. In the place I hope will someday be her home.

I shove him off me. "And I don't fucking care!" He

responds by knocking me back against the broken glass. "You're a hypocrite. The very thing you speak against. You were murifri once, like she is. Why should you get a choice and not her?!" The moment his grip loosens, I shove his hand away. "I will make her my princess, and not you, Uncle Michael, or anyone is going to keep that from happening."

He looks me up and down as though I repulse him. "What exactly are you trying to say, Son?"

"I'm not trying to say anything. I am telling you." I glance back to her, our eyes meeting when I say the words I should have said the moment she came here. "I love her."

ลฑฌๅ
28

Antiprayer for an Angel

Mishka

I can't tear my eyes away from him. Tears are on the brink of falling, but only because there are so many emotions storming in my chest.

"Then this is your mess. I will have no part of it."

The man, who I assume is Asmodeus, slams the door behind him before Loch stalks toward me, cupping my face. "Are you okay?"

"I love you too," I blurt.

His gorgeous smile has me fisting his shirt to smash my lips to his. He reaches down to hold my ass, picking me up and carrying me to his bed. Now that my angel side has been released, I can handle so much more of what he has the power to sexually give me. On the flip side, the thing about screwing an incubus is that they can keep going forever, and although I can now take a lot, I still have my limits.

By the time we finish, we're into the next morning, and I'm exhausted. I really want to sleep, but I know he'll want to go again once I wake up. I didn't expect to stay here this long, so I'm sure Leena is freaking out.

I have more feathers than yesterday, and the bones poking out from my back are starting to resemble the skeletal frame of actual wings. The problem is, I still haven't learned how to bring back my mortal appearance. I won't be able to leave my house until I do either.

Loch flies me to Lucifer's elaborate castle, making me anxious. "What if he says no?" Asmodeus already made it clear he has no intention of helping us.

"You don't need to worry. As self-absorbed as he is, he's also a romantic and a rebel. This is the shit he lives for."

We land outside of the room I arrived in a couple days ago with Vilum, the same symbol from the necklace burns above the door. Loch barely knocks when it swings open, revealing Lucifer who stands inside wearing a dark blue tunic and pants with a chalice in his hand.

"Your father is quite displeased with me at the moment."

Loch rubs the back of his neck, his half-laugh void of sincerity. "We need your help, Uncle." Lacing his fingers with mine, he kisses the top of my knuckles.

Lucifer places his cup on a small, twisted black table, making his way toward us with his hands behind his back. His eyes stare directly at me. "I assume you desire to return to the mortal realm?"

"Yes." I hate that the answer not only makes me feel guilty but also a bit morose. If it weren't for Leena, I would never leave this place.

"You require my gohed to do so." I nod even though it

wasn't a question. "There's also the complication with my brother." With a slight turn of his head, he smiles. "I have a proposition for you." He lifts his hand, gesturing behind him. "The vial, my love." Like a shadow appearing with a change of light, Lilith walks into the lavish room, her nails tapping the clear bottle in her hand. "I must ask that you are certain, daughter of Earth. Do you truly desire to remove any power Michael has over you as his offspring?"

I don't know what is happening. Nonetheless, I know it's precisely what I want. "Yes. Absolutely."

Lucifer stands toe to toe with me, leaning down so our faces are level. "I have an antiprayer that will make it impossible for Michael to physically be in your presence. This is permanent and can never be undone." He waves his hand, wafting his next words from his lips. "Think of it as a celestial emancipation."

I wish I would have known this was possible before, but I'm still not sure what this means exactly. "What will it do to me?"

Straightening, he appears taller as Loch squeezes my hand. "It will not alter you in any way that you will be aware of. It will simply make you a beacon of agony for Michael and Michael alone."

I've seen antiprayers done before, like the one with Pygmy and that seemed simple enough. "That's it? There are no other side effects?" He shakes his head, making my insides tight and tense. "What do I have to do?"

He motions for Lilith to come forward, and when she does, she unscrews the lid of the vial in her hand. Reaching her nails into the bottle, she removes three strands of clear hair. "The day your father dragged me back into the arms of Adam, I tore these from his head, vowing to someday repay him for the abuse he forced upon me." Her solid black eyes somehow get deeper and darker, a wicked smile crossing her lips. "This will keep that vow." My father was the angel who brought her back? It's a wonder she doesn't hate me too. "Hold out your right arm."

The moment I do what she says, her nail punctures my much more resilient flesh, tearing it open all the way to my wrist. The inside tissue is bright red, thick blood dripping down my arm. While the pain isn't unbearable, it still stings enough that I suck in air through my teeth. Placing the hairs inside the open wound, she bares her fangs, tracing her forked tongue around my split flesh.

What the hell? That's disgusting. If Loch's attempt at hiding his smile is any indication, I did a poor job masking my repulsion. However, within seconds, the gash closes, healing over the strands.

Lucifer bends over, bringing his mouth to my ear. "At the time Michael inevitably comes for you, recite this antiprayer: Michael, formurifri a balit, lrasd oi basgm gaspt ol zamran trian aai crip od mir."

It's such a trip that I can suddenly understand an ancient mystical language. The translation of the antiprayer is pretty straightforward.

Michael, archangel of virtue, from this day forth, my presence will bring you only torment.

I just hope I can remember it if and when the time comes. "Thank you, Your Highness."

Lucifer shows his perfect teeth as he smiles at me. With a wave of his hand, a drawer in his raised bedchamber opens and an elaborate jeweled box floats out of it. It carries itself across the room, stopping right in front of him. Opening the lid without touching it, he twitches his fingers, raising the necklace out of the box and sending it to Loch.

"I hope to see you again soon, Earth child."

"I do too."

Loch grabs the necklace suspended in midair, draping it over his neck before Lilith kisses him on the cheek and tells him to be careful around my father.

His hands hold my face. "Where do you want the gohed to take us?"

"My house."

Taking one hand from my cheek, he wraps it around the pendant. His lips brush against mine, whispering in Enochian, "Carry this divine jewel to the place where the angelic mortal sleeps."

Lucifer's castle melts away like paint being washed from a canvas, and the sensation of falling consumes me. One moment, I'm plummeting, and the next I'm in my room, somehow smelling the floral scent of my own home for the first time.

Pygmy is asleep in my bed, and Loch immediately leans down to kiss her cheek, brushing her dark curls off her forehead. The clock says it's past seven. It's late for her to still be here.

Tearing open my bedroom door, I run to my living room, stopping abruptly at the sight of Leena and Philip on the couch, clearly having a moment while his fingers caress her face.

I don't exactly want to interrupt, but I want her to know I'm here and okay. I'm about to turn around and wait for her in my room when Loch clicks his tongue.

"Hey."

They both scramble off the couch in surprise. The moment Philip's eyes land on me, the horror on his face makes me feel monstrous. I despise that I can't hide this side of me the same way Loch can.

His mouth opens and closes in between screams as if he's

forgotten how to speak. Leena reaches for him when his eyes roll back, and he crumples to the floor. "Shit! Philip."

"Oh, God. I'm so sorry."

She shakes his shoulders and squints at me. "Girl, I could kill you. I've been worried half to death!"

Philip starts mumbling, and she waves at us to get away. Loch presses his chest against my wings, wrapping his arms around my waist before resting his chin on my shoulder. A barrier raises from the floor, making the room and everything around us appear to be behind dirty glass, not perfectly clear.

"They can't see us." He kisses down my neck and across my shoulder. "Your biggest strength is your willpower. You have to urge these things with your mind." He leads me over to Leena helping Philip sit up. "To use your shield, imagine pulling it from the ground with them on the other side. Manifest it." So that's what bransg translates to. Shield. "Watch this." Suddenly Leena is on this side of the smudged glass while Philip remains outside of it.

Her eyes widen, glancing between us and Philip. "I thought I saw..." Philip's voice trails off.

Leena clears her throat, helping him to his feet. Her arms appear as if they are reaching through the glass as she keeps glancing at us. "He can't see us," I tell her.

She runs her hands down his arms. "Okay, I think you need to take Lilac home and rest. We have some things to talk about, but I think it should wait until tomorrow."

He rubs his head, his gaze shifting to where he saw me. "Are you going to be okay? You were pretty upset about Mishka earlier."

"I'll be fine, I promise. And I'll see you in the morning. Come early, and we'll talk then." Leaning forward, he kisses her. "I had a nice time with you tonight." Her bashful smile forces my own to cross my face. Whatever's happening between them sure happened fast. Not that I have room to speak on that. "I'll go get Lilac."

"That won't be necessary."

Sharp pins tingle up my arms at the sound of his voice. Loch's eyes connect with mine, Philip's screaming breaking me out of my frozen stance. My heart pounds in my ears. I spin around to find Michael holding a still sleeping Pygmy. His halo is held inches from her neck, and I can't help but blame myself for her little life being in danger.

"Put her down. Now." Loch bares his fangs, his voice dropping to the scary, borderline roaring tone I've only heard from him once.

Moving the halo closer, Michael keeps his focus on me. "Come with me, and the human child will be spared."

Every molecule of my body is about to pull apart in a million different directions. "You're a fucking psycho."

"I am a father."

Loch's saziamiin, that I now know means 'origin,' burn bright as the feathers of his wings raise like the hairs at the nape of my neck. He's going to get all of us killed if I don't do this immediately.

"If you put her down unharmed, I'll come with you." I want to tell Loch that I'll use the antiprayer, but I don't know if Michael could hear it too, and I have little control over any of the new things I can do. "Please."

"Mishka, no." Loch's jaw clenches along with his fists when Michael materializes next to Leena, holding out Pygmy. Philip immediately rips her out of his arms, pressing her against his chest.

Before I can sigh in relief that she's safe, Michael's large hand grips my arm, a blinding light obscuring my vision. A sharp coldness slides across my throat as my eyes settle on the halo in his hand. Grabbing my neck, I feel the slickness of split skin beneath my fingers.

Loch's body illuminates brighter than I've ever seen, and all I can think of is how beautiful he is.

"NO!" His roaring voice sounds so far away even though he's right next to me.

He lunges at Michael, sending them both sliding across the floor. I open my mouth, but I'm unable to get a single word out.

Leena's screams weave together with Pygmy's cries, the vinegary stench of terror stinging my nose. Every time I attempt to speak, I'm met with gargling. Slippery blood gushes between my fingers, warm to the touch.

The light of the halo leaves a phantom trail behind with every slice through the air. Grey liquid splatters across Loch's face and arms, taking me a moment to realize it's leaking out of him. The halo is cutting him. I've never seen him bleed. I never knew he could.

A wave of cold air folds over me, and I know this may be my last chance to say it. *Loch. I love you. Please know, no matter what, I always will.*

His head jerks toward me, his eyes shining bright when they snap to meet my stare. My heart thrashes in my chest, and I force every ounce of energy I have left toward my father. I fall to the floor, the wooden boards crashing against my knees. It's so hard to breathe. I don't know how the precision works, so I keep my eyes on my father's forehead, attempting to propel the words.

Michael, archangel of virtue, from this day forth, my presence will bring you only torment.

His screams reverberate down my spine, traveling all the way to my toes. His halo falls from his fingers, rolling across the floor as he clutches his ears. Climbing off Loch, he struggles to get on shaky knees.

Blurry blackness closes in around the edges of my vision, Loch's wide, glowing eyes are the last thing I see before the darkness swallows me whole.

Am I breathing? I don't think I am. My chest doesn't rise when I inhale. This should be terrifying. I should feel something, yet I don't. A soft whistle draws my attention to what I guess is a river, but the water is weird. I kneel on the glass pathway, dipping my hand inside, and while I can see it falling through my fingers, it's void of texture. It doesn't feel like anything. Toward the middle of the body of the strange substance, is what appears to be a waterfall. It rushes downward from a solid white sky. There are no clouds. Well, if there are, I can't see them.

How did I get here?

Where exactly is here?

"I was hoping we'd meet one day."

Looking next to me, I see the man who spoke. I think it's a man anyway. His face is covered by the hood of the robe he has on. Even his hands and feet are hidden by the impossibly sheer fabric. How can I not see through it?

"What is this stuff?" I ask running my fingers through the unexplainable element.

"Ialzo. Air's liquid form." Standing to my feet, I try to see his face, but I can't see beyond his hood.

"Who are you?"

He turns from me, and I follow beside him. "I have endless names. Though, you can call me Grandfather."

I should be stunned, angry … something. "Am I in Madriiax?"

"For the moment." Somehow, we're sitting on a hovering bench. My feet dangle beside the flowing material of His robe.

"Am I dead?" The question should be terrifying, yet I don't feel an ounce of trepidation regardless of His answer.

"In some ways, yes. The part of you that was human is no more. However, you won't be staying here. Your heart and essence have tethered you elsewhere."

"Loch." It's as if my memory has been on pause until his name crosses my lips.

I would say the sound He makes is a laugh, only because it's the closest thing I know of to compare it to. "The boy has so much of his uncle in him."

"You mean Lucifer. One of the many children you damned."

He holds out his arm to a circular creature of some kind who perches there. The revolving circles of its shape make it appear more mechanic than living, aside from the single blinking eye in the middle.

"I am sure you've heard many different versions from many different sources. I did not damn them. I simply gave them the freedom they longed for. I could have easily forced them to stay. Instead, I allow them to thrive in worlds of their making. Even eternal beings have a tendency to place blame on those who gave them life. Regardless, I love all my children."

"Not my mother. You killed her because of Michael. Not Loch's mother. You allowed her to be raped and then mutilated her."

Whatever the creature is on His arm, it lifts back into the air then spins off. Still not showing His face, the hood shakes with what I assume is His head moving inside.

"Lilith's abuse at the hand of Adam was necessary for her to become the orseiinak she is now. It was her destiny. Her 'mutilation' as you put it was a gift to my son. A physical symbol that marked her belonging with him in Maelprog." He stands, floating inches from the ground. "Your mother died because humans are not built to withstand birthing a murifri child, not because of what my son did. Michael being separated from her is punishment for his choices." He lifts His head, but still His face is hidden. "I will eventually grant him the permission to see her. It's my job as a father to teach my children lessons through discipline." So many questions flood my mind. I try to filter out which ones are most important when He says, "Your time here is coming to an end, child. I am pleased we could have this chat. I desire your eternity to be graced with fulfillment."

I turn to Him only to see that He's vanished. I jump off the bench, searching for Him over my shoulder. As though they all emerged from nothing, people and angels spring up around me, talking and laughing, walking along the glass pathway like they've been here all along.

Something soft and gentle wraps around my hand, making me turn to see a woman with short, blonde hair and the bluest eyes I've ever seen. Her tan halter gown blows in the non-existent breeze. Reaching up to my face, she kisses my cheek before wrapping her arms around me. I have no recollection of her, yet her embrace feels safe and familiar.

"You are more beautiful than I ever imagined. I'm so proud of you. I love you so much, Mishka."

TWEE
29

Crown of Crystal

LOCH

S he's dying. The light of her eyes and saziamiin grow duller with every second that passes. I'm losing her, and I can't even go to her because I have to try to stop Michael from doing any more damage.

I've never been worried about dying since there are very few things that can kill me. A halo is one of those things. Dying as an orseiinak means I evaporate into nothing, ceasing to exist in any form. I don't have a soul to carry me into the next realm. That's a risk I am gladly willing to take to keep her out of Madriiax. In her celestial state, she wouldn't be free there.

A freezing line of pain sears across my cheek from the slice of the halo. I push out the maximum level of heat I can muster from my fingertips, uselessly attempting to burn his chest. Every time, the air he releases from his hands snuffs it out. It's impossible to concentrate on this fight when my thoughts are with my murifric human being stripped of her mortality.

I've never considered myself as having a heart, and I don't technically, but in a way, I've developed the concept of one. That's because of the girl bleeding out a few feet from me. More than anything, I wish I had her power so I could whisper in her ear to hold on. That I love her more than I've ever loved anyone, and I will figure this out.

Continuing to swing at me with his weapon, he cuts my arm and slices through my shirt, singeing the flesh of my abdomen. With every ounce of strength I possess, I'm able to shove him off me for seconds at a time, but his power engulfs mine. We roll over each other while Pygmy's frightened cries pierce my ears. The smell of terror is so thick, it must be coming from more than one source.

Loch. I love you. Please know, no matter what, I always will.

My gaze snaps away from him to look at her. Wetness drips from the corners of my eyes, rolling down my cheeks at the sight of her life force dimming. I wrap my hands around Michael's throat, and he shrieks in agony. I can't believe my ability to inflict that kind of damage on a being of his stature. Quickly glancing to Mishka, I see that her illumination has increased tenfold. Her mouth moves, but no sound leaves her lips. It's then I comprehend she's saying the antiprayer.

Michael rolls off me in time for me to see her light go dark. The pink tint of her soul floats from her body, rising to the ceiling.

FUCK! No, no, no. NO! I shigmir to her just in time to catch her before she falls forward to the floor. Glancing back toward Michael, I realize he's nowhere to be seen. All that remains is his halo left glowing on the ground.

"Mishka! Come on, come on! Fuck!" Leena covers her mouth, the overflow of her fear and sorrow magnifying my own. I hold Mishka's limp body against my chest, kissing her hair, chanting every antiprayer I can remember that might bring her back to me. Gripping her neck, I lick around the gaping wound. My mother's tongue has healing properties, though, I've never had the thought or need to see if that trait was passed to me. I watch as the gash on her neck closes, but there's still no sign of life.

Leena's red, watery eyes widen, and I know it's because of my tears. I wipe the coal tinted liquid from my cheeks just for more to fall. I sob into Mishka's hair, soaking the translucent strands in black.

No breath leaves her lips. No essence flows in her saziamiin. My body has become so heavy that it feels impossible to operate. As I look at her, my throat swells. He destroyed her. I've never seen a divine being die, but she was still part human. I watched her soul leave her body. That has to mean the part of her that I love is still in existence.

When I open my eyes to look at Leena, I become too stunned to make a single movement. The pink-tinted ball of Mishka's essence hovers above us before bursting into a million tiny particles, raining down on Mishka's lifeless body. Her saziamiin flicker into illumination, making me too scared to hope and too scared not to.

Her healing wings flinch, attempting even in their damaged state to fly, making me choke on my unsteady inhale. She barely shifts, but then her soft moan has me laughing uncontrollably.

"Mishka?"

Her weakness is apparent, so I should be gentle, but I'm

too consumed by a joy I've never felt to control myself. I yank her into my lap to kiss her, running my fingers over the now closed wound across her neck. More tears pour down my cheeks when her silvery lashes flutter open.

Did I do it?

My body doesn't know whether to laugh or cry, so I do both, kissing her hair tinted in raven tears. "Yes, you did it, tin nanba."

"You can hear her?" I nod, and Leena gasps with wide eyes, taking Mishka's hand. "Oh my God." Human, clear tears drip off her jaw as she hugs Mishka. "I love you too." I smile at the fact that Mishka obviously just spoke to her friend's mind for the first time.

Mishka's fingers softly caress my cheek, her eyebrows scrunching together. "Your face," she rasps.

"Don't talk right now, okay? I'm fine."

"W-what the fuck just happened?!" Philip finally speaks, and from his tone and flavor of his emotions, he's not taking this well. He points at me with a shaky finger. "Are ... are any of you human?!" His voice becomes shriller with every word, and he's gasping for air, so I wouldn't be shocked if he passed out again.

Hesitant to step away from Mishka, Leena stands up to place a hand on his arm. "I know this is a lot. It was a bit rough for me to digest too. I—"

Pygmy starts squirming in his arms, reaching for me and screaming, "Pig mee! Pig mee!"

"Lilac, it's okay, sweetheart." His fear is controlling his emotions, yet as he gazes at Leena, there's true fondness there even now. "I need some space, okay?"

Finally, the child worms her way out of his grasp to the point he's forced to let her down. She waddles toward me, her little arms reaching around my neck, trying to get in my lap.

"I missed you too, Pygmy." I haven't gotten to hold her since she was at the 'foster' home, so I squeeze her tight.

Philip gives me a dumfounded stare. "That's the first time she's walked. Rubbing his hands down his face, he holds them out like he desperately needs something to keep him upright. "You call her Pygmy too. I've never once heard that, so I call bullshit on it being a 'common' nickname." He spins back to Leena. "What the hell are we involved in?"

Leena swallows, tentatively reaching for his hand. "If you calm down, I swear I'll explain all of it."

Wrapping my arms around Mishka, I shigmir into the washroom, gently laying her on the floor before I turn on the water to clean her up.

I kinda wanted to hear that conversation.

"I'm sure Leena will retell it to the point of exhaustion later." She smirks, yet even that appears to be painful. I help her stand up, kissing her forehead. With the explosion of events over the last few minutes, I'm feeling a bit disoriented myself. "You need to get some sleep. I just wanted to get you clean first."

After I help her wash her hair and soap off in the shower, I stare at the thick scar adorning her throat. I'm not surprised. All my uncles and my father have a few halo scars, and they'll never go away. Although I'm not sure how she'll feel about it, I love seeing the tangible proof of her bravery and what she did for us both. Now I'll have some too.

While she insists she can walk, I don't really give a shit and carry her to her bed. I pull the blanket over us, being mindful of her wings as I hold her to my chest.

She sighs. "I'm not half human anymore." I think part of me had considered that since seeing the way her soul changed, but it's not something I've yet had the chance to ponder. "How do you know?"

"I can't feel my heart anymore, and I think I … I think I talked to God." Wait, what? I jerk up to look at her when my wings go stiff in my back. Her trembling fingers cover her yawning mouth.

I don't know what to feel. I have so many questions. Is that possible? Of course it's possible, but… "What was He like?"

Closing her eyes, she pushes her body against mine. "Mmmm. I don't know exactly." Barely awake, she murmurs, "Kind. He was kind." A slow breath blows between her lips. "I saw my mom too. She told me she loved me."

Before I can ask her more about our grandfather, she slips into sleep, lying still beside me. Even with my curiosity itching my brain, I've never been more grateful for any moment more than this one.

Six months later

"How do I look?"

The full skirt of her new gown falls to her thighs, flying out around her as she spins. Her pale pink feathers perfectly match the satin beneath the black lace. I see why she loves it so much. It's a perfect mesh of her mortal style and Maelprog fashion. Even though I personally prefer her hair down, I do like the braids and curls she got done in Rorvors Comselh, and all I can think about is messing it up.

"You're sure Leena would be upset if we skipped this?"

Reaching out to run her hands over the belted buckles across my chest, she quirks her lips. "She would absolutely find a way to kill me if I missed her birthday. Besides, I already don't get to see her enough."

Birthdays are not something celebrated in Maelprog, so I'll admit the ritual is interesting. However, I'm not at all comfortable in large human crowds. The festivity is what Mishka calls a 'costume' party, so we don't have to wear our priidzars. Given the chance, Leena isn't one to pass up the opportunity to dress up.

I reach down to touch over Mishka's pink netted stockings. I'm going to demolish these later. "Fine, but you have to make it up to me before we go to dinner."

She wraps her hand around the waist of what she calls my 'distressed' black pants. Distressed is what I'm going to be if I'm not inside her soon. Kissing me, she stands on the tips of her black boots, running her fingers through the top of my hair. *I promise.*

Since the time difference between here and the mortal realm is so different, we're both getting used to minimal sleep. The worst is when we work. Her shifts at the doll shop are directly opposite of mine at the sorting office. The job isn't as exciting as it was being a guard. Still, I enjoy it so much more than I thought I would. With the help of my mother, my father has come around to us being together, and between his and Uncle Lucifer's gohed, we've been able to live dually between here and the mortal realm. It's unquestionably the most fulfilling my life has ever felt. All one hundred thousand years of it.

We shigmir to Uncle Lucifer's office where my mother lounges on the balcony with Ors. He loves Mishka, flying up to her the moment we walk in.

"Hello, my wickedling. Your uncle is meeting with his brothers. He left the gohed in his desk for you." I lean down to kiss her, and Mishka smiles. They have surprisingly gotten along quite well. Mishka giving her Michael's halo certainly didn't hurt anything either.

The Ammalok Qew sits in a glass case on a table next to my uncle's desk. It always makes me feel good to see it. Without its weathered pages, I would have never known her. My life would still be on repeat decade after decade. I made sure she brought it back with us so nobody could pull me or any of my family members away from our home ever again.

Sliding open the drawer, I find the gohed in a small granite box. After I drape it over my head, I walk back to her, brushing my lips over her cheek and murmuring the antiprayer.

When we arrive in the bedroom of our Earth residence, I slip the gohed in my pocket. From the sound of the blaring music and the overstimulating aroma of excitement, lust, and joy, it's apparent the party is in full swing.

Pygmy's uncle took some time to warm up to us after he learned the whole story of how I found her. Now I taste his fear and apprehension less and less. He's also in love with Leena and has introduced her to a whole new group of friends. I think sometimes Mishka feels a little left out. Even so, she's happy for her. With us living in two worlds, it's only fair for Leena to have her own comrades.

It's a bit odd being in my natural form in front of so many humans, but when we emerge from the hallway, we seem to be the most average ones. Apparently, these mortals take their costuming quite seriously.

Leena spots us within seconds, grabbing Mishka's arm to pull her into the crowd. I'm perfectly happy lurking in corners, becoming part of the background as I watch Mishka laughing and dancing with the music. Although in comparison to orseiinak, what mortals equate to dancing is vastly different.

Later in the evening, when our time to return to Maelprog arrives, I search for Mishka. She's not hard to find with her wings, yet once I do, my saziamiin glow in the darkened room.

I attempt to dull them, but my desire to break every single finger of the man with his hands on her is overpowering my restraint. Their bodies aren't touching, which is the only thing saving him from becoming a blood streak across the floor.

Slipping into the hall, I pull up my bransg and shigmir behind Mishka, who's dancing with the flesh bag dressed in what I assume is his interpretation of an Egyptian pharaoh. Mishka's arms are slack on his shoulders while his hands sit on her hips. They bounce back and forth to the beat, and I can't watch another second of this.

My hand grips the front of her neck, feeling her scar beneath my fingers. "Get away from him, now." For the moment, I'm able to keep my voice from sounding too angry, but it won't last long.

She immediately steps back, her nervousness apparent in her laughter. She should be nervous. "Thanks for the dance."

Turning around, she meets my gaze with widened, white eyes. "Tell Leena goodbye. We're leaving."

After doing what I tell her, she hugs her friend, following me into the hall where I throw the gohed over my head. She opens her mouth, but I speak the antiprayer before a word can escape her lips.

The moment we land in my uncle's office, I reveal the full extent of my fury. "Do not ever let someone lay hands on you again!"

She tilts her head. "Loch, it was a harmless dance. I don't even think he's straight."

"I don't care if he's straight or curly! He shouldn't have touched you."

"That's not—" she presses her lips together, clearly forcing herself not to smile, and I can't help wondering if she's purposefully trying to piss me off. "That's not what that means."

My mother, leans over to my uncle, tapping her nails on

her glass as if this is somehow amusing. "Sometimes he's more like you than his own father."

I storm over to her. I'm not waiting for dinner. I need to know. "Where is it? I want it now."

She places her hand on my arm. "Wickedling, I don't think now is the time—"

"Give it to me."

My uncle nods to her, and she sighs, taking a drink of her teloc juice. With a wave of his hand, he uses his powers of object manipulation to open the doors of an armoire and pulls out a drawer. A circular, satin box lifts in the air, flying to him as though pulled by a string. When the box lands in his grasp, he gives it to me.

Ripping off the lid, I pull out the jeweled crown I had fashioned from crystal. Mishka gasps, her mouth dropping open at the sight of it.

"Loch..." Her throat bobs, her eyes blinking at me.

"If this crown is placed on your head, no human, orsei-inak, or murifri is to ever lay a single finger on you. Ever. You are mine and mine only. My lover, my partner, my princess. For eternity."

It isn't until this moment that fear of her rejection falls like a stone in my gut. In my mind there is no doubt, no question.

She lifts her pale lips into a delicate smile, her head lowering into a subtle bow. The elation that courses through my entire body forces the illumination to radiate from my sazi-amiin while hers do the same.

Does that mean she...

Only yours. Forever, my prince.

Epilogue

MISHKA
5 years later

He's going to kill me with this. My body tenses, preparing to release the pent-up pressure when he once again puts a stop to it. "Please, Loch. Please!"

Naked demonic bodies writhe around us, yet his attention and his gaze has and always will remain on only me. He would prefer we stay locked away in the castle together for days on end, but I want to be social with the people who are now my family. I think he enjoys watching their eyes on me. He revels in other's desiring what's his and his alone.

My feathers tickle my back, fluttering in the hot wind blowing through the open doors of the lounge room.

Orgies are a common occurrence in Zibiidor Comselh, and even though we only ever touch each other, I still enjoy being included in all Maelprog customs.

He tugs at my nipples, his thick erection plunging deep inside my ass. The prickling build presses against my stomach, and I cry out loud enough I'm sure I can be heard above all the other moans in the room. "Fuck, Loch. Let me come."

My murifri body can take so much more violence than my mortal one could, something he's taken full advantage of. Knowing that he can make me bleed and I'll heal within moments has its perks. Slicing the tip of his horn down my back and between my wings has me fisting the fabric of the lounge couch. I push my ass against his abdomen, forcing him deeper. His fingers tap my clit until finally, he allows the orgasmic sensations to explode through my body.

I reach over my shoulder to clutch a fistful of his hair, arching my back as I ride my pleasure high. If he allows this to go on much longer, I'll be wiped out for the next couple hours, and we still have Pygmy's birthday tonight. I may be divine, but as he is a demon of lust, I am an angel of virtue. I'm not naturally equipped to have as much sex as we do.

"I don't know what I love wrapped around my cock more. Your tight pussy or tight ass." He sinks his fangs into my shoulder, my orifices clenching at his words. The heat of him emptying himself floods my body for the fourth time since this morning.

Sliding me off him, he throws me onto the enormous pillows on the floor, his ravenous eyes devouring every inch of me. He falls to his knees between my legs, his fingers clawing at my thighs to push them as far apart as they'll go. The tips of his tongue curl up inside my hole making me pant his name.

When I am completely spent and my body has the strength of gelatin, he stands, taking my hand to help me to my feet. He brings his lips to mine before we shigmir back to our room in the castle. While we clean ourselves up, dressing in our mortal clothes for Pygmy's party, Ilzmort's nanny, Myrnette, chases him into our room.

It's a rule in our home that the word 'slave' is forbidden. All the orseiinak whose jobs include making our lives easier are to be respected and treated equally to us. Loch is still struggling with that, it's a hard mindset to break, but I'm proud of the effort he has made. I've tried to fight for them, and at least in Zibiidor Comselh, advocate for them to be fairly compensated for their work and not to suffer physical punishments at the hands of the royals. I'm far from making a difference, but I refuse to back down until there are significant changes. No matter the level of demon, they don't deserve that.

"Mommy!" I pick him up, swinging him around as I kiss his sweet little nose.

I wipe the ash off his little jacket and ask Loch, "Did you get the gift? And a change of clothes for Ilzmort?"

He holds up the black leather satchel. "And ram's blood in a no-spill sippy cup. We're good."

I kneel in front of my child who is so much more like his father than I can handle sometimes. I'll never forget the day I laid him. I had never been informed that divine beings are hatched, not born the way I was. That was a terrifying experience, so I'm grateful I had Lilith to guide me through it, and she even helped me and Loch build his nest.

"Okay, Ilzy. Mommy and Daddy are trusting you to be a big boy orseiinak today and letting you go to Lilac's human birthday party. Can you tell me what the rules are?"

He slits his eyes at me in frustration before flipping his gaze to Loch. "Don't look at me, bud. This is important."

I'm so scared he'll get tired and out us to a bunch of first graders and their parents. With a huff and crossed arms, he rambles off what he's already told me a hundred times in his cute little voice. "Always wear my priidzar in front of strangers, don't bite, don't shigmir, and remember my manners."

"That's my little darkling. Good boy." I lift him into my arms, lacing my fingers with Loch's as he wraps his hand around Asmodeus's gohed.

Leena and Philip got married about a year and a half ago, moving into this bougie neighborhood she loves to talk shit on, even though I can taste the pride she has in the place. Her daycare, *Leena's Little Ones*, has now expanded into three locations across Oregon, and I couldn't be happier for her.

Once we land in their living room, Ilzmort flaps his little silver wings to fly upstairs to Lilac's room. Loch hollers behind him. "Don't you dare poke another hole in their wall with your horn, Ilzy!"

Seconds after Leena's squeal sounds from her kitchen, she runs up to me in her high heels and tea dress. These days she's more Stepford than the edgy Leena I grew up with. I give her crap about it, but I am so grateful for her happiness and that she found someone who treats her the way she deserves.

"Ahh! What's up, whoresickle!" She nearly knocks me over with her hug. It's been a little more difficult to get together like we used to with Ilzy and Lilac getting older, and I worry it'll be worse as more time passes because Ilzmort's aging will get slower and slower the older he gets. People already think he's an extremely gifted toddler.

Ilzy and Lilac can be heard laughing while she chases him down the stairs. "No fair! I told you flying breaks the rules!"

Lilac's eyes land on Loch, and she runs to jump in his arms. "Loch!"

Bopping her on the nose, he pecks her on the forehead. "Happy birthday, Pygmy."

Philip comes in from the garage, holding a hand up in a wave and kissing Leena on the cheek before he picks up more presents to load into the car. "Hey, guys. It's good to see you. Is everyone ready to go? This is the last of it."

Clapping my hands at Ilzmort, I say, "Okay, it's time, my darkling. Put on your priidzar."

He does this adorable shudder thing whenever he takes his priidzar on and off. It does have an odd weight to wearing it, so I think it's his little body adjusting. In his natural form, he has Lilith's black eyes, but his wings and hair are both silver. His horns and saziamiin are the same as Loch's, though.

Once we arrive at the park, I help Leena set up. I'm taping balloons to the present table when I catch something in the corner of my eye. Gazing up at the blue sky, my breath lodges in my throat. I've seen Michael a couple times since Ilzmort was hatched, but because of the antiprayer, he's unable to get any closer than he is now, forced to watch his grandson from a distance.

He's here, I speak to Loch's mind.

Loch comes to stand beside me, wrapping his arms around my waist and resting his chin on my shoulder. Sometimes I wish things could have gone differently with Michael. Regardless, I don't think I could ever trust him again, especially around Ilzy. He made his choices and will have to spend eternity paying for them. However, the more time that passes, the more memories I have of being in Madriiax, and I do hope someday it becomes possible to visit again.

"Are you okay, tin nanba?"

Spinning around, I hold his face in my hands to kiss him. "I'm perfect, my prince." Nipping at his ear, I decide to tell him what I've kept to myself all week. "But we should try to get back home fairly early."

He raises an eyebrow with a smirk, "Oh, yeah?"

We have a nest to build.

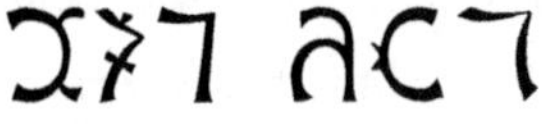

(The End)

PLAYLIST

I *Dolly Song (Devil's Cup)* // Vize & Leony

II *Wicked Ones* // Dorothy

III *Unthinkable* // Cloudy June

IV *Lust* // The Raveonettes

V *What's Wrong* // half·alive

VI *Angels & Demons* // Jxdn

VII *Prelude 12/21* // AFI

VIII *Fly Away* // TheFatRat ft. Anjulie

IX *Hurt* // Oliver Tree

X *Bed Head* // Manchester Orchestra

XI *Oh Lord* // In This Moment

XII *Bloody Valentine* // Machine Gun Kelly

XIII *Take It All Back* // Judah and the Lion

XIV *Destroyer* // Of Monsters and Men

XV *Born to the Night* // Ava Max

XVI *Love Race* // Machine Gun Kelly ft. Kellin Quinn

XVII *To Hell and Back* // Maren Morris

CHARITY B.

Series

Candy Coated Chaos (Sweet Treats #1)

Sweetened Suffering (Sweet Treats #2)

Cupcakes and Crooked Spoons (Sweet Treats #3)

Standalones

Anointed

R.I.P.

Featured

(Can be read as standalones)

Skeleton King (Dirty Heroes Collection #9)

Desiccate (Inferno World)

ACKNOWLEDGEMENTS

I am so lucky to have such a wonderful group of people who have been there for me and helped make this book what it has become. It's impossible to thank everyone who has supported me, read my books, and promoted me, but I do see you, and I couldn't do this without you.

The first ones to ever read my books are my beta and sensitivity readers. Good, honest betas are not easy to come by, so you guys are priceless. Thank you so much for all your help.

Niki Murray, you are always there to have my back, and I can't begin to thank you enough. You not only help me make my books the best they can be, but you have also been a sounding board for me and an amazing friend. Thank you for always lending me your ear and allowing me to have someone to talk to when I get frustrated or excited. I'm immensely lucky to have you.

Salina Donovan, my first ever OG. You know I wouldn't be here right now if you wouldn't have given me the encouragement and confidence to keep going after that first manuscript. It all started with you, the first EVER to read anything I had written, and I really can't thank you enough for being such a large reason for why I am on this path to following my dreams.

Mahjabeen Careem, I cannot even imagine this book without you! You were the first person to read this book, and you know I was so nervous! Your love and excitement for Leena and all the characters really allowed me to breathe for the first time since writing this. You have been nothing but an incredible cheerleader, and every single one of your messages put a huge smile on my face. I am so thrilled to have met you and adore that you're part of my team.

Kathi Goldwyn, I can always count on you to tell me exactly what I need to hear. You have been by me since the beginning of this journey, and I wouldn't be where I am without you. You never fail to pump me up and promote my work, and I will never be able to repay you for everything you've done for me in and out of this business. Thank you for always being there for me.

Rachelle Anne Wright, you are the queen of epic ideas, and you truly helped bring this book to the next level. I can't imagine this book without some of the 'extras' put in because of your brilliant mind. Our conversations had me rolling, and I am so grateful that our paths crossed. Now, you're stuck with me! I am so excited to work more with you in the future.

Cassandra Nelson, you were such a help on this book and probably saved my ass on a couple things! I really appreciate the time and care you took with your feedback. Your honesty and encouragement really made such a difference. Thank you so much.

Sarah Peña, I love how our relationship has grown over the years. You have had my back through all sorts of things and have pulled me off the edge a few times. Not only did you help me so much with incredible feedback for this book, but you are just always there for me and have been since my debut. I am so glad I have you in my life.

Kween Corie, my second OG! You have had my back, reading and encouraging me since before I had a single thing published. We go way back, and I love that you are still a part of my life. You are always singing my praises and have been a source of helping my confidence since before I knew this life was a possibility. There's no way I could encompass my gratefulness for everything you have done for me over the years.

Lilith Roman, while this has been a rough year for me, one of the best things to come out of it, is our friendship. You have not only been a good listener and understand my smorgasbord of emotions, but you have been a huge support as well as helped me with business decisions. I am so grateful that we met and that I have you in my life.

Thea Van Eijmeren, all the teasers you've made for me have been gorgeous, and I have loved every single one. You have been such a huge help to me and allowed me the time to focus on other things which is priceless. Thank you for everything. I've had such a wonderful time working with you!

Christine Iannone Schuller, I am so appreciative of the time you took to read and help me out on the sensitive topics of this book. It really gave me a lot of relief. You have read and supported me for years, and all of this just means so much to me!

Ann Rachelle, thank you for your friendship and all your help with not only this release, but past releases as well. You know I really struggle with the 'business' aspect such as marketing and you have been so kind with your time and patience assisting me along this journey. Thank you so much for everything you do!

Dirty Little Secret Book Club, you guys have been a big support ever since Candy Coated Chaos and it truly means a lot. Thank you for all of your promotions and allowing me to celebrate the release of Incubastard in the group. You guys are seriously awesome!

To my Babydolls, sometimes I can't believe you're all still here with me! You have given me a place where I can truly be myself, and you welcome me with the widest of open arms. You guys have truly given me an online home and no matter what have stuck by and supported me. You've been patient with how long it takes me to release and are always there to voice your excitement for each one, never making me feel bad or guilty for the timeline. I got so lucky with you guys. I could never have dreamt up a better group.

To my wizard of an editor, Kim BookJunkie, I am so freaking lucky to have you in my life on multiple levels. You always make my books the best they can be, and I love that I don't have to stress about the quality of your work because you always do an impeccable job. You have been there for me through the ups and downs of my personal life. I really love you for that. You are not only an amazing editor but a dear friend.

To the bloggers and readers who read and review my book, you guys are why us authors are even able to do this at all. It means so much that out of all the books, mine was one you chose to spend your time on, and then to go on and review it for others to learn about has such a huge impact on helping me grow. I can't tell you the serotonin I get from seeing that you read my words. This entire publishing journey would quite literally be impossible without you, so from the bottom of my heart, thank you for showing your support and choosing to read my stories.

Cassie at Opulent Designs, you really saved my ass on this one! You seriously knocked this out of the park. I know I'm not the easiest client, but you exceeded my expectations. You listened to me and gave me something that I am madly in love with. Thank you so much for putting such an amazing face to a story that I love so much. I truly appreciate you working with me when I was in a crunch. Thank you for everything that you did.

Stacey at Champagne Formats, it's so nice to not have to stress about anything I send to you. I always know that my words will look beautiful by the time you finish with them. You are always such a joy to work with. Thank you for helping make my books as gorgeous as they can be.

To my husband and son, if I didn't have you in my corner, I wouldn't be able to do any of this. I know it takes away from our time as a family to follow my dreams, and I know how hard that can be sometimes. If I didn't have your support, none of this could have ever happened. I owe you both so much more than I can ever express, and I love you with my whole heart. I am so lucky to have the both of you.

ABOUT THE AUTHOR

Charity B. is a dark romance author who writes in horror, taboo, and most recently, paranormal romance. Charity has always had an interest in the more disturbing and horrific side of life, while also being an incurable romantic. The Sweet Treats Trilogy was her debut series, and she is constantly preparing for her next release. She lives in Wichita Kansas with her husband and ornery little boy. In her spare time, when she's not chasing her son, she enjoys reading, the occasional TV show binge, and is deeply inspired by music.

For up-to-date information on upcoming releases and events visit www.authorcharityb.com

Printed in Great Britain
by Amazon

41251399R00169